# TANGERINE

## CHRISTINE MANGAN

LARGE
PRINT

First published in Great Britain 2018
by
Little, Brown
an imprint of Little, Brown Book Group

First Isis Edition
published 2018
by arrangement with
Little, Brown Book Group
An Hachette UK Company

A catalogue record for this book is available
from the British Library.

ISBN 978–1–78541–620–0 (hb)
ISBN 978–1–78541–626–2 (pb)

Published by
F. A. Thorpe (Publishing)
Anstey, Leicestershire

Set by Words & Graphics Ltd.
Anstey, Leicestershire
Printed and bound in Great Britain by
T. J. International Ltd., Padstow, Cornwall

This book is printed on acid-free paper

# TANGERINE

The last person Alice Shipley expected to see when she arrived in Tangier with her new husband was Lucy Maso

the tw

haven

there,

shoul

Moro

medi

and i

and e

starts

stifle

John,

arour

For my parents, who always believed this
was possible.

And for R.K., always.

# Prologue

## SPAIN

It takes three men to pull the body from the water.

It is a man — that much they can tell, but little else. The birds have been at him by then, perhaps attracted by the glinting piece of silver that adorns his tie. But that's only magpies, they remind themselves. *He must have seen three*, one of the men says to the others — a crude attempt at humor, that line from the old nursery rhyme, *Three for a funeral*, echoing in his head. They lift him, startled by the weight. *Do dead men weigh more?* another wonders aloud. Together they wait for the police to arrive, doing their best not to look down, to avoid the empty sockets where once the dead man's eyes rested. They are strangers to each other, these three, but they are bonded now by something deeper than kinship.

Of course, only the first bit is true — the rest I have simply imagined. I have time for such things now as I sit and gaze: across the room, out the window. The scenery changes, but nothing else. I suppose some would call it watching, but I would argue that it is not the same at all — that they are as different as daydreaming and thinking.

1

It is a warm day; summer is fast approaching. The sun has begun to fade and the sky has turned a peculiar shade of yellow, warning of storms on the horizon. It is in these moments — when the air is thick and hot, *threatening* — that I can close my eyes and inhale, when I can smell Tangier again. It is the smell of a kiln, of something warm, but not burning, almost like marshmallows, but not as sweet. There is a touch of spice, something vaguely familiar, like cinnamon, cloves, cardamom even, and then something else entirely unfamiliar. It is a comforting smell, like a memory from childhood, one that wraps you up and swaddles you and promises a happy ending, just like in the stories. Of course, this is not true. For underneath the smell, underneath the comfort, there are flies buzzing, cockroaches stirring, starving cats gazing meanly, watching your every movement.

Most times, the city appears as a fevered dream, a sparkling mirage that I can just about convince myself was real once, that I was there and that the people and places that I recall were tangible and not translucent ghosts that my mind has conjured up. Time moves quickly, I have found, turning people and places into first history and then later stories. I have trouble remembering the difference, for my mind often plays tricks on me now. In the worst moments — in the best moments — I forget about *her*. About what happened. It is a peculiar sensation, for she is always there, lurking just beneath the surface, threatening to break. But then there are times when even her name escapes me, so that I have taken to writing it down on any scrap of paper I can find. At night, when the nurses are gone, I whisper it to myself, as though it were a catechism learned as a child, as if the repetition will help me to remember, will stop me from forgetting — for I must never forget, I remind myself.

There is a knock at the door and a young red-haired girl enters the room, a tray of food held between her hands. Her arms are covered, I notice, with freckles, so heavily that the tiny brown flecks overwhelm the pale skin underneath.

I wonder whether she has ever tried to count them.

Looking down, I find a name scrawled across a piece of paper on the nightstand next to my bed and the name nags at me, for although it is not my own, it feels important, as if it is something that I should try to remember. I let my mind relax. It is a technique I have found useful: trying hard not to think while secretly thinking as hard as I can.

Nothing happens.

"Ready for breakfast?"

I look up, confused to find a strange girl with dark red hair standing just in front of me. She cannot be any more than thirty, so there can only be a handful of years between us. *Redheads are bad luck*, I think. Don't they say to avoid redheads when preparing for a sea voyage? And I think I'll most likely be at sea soon — to Tangier. I feel anxious now, eager to have this redheaded ill omen gone from my room. "Where did you come from?" I demand, angry that she has not bothered to knock.

She ignores my question. "Aren't you hungry today?" In her hand is a spoon full of some gray substance — I reach for its name, but my mind refuses to yield. Angry now, I push it away and instead point to the little slip of paper by my bed. "Put this in the bin," I tell her. "Someone is leaving me notes with nothing but nonsense written on them."

I settle back onto my bed, pulling the covers up close to my chin.

It's summer, I think, but my room suddenly feels as cold as winter.

# I

## TANGIER 1956

# CHAPTER
# ONE

## ALICE

Tuesdays were market days.

Not just for me, but for the entire city, the Rif women parading down from the mountains heralding the start, their baskets and carts overflowing with fruits and vegetables, their donkeys flanking them on either side. In response, Tangier came alive: crowds emerged, the streets flooding with men and women, foreigners and locals alike, pointing and ordering, arguing and bartering, exchanging coin for a bit of this, a bit of that. The sun seemed somehow brighter on these days, hotter, the scorch of it burning the nape of my neck.

Standing at the window now, looking down upon the swelling crowds, I made the silent wish that it was still Monday. But then, Monday, I knew, was always a false hope, a false comfort, before Tuesday would eventually come again and I would be forced to stand in the chaos swirling below me. Forced to stand before the impressive Rif women, adorned in their bright colors that caught and fought for attention, their eyes evaluating my own drab, ordinary dress that could not measure up, and seized with a sense of worry — worry that I would pay an exorbitant price without realizing it, that I would give the wrong coin, that I would say the wrong words, that I would make a fool of myself and they would all laugh and it would be evident what a mistake I had made in coming here.

*Morocco.* The name conjured up images of a vast, desert nothingness, of a piercing, red sun. The first time I had heard John mention it, I had sputtered and coughed on the drink he had pushed into my hand. We had met at the Ritz in Piccadilly, and only at Aunt Maude's insistence — which I could feel in those weeks after I returned from Bennington College, pushing, a headache that I could never quite manage to escape. I had been back in England for only a few months, had known John for less than that, but in that moment I was certain I could feel it — his excitement, his energy, filling the space around us, pumping through the warm summer air. Leaning in, eager to grasp it, to hold it, to claim some of it for my own, I had let the idea settle between us. Africa. Morocco. A few weeks earlier I would have balked, perhaps a week later I would only have laughed — but on that particular day, in that particular moment, listening to John's words, to his promises, his dreams, they had felt all too real, all too attainable. For the first time since Vermont, I found myself *wanting* — I didn't know what exactly, and I suspected in that moment that it might not even be the man sitting before me, but wanting something, all the same. I had taken a sip of the cocktail he had ordered for me, the champagne already warm and flat, feeling the acid on my tongue, in my belly. I had reached over,

8

before I could change my mind, clasping his hand between my fingers.

For although John McAllister was certainly not what I had once dreamed of for myself — he was loud and gregarious, brash and oftentimes reckless — I had found myself reveling in the opportunity that he had presented: to forget, to leave the past behind.

To not think each and every second of the day about what had happened in the cold, wintry Green Mountains of Vermont.

Over a year now, and it was still cast in a hazy fog that I could not seem to work my way out of, no matter how long I tripped through the labyrinth. *It's better that way*, my aunt had said afterward, when I had told her about the vaporous sheen my memories had taken on, how I could no longer remember the details of that horrible night, of the days that followed. Leave it in the past, she had urged, as if my memories were objects that could be packed away in boxes secure enough to ensure they would never let loose the secrets held within.

And I had in a way, had shut my eyes to the past — had opened them to John, to Tangier, to the blazing sun of Morocco. To the adventure that he had promised — with a proposal and a proper ring, though not an actual ceremony, just a signed slip of paper.

"But we can't," I had protested at first. "We hardly know one another."

"But of course we do," he had assured me. "Why, your family is practically related to my family. If anything, we know one another too well." He laughed, flashing me that wicked grin.

There would be no name change — I was adamant on that point. It felt important, somehow, to retain some part of myself, my family, after everything that had happened. And there was something else too, something I had a harder time explaining, even to myself. For although my aunt's guardianship would technically dissolve upon my marriage, she would still retain control of my financial trust until I turned the age of twenty-one, at which time my parents' estate would at last be released into my own name. The idea of being doubly covered seemed entirely too daunting, and so, when I reached for my passport, it was still Alice Shipley written there.

And at first I had told myself that Tangier wouldn't be so terrible. I imagined days spent playing tennis under the hot Moroccan sun, a team of servants to wait on us hand and foot, memberships at the various private clubs throughout the city. There were worse lives to live, I knew. But then, John wanted to experience the real Morocco, the real Tangier. So while his other associates hired cheap Moroccan help and their wives spent days languishing around the pool or planning parties, John eschewed it all. Instead he and his friend Charlie went gallivanting around the city, spending hours at the hammam or the markets, smoking kif in the backs of cafés, always trying to endear themselves to the locals rather than to their fellow coworkers and countrymen. Charlie had been the one to convince John to come to Tangier in the first place, plying his friend with tales of the country: its beauty, its lawlessness, until John was half in love with a place he had never seen. And I had done my best in the beginning, going with him to the flea markets for furniture, to the souks to shop for supper. I had sat in the cafés beside him and sipped café au laits and tried to rewrite my future in the hot and dusty city that he loved at first sight but which continued to elude me.

But then, there had been the incident at the flea market.

Amid a frenzied collision of sellers and stalls, of antiques and junk piled haphazardly, one careless layer after another, I had turned around and John had been gone. While I was standing there, strangers passing me, jostling me from either direction, my palms growing clammy with the familiar beginnings of anxiety, shadows had played at the edges of my vision — those strange wispy apparitions that the doctors had whispered were only manifestations but that to me felt real, visceral, tangible, so that they seemed to grow, until their dark shapes were all that I could see. In that moment I was struck with the notion of how very far away I was from home, from the life that I had once envisioned for myself.

Later, John had laughed, insisting he had only been gone the space of a minute, but the next time he asked me to go out, I shook my head, and the time after that, I found another excuse. Instead, I spent hours — long, lonely tiresome hours — exploring Tangier from the comfort of our apartment. After the first week, I knew how many steps it took to get from one end of it to the other — forty-five, sometimes more, depending on my gait.

Eventually, I began to feel John's regret looming above us, growing, our exchanges limited to matters of practicality, of finances, my allowance our main monetary support. John was bad at money, he had once told me with a grin, and at the time, I had smiled, thinking he meant that he didn't care about it, that it wasn't a concern for him. What it really meant, I soon learned, was that his family's fortune was nearly gone, just enough remained to keep him well dressed, so that he could play at pretending to still claim the wealth he had once had, that he had been born into and still felt was rightfully his. An illusion, I soon realized. And so, each week I handed over my allowance, not really caring, not really interested where the numbers disappeared to in the end.

And each month, John continued to vanish as well: into his mysterious city that he loved with a fierceness I could not understand, exploring her secrets on his own, while I remained inside — my very own captor and captive.

I glanced at the clock now and frowned. It had been only half past eight the last time I had checked, and now it was ticking steadily toward noon. I cursed and moved quickly toward the bed, toward the outfit I had laid out earlier that morning, before I had lost all the hours in between. For, today, I had promised John that I would go to the market; today, I had promised myself that I would try. And so I looked to my costume, such as it was, the semblance of an ordinary woman about to do the week's shopping: stockings, shoes, a dress that I had purchased in England just before moving to Tangier.

Pulling the dress over my head, I noticed a slight tear on the front, at the bit where the lace met the collar. I frowned, bringing it closer to my face for inspection, trying not to tremble at the sight of the damaged material, telling myself that it was not a sign, that it was not an ill omen, that it did not mean anything at all.

The room felt too warm then, and so I stepped out onto the balcony, needing, in that moment, to be free of its imposing walls. Closing my eyes, desperate for any hint of a breeze, I waited, but there was nothing, except the still, arid heat of Tangier as it bore down on me.

A minute passed and then another, and in the quiet, listening to the rise and fall of my breath, I became aware of the peculiar sensation of being watched. Opening my eyes, I cast a hurried glance toward the street below. There was no one. Only a handful of locals making their way to the market, their steps rushed, the hour when the market would end slowly approaching. "Pull yourself together," I whispered, heading back into the safety of the flat. Despite these words, I closed the windows firmly behind me, my heart pounding. Glancing at the clock, I saw that it was now half past one. The market could wait, I told myself.

It would have to, I knew, my hands shaking as I tugged the curtains closed so that not even the tiniest trace of sunlight could filter through.

# CHAPTER
# TWO

## LUCY

The sun beat down heavily as I leaned against the railing. I felt the rocking sensation beneath me grow stronger, a lurch in my stomach as the ferry started and stopped, inching awkwardly to its final destination: Morocco. I hurried to grab my suitcase, the past few months already marked by dreams of grand, sweeping displays of Moorish architecture, of the intricate twists and turns of the lively souks, of colorful mosaics and brightly painted alleyways. Joining the queue that had already begun to form, I craned my neck, impatient now to grasp my first, real glimpse of Africa. For already, there was the smell of her, beckoning us from the shore — the promise of the unknown, of something infinitely deeper, richer, than anything I had ever experienced in the cold streets of New York.

And Alice, she was here too, somewhere within the beating pulse of the city.

Stepping off the boat, I scanned the crowd for her face. In the few hours between land and sea, I had managed to convince myself that she might be there to greet me, even after all that had transpired. But there was no one. Not a single familiar face. Only dozens of locals — young boys and old men alike — trying to entice me, along with the other tourists who had disembarked, into purchasing one or another of their services. "I am not a tour guide — only a local that everyone knows. I will take you places other tour guides do not know about." When this did not work, wares were displayed: "Madame needs a purse?" To the gentleman trailing behind me: "Monsieur needs a belt?" Coats were opened and other items were taken out and passed beneath the eyes of each and every unassuming newcomer. Jewelry, small wooden carvings, and strange musical instruments that were foreign to the sight. I, like everyone else, waved away these trinkets with impatience.

There had been few travel guides on Tangier, but I had hunted down whatever literature I could find, reading line after line about the city that I would soon call home, however temporarily. I had read Wharton and Twain, and once, in desperation, some pages by Hans Christian Andersen. He had, quite surprisingly, been the most helpful in preparing me for this onslaught of eager guides, the crushing tidal wave of faces who descended upon the arriving boats like locusts, ready and able to provide services to the naive and inexperienced traveler. The latter I could be described as, certainly, but the former, never. So I was ready, prepared, armed with words and research to protect me against this scene of chaos. I knew precisely what it was that I would be stepping into from the safety and relative quiet of the ferry. And yet, nothing could have prepared me for it. Wharton, Twain, and even Andersen — their words failed to act as swords and shields in the end.

I tried to move away from the hawkers, a map held firmly between my hands — as if to prove my determination. A shake of the head, then a murmur of first French, *non, merci,* followed by Spanish, *no, gracias,* and then, out of frustration, the minuscule Arabic that I had learned prior to my journey — *la, choukran.* Nothing helped. I pushed on, determined to make my way out of the port and into the medina. Most dropped back, but a few still persisted, following me from the water's edge and up onto the hilly path that led into the old city. "You are lost? You need help?" Finally, there was just one solitary man who refused to leave. He was unobtrusive at first, insisting on following me slowly, relaxing his gait so that he mirrored my own. His command of English was better than the rest, and he put it to good use, rattling on about all the places that he would take me — places that no other tourists would ever see.

I tried to ignore him, to shrug off the crushing heat that already caused my cheeks to flush red and hot, to look away from the swarm of flies that seemed to lurk in every corner as I made my way into the city's twisting labyrinth. But then, after several minutes, he moved in front of me, cutting me off so that I stopped in confusion, grasping at my single bag. I tried to push past, but he stood, insistent.

"Yes," he said, smiling, "I am a mosquito, I know." He leaned in closer and I could feel his breath, hot and moist, against my face. "Lady, listen. It is better to have

**16**

one mosquito with you, do you know why?" He paused, as if waiting for a response. "One mosquito will keep all the other mosquitoes at bay." He smiled, threw back his head, and laughed, the sharp, unexpected noise echoing off the walls that now surrounded us, so that I started, stumbled, my bag landing heavily beside me as my knee connected with the hard, dusty road beneath.

I let out a sharp exclamation, moving to assess the damage while recoiling from the outstretched hand of the Mosquito. My new taupe stockings — which I had paid a dear one dollar and fifty cents for after the shopgirl's insistence they were top-of-the-line — were ruined. There was a tear just above my knee, with a run trailing downward, and I noticed with increasing dismay an angry-looking red spot that threatened to bleed. "Of all the rotten luck," I murmured.

The Mosquito, as if sensing my discomfort, my unease, moved closer still. "You look lost," he whispered, his voice suddenly low, insistent. As if my newly subjected stance required such theatrics. "Do you know what you are looking for, mademoiselle?"

At his words I paused for a moment — just a moment — wondering what it was that I was actually doing in this strange foreign land that I had dreamed of so often that it had begun to take on a shiny, unreal quality each and every time I conjured it in my mind. So that even now, as I rested on the hard truth of its existence, it still failed to be real. My breath caught in my throat — but then, there it was: a hazy image of *her*, just before me.

That was all it took, and then I was myself again.

"Yes," I told him, the Mosquito, my voice now hardened with determination, with purpose. I stood, abruptly pushing past him so that our shoulders collided, so that he felt the weight of the impact, felt the weight of my body thrust against his own. I saw the shock on his face. "Yes, I know exactly what I'm looking for."

The Mosquito gave a quick shrug and began, at last, to amble away.

*Affinity.* I had looked up the word in a dictionary during my first year at Bennington College — that strange little cluster of buildings that sat, hidden, or so it seemed, in the heart of Vermont's Green Mountains. *A spontaneous or natural like or sympathy for something. A similarity of characteristics suggesting a relationship.* I began to search for other similar words. *Similitude. Inclination.* I wrote them all down in my notebook, carrying it with me as I moved between the library and class and back again. I clutched its fraying blue leather to my chest, careful to guard it, to remember it, so that it would never be left behind: my treasury of found and cherished words. I took them out to read often — in the morning before class, at night before I fell asleep. I whispered them to myself, as if the memorization of these words were something I would later be tested on — as if they were integral to my education, to my survival at the college.

I had stumbled across that particular word — *affinity* — a few weeks after I had first met Alice. The moment had seemed poignant — a description for something I had not yet known I was looking to describe. The relationship that Alice and I had formed after only a few short weeks, the partiality that we felt for each other — it went beyond any rational description. Affinity, I decided, was a good enough start.

We had met on our first day at college. Alice was standing in the hallway of our assigned clapboard house — each one consisting of two floors with nearly a dozen or so rooms per level, a common living space replete with fireplace on the bottom floor — searching for our room, arms clutched around a stack of books, looking as if there was nothing more she wanted in all the world than to disappear. And she almost did — her upper body and face nearly vanishing behind the books that were obviously too heavy a burden. I knew already that she was my roommate — we had earlier arranged to meet, a flurry of letters sent back and forth before we arrived at school, a picture included so that we would recognize each other — and yet, I couldn't help waiting, stalling, drawing out the moment for as long as possible. I didn't want to go up and help her, to introduce myself — not yet.

And so I waited. And watched.

Her ankles and wrists were the most delicate things I had ever seen. It was still summer, and her ballerina-style skirt, which floated against her calves, and her thin short-sleeved camisole revealed them in startling clarity. Her hair was long and blond, with curls that looked like they had been created rather than organically grown. When she finally approached, I saw that her nail varnish was a soft pink, almost too subtle to be noticed. The same could be said about her makeup. For a moment I wondered whether or not she even had any on, but it was there, I decided, nearly invisible, but still there all the same. She was put together nicely, with the intention of others not noticing. There was nothing about her that clamored for attention, nothing that demanded to be seen, and yet, everything was done exactly in anticipation of such notice.

That was how I knew she was used to people looking at her, used to having to present herself in front of others. And it was the way she chose to do so that told me she had never had to scrape together money for rent, had never worried about what was in the cupboards and whether it could be made to last a week rather than a day or two. And yet, I didn't resent her the way I did some of the other girls I had already met. There was nothing gloating or spoiled about this girl, nothing that reeked of superiority. The other girls at college were always so keen to prove themselves better than one another, boasting about family holidays or dropping names they knew would inspire fear and awe in others. Alice, I would soon learn, wasn't like that at all. While the other girls stuck up their noses at the *shippers* — their word for the scholarship girls — Alice had treated me, a shipper from the next town over, the same. Watching her that day, before we had exchanged so much as a greeting, I thought she seemed kind, lonely even.

I moved back into the room then, pretending to observe the barren white walls, all the while holding my breath, waiting for her to approach, frightened, in that instant, that I might lose her to someone else if I stalled too long, if I waited for just one moment more. At last, she appeared in the doorway, and I smiled and began. "I'm Lucy Mason," I said, holding out my hand as I walked toward her, feeling as if each and every word I wanted to say were twisted and tangled into that one small gesture, so that everything — the very future — depended on it. I waited for what seemed an infinite amount of time, though it was likely only a hairbreadth, wondering whether she would accept my outstretched hand, wondering where it would lead us, how our journey together would unfold.

She shifted her books to one side and an instant smile broke across her face. "I was worried you'd forgotten," she said, blushing at the words, her accent British, clipped and polished. "I'm Alice. Alice Shipley."

Her hand was warm. "It's nice to meet you, Alice Shipley."

The next morning, I dressed carefully.

I gathered up all my belongings from the *riad* that I had rented for the night — wanting after the journey a chance to change, to refresh myself, not wanting to appear at Alice's doorstep with my stockings torn, my hair a mess. I checked the room once, twice, until satisfied that I had left nothing, before closing the door behind me.

In the medina, I waited in line at one of the stands and ordered breakfast — a braided bread I did not recognize, sprinkled with sesame seeds and stuffed with a paste that tasted of dates. Standing against a wall, feeling the strange stale texture of the dough pressing against my tongue, my cheek, and pausing every now and then to take a sip of the café au lait I had also ordered, I let my eyes roam the street.

I watched the tourists sipping mint tea at the cafés, watched a group of locals as they unloaded goods, transporting them from donkey to person to store, before finally, my gaze met his.

He was several feet away, seated at one of the numerous cafés that lined the square. Tall, dark, although not as handsome as some, a local, I guessed, though I couldn't be entirely certain. He wore a fedora tipped low over his face, the base of the crown encircled with a vibrant purple ribbon. I stood a moment or two longer, feeling his eyes on me, wondering what it was that he saw, what had caught his attention. It was true that I had taken extra care that morning, selecting the one decent dress that I had purchased before my voyage across the ocean, the price tag depleting the small savings I had left. I smoothed the skirt with my left hand, finished my coffee, and moved away from the medina, from the man's inquisitive stare.

After nearly an hour of walking and retracing my steps, ignoring the smirks of waiters — dressed formally in suits and small cravats, despite the blistering heat — as I passed by the same restaurant, once, twice, three times, believing for one mad moment that all roads literally led back to the Petit Socco, I had found it. Past the medina and west of the Kasbah, Alice's flat sat just outside of the chaos that I had first descended into. The

Quartier du Marshan, my guidebook told me. I sensed the strange shift long before I became aware of any actual change. It was greener, with trees lining the streets, although they were still scarce and entirely unfamiliar to my eye. And there was a general feeling of lightness, as if all the tension that existed in my shoulders, or no, rather, just there, between my shoulder blades, began to dissipate the closer I got. Perhaps it was simply that I was nearer to her, I thought, stopping then to set my bag down, to take a breath.

The building itself was unremarkable, blending in easily among the rest: it would not have looked out of place in Paris, I thought, a pale stone block that had been embellished with wrought iron balconies and generous windows. Its familiarity was to be expected, of course, but I still could not stop myself from feeling a bit of disappointment. It had taken me so long to get to this point — months of planning and saving, hours spent traveling on boat, train, and across the ocean once again. My clothes were covered in dirt, my mind tired and frayed in exploration of this new land. I had come to expect something more at the end of my long journey — a glittering door, a magnificent palace, something that said dramatically and definitively: *here is your reward — you have found your way at last.* I pressed my finger against the buzzer.

For several moments, nothing happened. I felt my heart begin to quicken — perhaps she had gone back to the Continent? Or perhaps I had the wrong address? I looked at the piece of paper between my fingers, the inky scrawl faded from so much folding and unfolding. I imagined having to turn around and head back to the port. I saw myself buying another ferry ticket, ignoring the derision of the workers who had only just ferried me across, laughing as I made my way, once again, across the ocean — this time in defeat. I shook my head. It was impossible. The thought of New York, of yet another dull gray winter looming ahead, of the tiny rooms I had rented in various boardinghouses spread across the city, of the sound of dozens and dozens of females, their heels trotting up and down the halls. And the smell. I shivered, even in the afternoon heat. That strange, heavily perfumed smell that seemed to trail each and every one of them, and which hung thickest within the walls of the shared toilet. There was always an overly sweet quality to the pungent odor, like something on the verge of being rotten. I grimaced. No. I would not go back, no matter what happened.

"Yes?"

I heard the word before I saw her. I tilted my head upward, but the sun blinded my view. Raising my hand, I managed to partially shut it out, so that her form eventually came to me, severed by bright strips of white.

"Alice," I said, not raising my voice, reveling, just for a moment, in the sound of her name. "It's me."

She was far enough away that I couldn't be certain, but I thought I heard a sharp intake of breath, and I struggled then to contain my delight, pleased to find that I had managed to surprise her. "Well?" I finally asked, raising my voice just a bit. "Do I have to scale the wall?"

A nervous-looking smile broke across her face. "No, no, of course not." She stood behind an iron railing, its dips and curves made to resemble some sort of ivy, that ended just below her waist. Her hands flew to her throat, the way they always did when she was nervous. "Hold on just a moment. I'll be right down."

As I waited, I became aware of a slight fluttering in my ear. As a child, I'd suffered from terrible earaches, and as I grew, there was always a season where I would feel that same pain return, and which would send me rushing to the doctor. But no matter how often I visited, they would always smile and shake their heads, assuring me *absolutely nothing is wrong*, as they ushered me toward the exit. One physician had paused long enough to instruct me how to lay my finger just above my earlobe and pull gently. *If you feel pain now,* he said, *that means there is an infection. Otherwise, it's just . . .* He had let his words trail, unfinished. Later, he suggested that he had seen similar symptoms among a specific set of patients, a nervous condition that seemed to affect only his more intelligent clientele — though I suspected that the comment was made more to flatter himself, a testament to the practice he had created, rather than from any great desire to help. Still, standing there, waiting for Alice to make her way down the stairs, I repeated this movement, checking for any source of pain, any indication that an infection had managed to take hold. There was nothing, and yet still, the fluttering persisted.

25

When Alice appeared in the doorway, she was slightly out of breath, two bright pink spots on her cheeks, a small heat rash creeping below her throat. She had always been prone to rubbing that same spot — set just between where the two clavicles met — whenever she was anxious. I wondered if she had done that before or after my arrival, or if, in fact, the pink spot was simply from the heat of midday, which pulsed around us.

She looked exactly as I remembered. True, it had been just over a year, but enough had passed between us since then that it seemed almost as though it were a different life entirely. She was still so small — she hated the word *petite*, I knew — but there was no other way to describe her. Short and blond, she still held the shape of a young girl, a fact that Alice had once frequently lamented. A string of pearls hung, hitting her just above her collarbone, and I was struck by how out of place they seemed, somehow incongruous with the scenery around us. I resisted the strange sudden urge to reach out and touch them, to tear them from her neck and watch the beads as they clattered to the ground, spilling out into the crooks and crannies of the street.

"You look wonderful," I said, leaning in and kissing her on either side of her cheeks. "It's been too long."

"Yes," she murmured, her eyes bright, but distant. "Yes, of course."

I felt the sharpness of her bones underneath my hands. She stepped back into the doorframe, behind the threshold, her movements betraying an anxiety that I suspected she would rather not have revealed. Alice motioned for me to follow her, and I did, watching as she led me up a narrow staircase, listening to her warning about what steps to take gingerly, her instructions quickly followed by an apology for the decay of the building, a rambling that she was always prone to when nervous. "It's absolutely gorgeous, of course, but in desperate need of some repairs. I've told John several times, but he doesn't seem to listen. I actually think he likes it. It's where all the artists live, he says. Writers, apparently. He's told me the names a million times, but I can never manage to remember them. But then, I suppose that's more up your alley. We'll have to ask him when he gets home from work."

John. The man that Alice had met after leaving Bennington, the man who was, I had only recently learned, responsible for her move to Morocco.

"Is he home?" I asked.

"Who?" Alice frowned. "Oh, John. No, no. He's at work."

"And how is he?" I asked, as if we were all old friends, though the words sounded hollow, and I hastened to cover them. "And you, how are you?"

"Good. We're both doing quite well." She said the words quickly, burying them underneath her breath. "And you?"

"I'm happy to be in Tangier." I smiled. *With you.*

I did not say these last words aloud, though I could feel them, beating steadily within my chest. In fact, half of me was convinced that she had heard them too — or if not *heard*, perhaps *felt*.

27

I became aware that by this time we had moved into her flat, were, in fact, standing in the foyer, the wooden floor covered with an intricately designed rug, my suitcase still hanging heavily from my hands. I wondered at her not reaching for it and showing me to the spare room, so that we could sit and relax and begin to trade stories, like we had done in the old days. It was perhaps too much to hope for, I knew, that things would simply revert back to how they had once been, before that terrible night. And yet still, I couldn't help myself. Hope still lived, however buried in the hollowed-out cavity of my chest. And yet, there was something in her stance, something in the way she moved — as though a caged and frightened bird, I thought — that led me to wonder whether the problem was not, in fact, the secrets that we held between us but something altogether different.

I had since wondered at Alice's move to Tangier, recalling the old worn map that had hung over my bed at Bennington. We had made a game of it, over the years, pushing pins into the wall, the tacky white plaster giving way with ease as we decided where we would go once we graduated. The adventures that we would have, together. Paris for Alice, or, on days when she was feeling particularly brave, Budapest. But never Tangier. My own pins were placed farther afield: Cairo, Istanbul, Athens. Places that had once seemed distant and impossible, but no longer, with Alice by my side.

*I'll take you to Paris after we graduate,* she said one evening, not long after we first met. We had sat, hidden behind the End of the World, that stretch of land at the end of Commons Lawn, where the earth appeared to abruptly give way — though if one was to look down, one would find only an unfurling of gentle, rolling hills. A mirage of sorts. An illusion. Night had already set in, the dampness of the grass bleeding through the cotton fabric of the blanket we sat upon, but still we remained, happy to ignore its encroachment.

I squeezed her palm in response. I knew by then about the trust that had been set up in her name, about the monthly allowance that she received — checks with her full name, *Alice Elizabeth Shipley*, written in a careful, old-fashioned script that appeared in her mail slot at the start of each month, precisely — but to make the offer, to extend such an invitation to a girl that she had known only a few weeks, it defied logic as I knew it. My heart had clenched, as if refusing to believe that such generosity, such kindness, truly lived in other people, as my own past had not taught me it was possible. Born in a small town in Vermont, only miles away from the college, I had always considered my hometown a place one drove through on the way to somewhere else, somewhere infinitely better. A scholarship had given me that chance, snatching me from the close confines of a stuffy apartment over a garage, transporting me only a few miles away, though it might as well have been to an entirely different world.

But then, Paris had never happened.

Instead, Alice had come to Tangier, to a place that she had never pinned on our map. And she had come without me.

"What are you doing in Tangier, Lucy?" Alice asked, shaking me from my reverie.

I blinked, startled by her words. "I'm here to see you, of course." I smiled, my voice catching on the words as I worked to hide the emotion behind them.

I looked at Alice then — *properly* looked at her — for the first time. She was, as I had noted before, slimmer than the last time I had seen her — paler too, which was strange, considering the climate. There were dark circles underneath her eyes and she looked, I thought, like she hadn't slept properly for quite some time. Her fingers were worrying at that spot just below her throat, which had turned a more threatening color since I had first arrived. She was wearing a housecoat, despite the hour, a yellow piece that tied at the waist with a simple sash and nearly touched her ankles. Her face was bare, without any trace of paint, and her hair — that once brilliant, thick tangle of golden curls — was shorter now and hung limply, its dingy color indicating that it was in need of a good wash.

"Is everything all right, Alice?" I moved closer, setting my suitcase down beside my feet.

"Of course, of course it is." Those rushed words again.

"You would tell me, wouldn't you? If something was wrong? If you and John —"

She flinched. "No, no. It's all fine. Really. You've just surprised me, that's all." She smiled, though there was an edge in her voice — something sharp, steely.

But then her shoulders seemed to relax, her smile became less tight, and for the first time, she seemed to notice me: from the new bouffant-style hairdo, held into place by a generous amount of hair spray — although it had already begun to frizz in the heat, I noted sourly — to the dark, belted shirtdress that had cost as much as one month's rent. It was a far cry from our college days, I knew, but conscious of the fact that I would be seeing Alice for the first time in more than a year, I had wanted it to be evident how well I had done since those days — not in a gloating fashion, the way that other girls behaved around one another, passively flaunting their success only in order to make the others green with envy. No, I wanted to show Alice just how much our days and nights spent together at college had meant, how all our dreaming of the future had not just been a fanciful way to pass the time. I had meant it, every single word. That was what I wanted to show her. That I had never lied, not about any of it, despite what had happened between us.

"You look well, Lucy," she observed, though I thought it sounded as though it were a concession, as though the words had left her lips despite, rather than for, something.

"So do you," I replied, eager to match her compliment — whether easily given or not — although I suspected we both knew the words were offered out of politeness.

She smiled again, that same inward smile I had witnessed often during those first few days of college, when she had been so shy and uncertain of herself. Toward the end of our four years, she had shed almost every one of those diminishing attributes, and yet here they were again, reemerging one by one. "I would offer you tea," she said, as though anxious to cover any patches of silence, "but John's forgot the bottle of gas again, I'm afraid. I won't be able to boil any water until he brings home another one. But why don't I show you to the sitting room. Then I can fix us another sort of drink," she suggested, reaching for my suitcase.

I stopped her, insisting that she let me carry it, fearful that she would buckle under its weight. I looked at her shoulders as she turned, the thin material of her robe doing nothing to hide the two jagged points underneath. I took in the sharp hollows of her cheeks, the bony elbows, the way her hands seemed to shake, almost imperceptibly, but still there.

"I can't quite believe how long it's been," I said, following her down the hallway. As we walked, I noted that almost every inch of the apartment was filled, so that it was nearly impossible to walk without tripping over the leg of a chair or the pouf of a cushion. Not even the walls were safe, I soon discovered, as on top of the layers of paint sat an additional one made up of various bric-a-brac. Plates seemed to be of a particular fascination, I noted. Silver, copper, china, some of them painted, some of them bare — there seemed to be no real pattern that I could decipher, row upon row of them affixed to the brightly colored walls.

"I know," she replied at last. "Bennington feels like a lifetime ago."

We moved into the sitting room, and I placed my suitcase down beside my feet, onto the carpet. A few seconds passed, both of us looking around the room, as if the way to reconnect, to find our way back to each other again, to that time, was hiding somewhere in its crevices, in the foreign city of Tangier.

"I'll just go and fetch us those drinks," she said, making her way determinedly to the edge of the room.

"Thank you, Alice." I reached out my hand to touch hers. At my gesture, she flinched, the small movement pressing against my skin. "Alice, are you sure everything is all right?" I asked, my voice dropping to a whisper.

At first, she would not look at me, but then slowly she lifted her thin, hollowed face, her eyes still shining and bright. "Of course, Lucy." She moved quickly away, back toward the hallway. "Everything is wonderful."

Later, I reflected on the fact that she had not mentioned the accident.

But then, neither had I.

I spent several moments in the bathroom, a towel pressed against my face, willing the color to disappear from my cheeks. When I emerged, my hair still matted to my face with sweat, I discovered a stack of pink, overly starched towels in front of the door, a few scalloped soaps sitting on top, and the sound of Alice, singing from the kitchen.

I left the towels, following the lyrics and smiling to myself as I walked through the hallway, my hands attempting to push my hair back into place. She was singing a song I recognized from the radio. The girls in my most recent boardinghouse had gone in together on a cream-and-gold-colored Silvertone, at first taking turns keeping it in their respective rooms, more to show it off than anything else, until it had at last ended up downstairs, largely forgotten, becoming a permanent fixture of the common area.

I hummed the melody. "I see you haven't improved your singing," I teased, my voice raised just a note or two, so that she could hear me more easily.

A sound of laughter escaped from the kitchen — no longer quite as hesitant, I noted. "Go ahead, take a seat. I'll be there in just a moment."

I returned to the sitting room, taking it in for the first time. Similar to the other rooms, it too was composed of dark woods and leather — the sweet, sickly smell of which was overpowering in the late afternoon heat. A few dozen books lay scattered throughout the room. I glanced at one. Charles Dickens. Another was by a Russian author I had never heard of before. Alice, I knew, was not a big reader. I had tried to encourage her during our four years as roommates, but try as I might to interest her, she had only stuck up her nose. *They're all just so serious*, she had complained. I remembered thinking that I would have detested the comment had it been made by anyone else, but with Alice, the words were strangely fitting. The idea of her trapped behind a heavy book seemed somehow wrong — she was made of lightness and air, she was made, it seemed, for living, rather than reading about the experiences of other lives. I had told her this once, and in response, she had laughed and waved me away. But it was true. It was Alice who would wake me early in the morning, when it was still dark outside, dragging me to the Adirondack chairs on the Commons Lawn, blankets slipping from

34

her arms and onto the dewy grass, insistent that we be the first to see the sun rise. I would always marvel, in those quiet moments, watching as my breath billowed out in great white clouds, that we had found each other. That Alice's mother, an American who had later moved across the pond and married a Brit, had been a graduate of our tiny Vermont college, which had, in turn, prompted Alice to attend her mother's alma mater, in her memory. That Alice had somehow managed, with her tentative smile, to pull me from the comfort of my hiding spot in the library, had exhumed me from the voices of the dead and thrust me into the world of the living. Pulling the blanket tighter, I would shift closer to the warmth of her body, willing those moments to last forever, knowing that they could not.

I ran my finger over the pages of a few books, noting, curiously, that the pages were still uncut. A portrait of the man Alice had married began to form in my mind.

"Were you surprised to see me standing outside your doorstep this morning?" I called out, settling onto the leather sofa, where almost immediately my skin began to sweat.

There was only silence from the kitchen.

"Alice?" I called again, frowning. I squirmed from side to side, trying to alternatively air out the parts of my skin in contact with the leather, hoping the sweat wouldn't stain my new dress. The air in Tangier, I had already begun to notice, moved slowly and without any real insistence. It seemed to hang: thick and humid.

*Languid.* That would be the right word to describe it, I decided.

"Oh, yes," she said, her voice muffled, sounding as if she were somewhere far away, and not simply in the next room. "Yes, quite."

Before I could ask anything more, I heard the turning of the doorknob from the foyer. "Alice?" a voice called out, deeper, somehow, than what I had imagined. "Are you home?" And then, somewhat more quietly, "I don't suppose you made it to the market today?"

Looking back, I'm quite certain that, in that exact moment, my heart stopped.

It often did, of course. A slight murmur, nothing to worry about — at least, according to the doctors. It didn't really affect anything, they assured me, except that there were moments, only once in a great while, when my heart refused to beat in rhythm. When it acted up — or out, I supposed — stopping for the smallest second, perhaps less than that, but long enough so that the next beat felt like a resounding thud inside my chest. Like something trying to trample me or push me underfoot. I could have reimagined it over the years, of course — my memories altered and changed by what eventually transpired — but I'm almost certain my heart skipped then. Perhaps in warning, perhaps sensing danger. There is no way to ever really know, but I believe my heart was trying to tell me something: to warn me of the man slowly making his way through the hallway and into the room where I sat.

I sometimes wondered what would have happened if I had listened.

★ ★ ★

A man stepped into view.

I took in the tanned face, splattered with freckles, the golden hair that was styled into a sweeping wave. He looked, I thought, like most men our age: vivacious, eager, not yet dulled by the monotony of everyday life. He was handsome, that much I could ascertain. And yet, while I suspected that his features would have been classically pleasing to some, I found them overbearing and difficult to look at for any great length of time. There was something else there too I could already see — something harder, more concrete. But then, I brushed the thought aside, reasoning that perhaps it was just the imposing line of his suit. Though I knew little about men's fashion, I could tell that his clothes were expensive. He wore a three-piece suit cut from a textured pattern that looked entirely out of place in Tangier and a tan fedora with a narrow brim resting atop his head. He seemed, I noticed with a touch of envy, unfazed wearing the heavy material in the unforgiving heat of Morocco.

"We have a visitor," Alice called out, in a strange tone. "It's Lucy." *Falsetto* — was that the right word? I wondered.

"Lucy?" he repeated, standing at the threshold of the room, a frown crossing his face.

"Lucy, darling. My friend from college." Alice let out a hollow laugh. "I've told you loads about her."

She hadn't, of course. I could tell from the start of confusion that clouded John's face when Alice first said my name. From the look of it, John had never heard of me at all.

"Any chance you made dinner tonight, Alice? I'm starving," John said, starting to remove his tie, a note of exhaustion evident in his voice. It was at that moment he noticed me: the stranger sitting on his couch. A flicker of annoyance flashed, but then he seemed to take in my figure — well dressed, reasonably attractive — and his features relaxed, growing into one of surprise, pleasure. "You must be the infamous Lucy, then." He smiled, smoothing out the tie in his hand and extending his other one. "It's so wonderful to meet you at last."

I offered my own hand, instantly regretting that it was so moist. "A pleasure to make your acquaintance."

He cocked his head to the side, his smile turning into something that resembled a smirk, though I suspected he imagined it to be charming. I could feel him reading the situation, trying to figure out if he knew me or, worse yet, was supposed to. He was waiting for my indication. I remained silent. A few seconds passed before he asked, "Thirsty at all?"

At that moment, Alice emerged from the kitchen. She was balancing a silver platter between her two hands, which I half rose to take from her, but then she was already setting it on the top of a wooden bar, tucked back into the corner of the room.

She had changed out of her housecoat from earlier and was wearing a daytime dress, despite the encroaching evening hour, of silk crepe, its full-hipped skirt suggesting that it was an older piece, though I didn't recognize it from our college days. But it was more than just her outfit that had changed, as she seemed strangely altered from the girl who had greeted me earlier. There was a giddiness about her; gone was the morose countenance of hours before, apparently shrugged off in the company of her *husband* — that word still catching somewhere in my throat. I watched as she moved to fill the glasses, her movements sharp, surreal, so that she seemed all at once incredibly fragile, and I found myself wondering whether she wouldn't shatter into a million pieces in front of us both.

"A visit from an old college friend, did you say?" John asked, addressing Alice. "This is quite the surprise." He reached out to take a drink from her proffered hand, the condensation from the chilled glass already beginning to drip down the sides. "I didn't know my Alice in Wonderland had any friends," he joked.

"Of course I have friends." Alice laughed, but I could see his comment had wounded her.

"Ice," he declared, raising his eyebrows. "Now I *know* this is a special occasion. We never have *chilled* martinis, Lucy," he said, the latter sounding like an accusation. I accepted my own drink from Alice. "I've been endeared to the idea of your presence already." He laughed, taking a greedy sip. "And speaking of your presence here, are you actually in Tangier, traveling on your own?" When I nodded, he smiled and asked, "Where from?"

"New York," I said, watching Alice's face.

He frowned. "And doesn't your fellow mind? Your traveling alone, I mean?"

My smile stretched tightly across my face. "I'm afraid I haven't one to mind."

Alice looked away at my easy admission, while John leaned forward, ready, or so it seemed, to seize upon the idea. "No fellow? None at all?"

I sighed. "I'm afraid not."

"Aren't there any left? Surely the war didn't do away with them all — or perhaps they're too frightened of you?" he asked with another laugh.

I saw Alice flinch. "Don't be awful, John," she murmured.

"I'm only trying to get to the bottom of this, that's all," he said, making a great show of scratching his chin. "To be single in the city of New York — the pictures would make you think it's impossible. And, well, look at her," he said, indicating in my direction. "I simply don't buy it." He leaned forward. "Perhaps you're too picky. Is that it? Or perhaps there's something else," he continued, a jeering tone entering his voice. "I've heard stories about you Bennington girls."

Alice flushed. "Oh, leave it, John."

"Well, anyway," John said, his voice light and jovial, though his smile, I noticed, did not quite extend to his eyes. "You're here now. Perhaps we can find you an interesting suitor in Tangier. Lord knows we've got enough of them. Though, of course," he said, shaking his head, "I'm not sure any of them have that on the mind at the moment. You've chosen an interesting time to come to Morocco."

I frowned. "What do you mean?"

"Haven't you heard?" he asked with a slight smirk, wriggling his eyebrows in what he seemed to intend as comedic effect. "The natives are getting restless, my dear."

"Oh, don't talk about it like that," Alice said, with a movement of her shoulders, as if she could draw herself further inward, away from the conversation.

"Like what?" John asked with mock innocence.

"Like that," she repeated, casting him a serious glance. "Like it isn't anything important."

He turned to me and gave a short laugh. "Sometimes I think Alice fancies she understands the plight of the locals better than any of us," he said, with a teasing voice, "even though she rarely leaves the house and never interacts with another person outside of myself."

"That isn't true," she protested.

"Not entirely, I suppose," he conceded. "Still, you're too sensitive about the whole thing."

I noticed the strained look that had settled over Alice's features. "Restless for what, exactly?" I asked, though I already had a vague idea, based upon the various newspapers that had passed under my eyes over the last fortnight or so.

"For independence," John responded, his eyes narrowing as he spoke. "They're tired of belonging to someone else, and I don't blame them, not at all. But it means the French are everywhere these days. Protecting their interests up until the very end. Their forces have only grown since the unrest first began, when they ousted Mohammed two years back. Of course, this is Tangier, so it's all a bit different. Or it's supposed to be, at any rate. Still, they're here, if you look closely enough. It almost looks like they are clinging to the hope that somehow things will revert back to their favor, what with their little spies running around everywhere."

"Spies?" I asked.

"Oh, stop it," Alice said, sipping at her drink. I noticed that her hand shook slightly. "John sometimes likes to pretend he's in a spy novel, I think. He's always convinced that someone is watching him, French or otherwise. Pay him absolutely no attention, please. You're perfectly safe here, Lucy." She stopped. "Well, as safe as anyone can be in Morocco, I suppose."

I had a sudden image of John lurking in unlit passageways, of Alice being watched, stalked, by her own husband, like some sort of damsel in distress, John cast as the villain of the film. I did my best to suppress a shiver.

"She's not French, she'll be fine," John said, waving his hand dismissively, breaking the spell. "I don't think she has to worry that any weapons being concealed beneath djellabas are intended for her. Well, not the sort reserved for the French at any rate."

I felt myself blush, felt tiny pinpricks of anger, of resentment, hot against my skin.

"But then, surely it *is* a sensitive subject?" I pressed, referring to John's previous slight at Alice. And before I could think better of it, before I could stop myself, I said, "We are talking about the oppressor and the oppressed, aren't we? What topic could be more sensitive than that?"

At my words, there was something mean that flashed there, in his sharp little eyes, so that I wondered what it was that he would say in response to my comment. But then it was gone, vanished, before I could fully say whether I had truly seen it to begin with. "Ah," he said. "I see it now. You're one of *those* women."

I held my face intentionally still. "Those women?"

"You know, *those* women," he said, taking a loud sip from his drink. "Out of the kitchen, and all that."

"John, don't," Alice said, looking miserable. Her voice was tight and strained, her face paled a shade or two.

"Don't what?" He laughed. "I'm just making an observation, that's all."

"Yes, well," I said, pausing to take a drink now myself. "I suppose your observation is correct. I am one of *those* women — out of the kitchen and all that." I smiled, refusing to cower.

"Ah," John cried, giving his leg a quick slap. "You see?" he asked, turning to Alice. "I was right."

"Yes," she responded, not meeting his eye.

I leaned forward. "So it's really happening, then?" I asked, anxious to leave the subject behind. "Independence, I mean."

John nodded, apparently content, or so it seemed, to move on as well. "Oh, yes. It's all been agreed already — the whole thing's been set in motion. The French have already relinquished their hold on Morocco, which means the Spanish aren't far behind. Tangier will most likely be next. It's a good thing, as I said before. Independence is always good. But I suspect we're all running on borrowed time here, as it were. Ticktock." He took another sip of his drink. "Things will change for those of us who decide to stay behind."

I frowned. "How so?"

He paused, looking at me as though he hadn't quite understood the question. And then, with another slap on his knee, he exclaimed: "Well, that's the question, isn't it?"

I nodded, taken aback. "Yes, I suppose it is."

We lapsed into silence then, the three of us staring into our drinks, leaving me to wonder how this could be the man who had stolen Alice's heart. I thought of the past, of all the plans that we had made, and wondered how it was possible that they had been exchanged for this, for *him*, though of course I knew it wasn't as simple as that.

"So," John's voice rang out, startling us all out of our reveries. "Just how long is Lucy here for?"

"I haven't quite decided," I responded.

He nodded. "But what brings you to Tangier, of all places?"

"Travel, of course," Alice answered quickly — too quickly, I couldn't help but think. "Perhaps you could provide Lucy with some recommendations," she said to John. She turned and looked at me, and I couldn't help but be reminded of a tennis match, with that dizzying back-and-forth motion that always made my head ache. "If you wanted to see anything other than Tangier."

I nodded but didn't respond. Instead I found myself preoccupied with the idea that she had mentioned it — the possibility of other cities — only in order to get me out of the apartment, away from herself and John. Though to what end, I was uncertain.

"I prefer Tangier myself," John said, though his interest seemed more directed toward the drink in his hand, which had since been refilled, although Alice and I remained on our first. "Most people will say Marrakech is the spot you should go to. Really, though, I don't like it much myself past three or four nights. And you can't stand even that, can you?" he asked without turning, though his question was obviously directed to Alice. "Chefchaouen is always worth a few days, and so is Casablanca, I suppose. I know a few who would swear that Fez is the best out of them all. The roadblocks can be a bit tiresome, of course, but once you show your papers, there's never any trouble," John continued. He paused, looking at me with a peculiar expression. "Are you really interested in any of this?"

"Of course," I responded, though I wasn't, not really. I had no intention of leaving Tangier anytime soon. My eyes moved between the two of them, the pair of them, and I decided that something was most certainly amiss — I could feel it, for it seemed to fill the very room around us, crackling and sizzling, calling out to be noticed. Watching her from the corner of my eye, I could not help but think how *haunted* she looked — a strange word, I knew, and yet it was the only one that seemed to apply. She was haunted by the ghost of her former self. "I'll keep that in mind," I replied. "But I think I'll focus on Tangier for now."

"A wise decision." He nodded. "And where will you be staying, during your little holiday?"

I shifted, feeling, in that moment, Alice's gaze upon me. "I'm not quite sure yet."

"Well, then you'll have to stay with us. We can't have one of Alice's friends staying in some suspect *riad*, not when we have an extra room here." He gave Alice a slight shove. "Right, darling?"

Alice blinked, as though startled, as though she hadn't been listening to our conversation but had let her mind wander, far and away from the room in which the three of us now sat. "Yes," she said at last, though the word was soft, muted somehow. She stirred a bit, and then her voice came more firmly, more resolute as she said: "Yes, of course." She turned to me, though her gaze seemed somewhat averted, as if pointed somewhere just above my shoulder. "Lucy, you must stay with us. It would be silly not to."

"Yes." John nodded. "After all, the spare room is just going to waste at the moment. It's become a sort of holding room, for papers from my work and such." He turned to Alice, who had, I noted, gone a particular shade of red. "Though that wasn't the original intention."

I gathered what he meant, of course — and which was, I suspected, the point of him bringing it up at all, for me to understand, for her to be embarrassed — and I found that the thought, the very notion, made my stomach churn in a way that I couldn't quite describe. I thought perhaps Alice must feel similarly, for it was not embarrassment alone that seemed to color her face, but rather a strange combination of emotions — something that spoke of her inner turmoil in place of the actual words that seemed to fail her.

"That's very generous of you both," I replied, my voice louder than I intended, perhaps in an effort to quiet the unease that had settled within the room, creeping and claiming every corner of the space until it seemed that was all there was.

"It's settled, then," John said, swirling the ice in his cup. "Say, if you're really keen on remaining in Tangier, then we'll go and listen to some jazz. Maybe this weekend. We can stop into Dean's for a round first." Alice started to respond, but John quickly silenced her with a shake of his head. "Oh no, my dear. There is absolutely no way we can let your friend visit this city without a trip to Dean's. It would be sacrilegious, and you know it."

I tried to conjure up an image of Alice at a jazz club in Tangier, at a bar, even, but failed. She had never been a fan of the raucous, smoky dens that our fellow classmates had gravitated toward, both on campus and off. At the start, I had dragged her to a few, confident I would be able to locate at least one that would suit her, though in the end I had been forced to concede defeat. Instead, we had mixed drinks from the bottles we kept hidden in our closet, listened to records as we danced around our tiny room, using the woven rugs to propel ourselves across the wooden floor, before collapsing into a heap of hysterical laughter. I smiled at the memory. "I'm happy to go if Alice does," I said, nodding in her direction.

Alice seemed flustered by my words. "I suppose. Like John said, it's where everyone goes."

By then, the drink had loosened my tongue. It seemed that Alice still made drinks the way I remembered — with an excessive amount of gin — and I could feel it working, relaxing me, so that the words I would normally keep contained threatened to release themselves. "But what do *you* want, Alice?" I pressed, refusing to acknowledge the look of discomfort that spread across her face at my question.

"Alice doesn't like to make decisions," John interjected. He said it with a smile, but there was something spiteful there, just beneath his words. A tone I hadn't noticed before, something more than a simple chiding.

I felt that same flutter in my ear from earlier, but I ignored it, shaking my head slightly, as if to dislodge the strange feeling of fullness that had settled there. I wondered briefly whether some sort of desert bug had managed to crawl inside — I had read stories about that, of water having to be poured down one's ear while others waited with bated breath to see the evidence float upward, emerging from the ear canal and into daylight. I imagined myself in the same prostrate pose, John standing above me, sneering.

Alice, for her part, looked determined to ignore the comment. Already she was up off the sofa, insisting on yet another refill. I obeyed, offering my glass to her as I noted, somewhere in the back of my mind, that I couldn't remember the last time I'd had anything substantial to eat. That strange bread earlier in the day, and the day before that, a handful of crackers prior to the ferry, my stomach too nervous to handle anything else.

"It's not true," she said, sitting down beside me once again. Several minutes had elapsed since John's remark, and I could tell he was confused by her declaration. She pushed against him, sharply, with her shoulder. "It's not true," she said again, this time louder. "In fact, let's go to Dean's tonight." Alice smiled, though her voice trembled. "To welcome Lucy properly to Tangier."

I noted again the strangeness in her sudden cheerfulness — such a change from the stoic calmness she had exhibited earlier that morning. It was almost frantic, as if at any moment it could all go horribly wrong. I wondered then if it would, so close to the edge did Alice seem to be approaching as she smiled, the sound of her laughter empty and hollow as she moved about the room, refilling glasses and hurrying to fill the empty spaces that emerged in our conversation. It was all so different from the girl I had once known. But then, if our senior year at Bennington had taught me nothing else, I knew there was no such thing as an absolute. Everything changes, sooner or later. Time moves along, without constraints — no matter how hard one may attempt to pause, to alter, to rewrite it.

Quite simply, there is nothing to stop it, nothing at all.

# CHAPTER
# THREE

## ALICE

I had been wrong: about the past, about the closed box. Surely.

As we walked toward the bar — night having fallen fast and quick, so that my eyes searched and sought for safe ground — my heart thumped loudly in my chest, berating me for my hastily spoken declaration. I should not have risen to John's taunt — for that was what it was, I knew, his words intending to harm, to injure. I should have remained silent, just as I always did. But then he had made that comment about the spare bedroom. About our stalled attempts — which was my decision, my fault. And then, *she* had been there, staring at me with that same queer, inquisitive gaze she always had, and which was so intimately familiar and yet now somehow so utterly foreign, the year in between the last time we had seen each other and the things that had happened since spanning an ocean between us, so that my breath had caught in my throat.

Lucy Mason. For a moment, earlier that morning, I hadn't trusted my own eyes, my own mind, when I first saw her. But it was her, standing on the doorstep of my flat in Tangier, the look on her face closing the distance, dispelling the darkness of that night, the fog threatening to retreat so that I was once again reminded of how entirely I knew her, how entirely familiar she was to me, so that it seemed at times as if we were one and the same person. And yet — and yet, there was always that strange sense of how little I actually knew her when it came down to facts and truths.

I thought of the few works of Shakespeare I knew and the line that frequently rattled in my brain — what's past is prologue.

And there she was: my past, made corporeal, made tangible, or whatever other fancy words I was certain she would use to describe it. Lucy Mason. I had started, grabbing the old housecoat that I had only just shed, my intentions for the day already forgotten, and headed for the door. And as I did so, all I could do was think of that collar from the day before, that stupid, awful little tear and what it seemed to mean, what it seemed to predict. Wasn't there a smarter word for it? I struggled to recall it then, under the heavy gaze of my former roommate — no, that wasn't an accurate description — of my once friend, the closest friend that I had ever known before it had all gone wrong.

We stood together in the front hall, and I remembered, in the space of our silence, the last words I had spoken to her that night. I had told her . . . no, I had shouted — the first time I could ever remember raising my voice to her — something awful, something wretched, something about wishing she would disappear, wishing I would never see her again. And then I remembered what had happened afterward, what I had

**51**

thought, what I had said — though not to her, not to Lucy, who had disappeared long before I regained consciousness.

I felt my cheeks go warm, felt her eyes watching me — certain, in that moment, that she knew precisely what I was thinking about.

She was different from what I remembered — although at first I was not sure how, my eyes searching her for any clue. Anything that would tell me why she was here, after all that had transpired between us. She was thinner, her features sharper, more defined. She was, I realized, more beautiful than I remembered — but there was still that strange quality, that penetrating gaze that made me blush and look away and that made me love her and hate her all at once.

I cleared my throat. "Lucy." Her name escaped me like a declaration, a single word that held so much meaning, and yet nothing at all. I had never, not once in the many moments that had occurred between the Green Mountains of Vermont and the dusty alleyways of Morocco, expected to see her again. Not after what had happened. Not after what I had said and all the questions I still had — about what she had done, about what I had only imagined. My heart began to pound.

I had stared into her face and wondered — for one mad moment — if, somehow, I had summoned her, if somehow, from across the Atlantic, despite my lingering mistrust, my anger, she had managed to feel my unhappiness, my desperation, and materialized in front of me, a genie I had unwillingly conjured up. I had looked at her, the early morning heat of Tangier beginning to pulse around us — a safety and a danger all at once, just like her. My knight in shining armor, always. I felt the truth of it, heavy against my chest.

I pushed through the door, into Dean's. *It was Tangier.* That was my first thought upon entering, the bar a strange mix of anyone and everyone. Locals, foreigners — French, Moroccan, and beyond — suits and ties, their more casual counterparts. It seemed that everyone flocked to this small, dingy bar, no matter who they were or where they were from. The noise was overwhelming. A loud sonic boom of voices shouting over one another, a cacophony of raucous laughter, the kind that grated and thrilled. I watched a man fall onto the ground, his face red with laughter and drink. His companion, a woman in a sleek black dress and large, glittering diamond earrings, threw back her head and let out what I could only think of as a barking noise, though I realized soon enough that it was meant to be a laugh. We moved farther into the belly of the place, and I felt the stickiness of one too many spilled drinks underneath my feet.

"I'll get us some drinks," John shouted, heading to the bar without bothering to ask what we wanted first.

There were few stools left at that late hour, at least placed together, though after several minutes of searching we managed to find a space toward the back, hidden away in the corner. When John appeared moments later, drinks in hand, he stared down, frowning. "Did you want to sit somewhere else?" I asked, suspecting — no, *knowing* — that John would want to be more in the center of it all. It was one of many things I had learned about him during our time together in Tangier: his enduring need to be in the spotlight, to be noticed by those around him. Or no, perhaps not *need*, perhaps that was too cruel, too calculating a word. It was simply what happened. Wherever John went, heads seemed to turn, gazes seemed to linger. It was the natural order of things, so that he began to expect it, so that even I considered it to be part of everyday life. And I had felt it too once, that strange pull toward him, the one that had led me to Tangier, to Dean's, to this particular moment in time, my past and present flanking me on either side as I sipped on a lukewarm gin.

In that moment, I wanted to rebel. To punish him for the way he was so obviously trying to punish me. John had resented my decision to come out — for the simple reason that it had not been his own, I suspected — grumbling about the long hours he had worked that day. "But who is she, even?" he had pressed, his eyes searching mine in the reflection of the bathroom mirror. "I'm quite sure I've never even heard you mention her name before today." By the time he had done a quick toilette, layering his hair carefully with cream — the powerful scent causing my stomach to turn — and we had left the apartment at last, his mood had shifted, the alcohol turning him sullen and petulant, though he attempted to hide it behind a large grin.

And throughout it all, I could feel her. Lucy. Sitting beside me, eyes peering through the darkness, watching

John, watching everything, just as she always did. She had only been in Tangier for the space of a few hours, but I could already feel that same effect she always had over me: strengthening and emboldening me, her presence serving as an armor I could somehow never manage to affix on my own.

John grabbed one of the stools. "This is fine," he said, his voice a bit harder than before. He swirled the amber liquid in his glass, its scent like smoke and dust and something ancient. "Well, what do you think?" he asked, turning to Lucy, sweeping his hand around him. "It's not much, but it attracts quite the crowd."

Lucy nodded but made no response. I did my best to smile, a sour taste on the edge of my tongue. There was silence, and I could feel the tension — thick, like the Moroccan air — huddling around us.

"So, Lucy Mason from America." John smiled. "What is it that you do exactly, out there in the real world, I mean?"

"I type manuscripts," she answered. "For a publishing company."

He nodded, though his expression was dull, as though he wasn't listening, not really, so that I suspected the real reason he had asked was only so that she would do the same. For while John had never been entirely forthcoming about his work to others, not even to me, he seemed to take pleasure in throwing around vague allusions, referencing the government, the insinuation that being in Tangier, at this particular moment, was affording him the chance to prove himself to his superiors. *The opportunity*, he had said to me, and various others, on more than one occasion, though he never actually bothered to explain what it was actually an opportunity *for*, and I, in turn, had never bothered to inquire.

I could see him now, waiting for Lucy to ask, for the chance to begin his monologue, but she only smiled and hastened to continue: "Yes, though it isn't the only job that I have." She took a gulp of her drink. "I'm also a writer."

His eyebrows raised in surprise, and I could see him casting aside his feigned interest. "Really?"

"Of sorts," she replied.

John looked at her with curiosity. "'A writer, of sorts,'" he repeated. "And what does that mean exactly?"

She hesitated, and I wondered then whether her initial declaration was as grand as she had made it seem, both hoping and dreading that it was. I knew it was wrong, that it only made me small and petty, but I felt sad, slightly resentful even, at the idea that she might have fulfilled the promises we had once made to each other, while I had — what? — become the opposite of the idea I had envisioned.

"I write obituaries for a local newspaper," she replied. I saw a flicker in John's eyes, a note of disappointment, and I saw Lucy stiffen in response. Her voice was tight as she continued: "There's a good deal of research involved, actually. A number of interviews have to be conducted, for background information, for quotes. It's no different from any other story that's printed in the newspaper." I could hear the defensiveness in her tone, could see that John had noted it as well. Lucy turned to me and smiled. "But what about you, Alice?" she asked. "Are you still working on your photographs?"

John frowned. "Photographs?"

I felt myself blush. I had never told John much about Bennington, about the accident — only what any of the newspapers had reported. Instead I had pushed away everything to do with my former life, including Lucy, and the camera that I had once considered my most prized possession and now sat, unused, the shutter release most likely rusted from disuse. Still, it had been among the few possessions that I had brought along with me to Tangier — a great *what if* rattling somewhere at the back of my mind. And while I hadn't yet released it from the depths of my suitcase, in the back of our bedroom's wardrobe, I sometimes thought I could feel its presence as I walked past, so that more than once I had hurried my footsteps in response.

"Yes," Lucy said. "Alice was quite the photographer at Bennington. I'm surprised you didn't know."

He raised his eyebrows. "Is that right?" He gave a soft laugh. "Well. My Alice is full of surprises tonight."

There was an edge to his voice. He was being cruel, I knew, most likely annoyed that this new piece of information, about his wife, his Alice, was being relayed by a complete stranger. I felt the knowledge of it pressing in, assaulting me from all sides, so that in that moment, I wanted nothing more than to have it out with him — something, a confrontation, perhaps — to complete what the two of us had started earlier in the night, with his jokes about my lack of friends, lack of fertility, a sparring that had seemed to blossom, to thrive during our first few months in Tangier so that now, at times, it felt as though it was all that was between us. I could feel the need, the desire for it starting to spill out of my pores. I wiped the sweat from my brow, trying to cool myself. It was suddenly too warm in the bar, too stifling, so that when I took a deep breath my lungs seemed to stop short, give way, refusing me that last refreshing, comforting breath. I could feel my cheeks start to warm and hoped that it was not visible.

"So why bother with a place like Bennington?" John asked, turning back to Lucy, his voice light, deceptively casual. "Surely you didn't need to in order to write a few snippets for a rag? That's an expensive school, from what I understand."

"I was on scholarship," Lucy replied.

As she said the words, I realized that was what he had wanted to know all along, what he had been digging for in the first place, with his questions about her profession, about her love life — the origins of this American girl that he had never heard of before. He had been wondering, I realized, whether Lucy Mason was worth knowing.

And now, it seemed, he had his answer.

He shrugged. "Still, even with the money."

Lucy fixed him with a smile. "Actually," she said, "I have always loved literature. That's why I decided to go to Bennington." She finished her gin in one final gulp and leaned close to him. "Have you ever read the Brontës, John?"

I stopped, glancing up from my drink, hearing the shift before I saw it, written just there, on her face. A quick look at John told me that he had not noticed it — but then, he did not know her as I did. Did not know that this was *her*, the Lucy that I remembered. Not the polite, perfect houseguest who had sat on our sofa trading banter over cocktails. This was the Lucy who spoke her mind, who knew what she wanted and took it.

John, still unaware, shook his head — though he was, I could see, unsettled by the question, the unexpected turn in the conversation. "No, I haven't."

She affected surprise. "What, never?"

He gave her a tense smile. "Never."

I became aware, in that moment, of my silence, of the fact that the conversation between them seemed to exclude me entirely. And yet I did not stir. Instead I only sat, watching them both: the narrowing of the eyes, the tilting of the head, the mistrust, no, *distrust*, that was already growing between them. I thought I could hear it. In my mind I saw them circling each other, slowly, testing out the boundaries that separated them.

"Not even a little of Jane?" Lucy was laughing, though the sound was sharp, jagged. "Heathcliff and Cathy, I can understand. They can be difficult even for the most ardent of admirers. Perhaps that's why Emily only ever published one novel?" She swallowed her gin. "Do you know, I once had a teacher in secondary school who absolutely hated *Wuthering Heights*. Called it the worst book in British literature, in fact. So

I can understand the aversion, the hesitation. But Jane? Sweet, orphaned Jane? You really haven't read it at all? Not even a sentence?"

His smile grew wider, the expression stretched tightly against his face, so that it fitted as though some sort of grotesque mask. "Not even one goddamn word."

She knew about the books, I realized then. Somehow, in the way that she always did, she knew that they were only for show, that they were only part of the carefully curated image John worked to display — nothing more. I supposed that I should be mad, that I should feel resentment for her then, for baiting the man that I had promised to stand by for all the rest of my days, for the way she had so carelessly stepped back into my life, as if Vermont and what had happened there were of no real consequence. I could feel it — the anger that should have been mine, hovering in the air around us, snapping questions and demanding answers, and yet, I could not reach for it, could not manage to claim it as my own. Instead I focused only on the bend that they, John and Lucy, were driving toward, dangerously, recklessly. I knew that were they to take the curve, there would be no turning back. I leaned in and said anxiously, longing for the comfort of the apartment and the safety it promised: "John has never been much of a reader."

It was, I quickly realized, the wrong thing to say.

"You both make it sound as though I'm illiterate." John frowned. "Just because I don't fawn over these Brontës," he said, pronouncing it Bron-tay.

"Brontë," I corrected him, without thinking.

John was silent, quickly finishing the rest of his drink and setting his glass onto the table with more force than necessary. I gave a little jump, though Lucy, I noticed, managed to remain still. "I've just seen Charlie at the bar," he said, abruptly. "I'll be back in a moment." Before I could respond, he had grabbed his empty glass and disappeared.

A few minutes of silence passed. "He struggled in school," I finally offered.

Lucy nodded, her face closed. "I'm just off to the toilets." She slid from her seat. "I won't be long."

She smiled, moving, for one moment, as if to touch me. But then she stopped and, turning, her eyes averted from mine, disappeared into the swelling crowd that surrounded us.

In their absence, I felt unmoored, untethered, so that my hands grasped the wooden table beneath me in a desperate attempt to find an anchor. I felt something brush against my leg then and I jumped, though looking down I could see that it was only one of the city's many stray dogs, wandered in off the streets. During my first days in Tangier, John had cautioned me that I could not be afraid, that I could not display my fear to the poor beasts, that it would only incite them further. I remembered walking with him along the port early one morning, passing by one dog after another as they lay, stretched out on the hot, unforgiving pavement beneath them. At the sound of our footsteps, they had raised their heads, their bodies braced, and I had retreated farther into John, despite his rebuke, fearing that one of the dogs would lunge, would bite, and I'd be stricken with rabies. In that moment, I had been petrified, but John had only pushed me away, whispering that it was for my own good.

Now, the dog sank to its haunches, finding comfort against the warmth of my legs. And I let him, grateful to no longer be alone.

I had met Lucy Mason on my first day at Bennington.

She was standing in our room, her single suitcase already situated at the bottom of the bed closest to the window, her eyes taking in the barren walls that surrounded her. I had paused in the doorway, quietly observing the girl I would be living with for the next year. And yet, *girl*, I thought, standing there, examining her, struck me as somehow wrong. I watched as she reached into the pocket of her jacket, pulling out a packet of cigarettes and a lighter. I had never smoked before, not even once, and I watched, fascinated, as plumes of smoke enveloped her, spreading throughout our room, as if hungry to mark the corners of it, to claim it.

Although we were both just seventeen, there was something about the stranger standing before me that seemed infinitely older — wiser perhaps — than myself. The difference was evident even in our clothing. I looked down at my dress, suddenly embarrassed by what seemed a childish frock, covered as it was with a pattern of flowers and ivy and reaching to the floor in a ballerina-inspired cut. In contrast, my new roommate wore a dark, emerald-green jacket with a peplum waistline, accentuating her enviable hourglass figure, paired with a slim black skirt. And while neither the jacket nor the skirt looked particularly new — there was a strange weariness about both of them, I thought, as if the owner had worn them once too often — she emitted a sophistication that I had only before seen in the pages of magazines.

I entered slowly, sounding a soft knock against the door. She looked up, fixing me with a thoughtful gaze that I could not read, but that caused me to turn away and blush.

"Hello," I murmured, placing a timid smile on my face.

She stared back, blinking.

"I'm Alice," I said, realizing too late that it looked as though I was waiting for an invitation to enter. I quickly closed the distance between us. "I was afraid you might have forgotten," I said, extending my free hand.

She accepted it, with a slight tilt of her head. "I'm Lucy."

There were no gloves on her own hands, I noticed, silently chiding myself for selecting the lacy ones that my aunt had purchased in anticipation of my matriculation to Bennington. They seemed somehow wrong, in the bareness of the room and against the plainness of my roommate. She wore no makeup, so that I felt foolish with my pink lips and wing tip eyes, like a little girl caught playing dress-up in her mother's clothes.

Lucy glanced behind me, in the direction of the door. "Are your parents with you?"

I looked down. "No, they're not," I said, taking a deep breath. It was a line that I had rehearsed in the bathroom mirror of my aunt's house countless times over the summer. I knew the question would eventually be broached, it always was, though I had since schooled myself on how to make the answer appear casual — or as casual as it could ever be. I was tired of the typical reaction: the scrunching of the nose, the furrowing of the brow, that expression that conveyed pity and yet something more as well. A fear. As if my parents' death was something that was catching and I, the sole survivor, a contaminant that threatened them. I had seen it happen, had experienced it firsthand. At school, they had all huddled around me at first, their bodies pressed against my own, conveying regret and sadness, hugging me tight with assurances that it would all be fine, that we would survive this together. But then a week passed, and then two, and one girl was gone and then another. Soon, their closeness was replaced with small, tight smiles as we passed by one another in the hallway, or a brief wave from across the grounds. By the time that school let out, their relief was palpable, surging underneath every interaction. I was not surprised when the phone calls and visits died away. By the time my bags were packed for college, not a single one of them was to be found. And so, I said the words again, bracing for the worst, expecting it. I imagined the reaction I would receive — a downward tug of the lips, a brief yet awkward hug, and then my roommate would move on, searching among the countless other

**64**

girls, looking for one that was not already damaged, tainted, marred by tragedy.

But then she only looked at me from beneath her heavy-lidded eyes and said: "Mine have passed away as well."

I blinked, startled, unprepared for such a possibility. And though I supposed it should have pained me, in that moment, I felt nothing but joy. Sheer and utter relief flooded through me, and it was all I could do to keep from smiling. I told her this, later, hours after we had known one another and had already marked each other as fast friends. She had produced a stolen bottle of sherry — "My aunt will never notice," she had assured me, referring to the relatives she had stayed with over the summer — and together we had set off to explore, passing the bottle of strange, burning liquid between us as we walked. I listened as our feet crunched against fallen leaves and branches, the sound seeming to stretch out and across to the trees that encroached upon us on either side. It was already mid-September. Bennington had a later start date than most colleges, and as we made our way across campus, the night already setting in, fast and dark, a cool breeze stole across so that we moved toward each other, instinctively, as if we were already a pair. As we walked I could feel my tongue loosening, could feel my stomach sound in hunger — most of the other girls would be at dinner, I knew, but I didn't mind, the newness of the relationship between us more important than a hot meal. The wall that had been erected upon my parents' death, like some great impenetrable

**65**

perimeter, at last began to yield, tempered by the alcohol, by Lucy's presence.

"How old were you?" I asked, tentatively, unsure whether her wounds were still fresh like mine, or even whether she would want to talk about it at all, recent or not.

"Five years old," she replied, that same nonchalant tone lacing her words, so that I found myself hoping I would one day be able to answer such questions in a similar tenor, that my voice would not shake and quiver as it fought to pronounce each word, to form sentences that conveyed who my parents had been and just how much I had lost with their deaths. "I don't really remember my father anymore, he's more of just a hazy impression — a suggestion, really," she continued, whispering. "I know he worked at a garage, but beyond that, I don't remember anything much about him. But my mother — sometimes I think I can remember everything about her, even the little things. Like a tube of lipstick, honey colored. Or the strange little glass bottle of perfume that she used to keep on her vanity — it was brown glass, with a clear top." She shifted. "Anyway, I try not to think of her anymore."

She stopped then, and I could feel the curls of her hair, so close, tickling my face.

"Does that work?" I asked.

"Sometimes." I could feel her shrug. "It's harder in the morning."

I knew what she meant. "Sometimes I forget," I said. "I wake up in the morning and it's like my mind has completely reset. And then I remember, and I have to live through it all over again."

She nodded, but I could see that something else had pulled at her attention.

"Look," she whispered.

Jennings Hall, the mansion that sat just beyond the main campus, unfolded before us. The college's very own Gothic story, made real. There were always whispers about mysterious footsteps, ghostly voices, and strange noises that could never be accounted for, stories about various hauntings that had occurred over the years since it had been donated to the college. Perhaps it was only the sherry, but I was struck in that moment with how ridiculous a notion the idea actually was. Its outside was covered almost entirely by ivy, which had turned a blazing autumnal red in the weather, highlighted further still by the setting sun. It was beautiful, I thought, the walk through the forest more frightening than anything the building in front of us seemed to promise.

And so when Lucy tilted her head toward the entrance, a silent invitation between us, I took a quick, deep breath and followed.

"Is this what your home is like, in England?" she asked, turning toward me as we made our way into the hallway, a queer expression on her face.

I frowned, wondering exactly what type of image Lucy had managed to sketch from the letters we had exchanged. Aunt Maude was well-off, that much was true, but she had lived alone prior to my parents' death — a spinster, they might have called her only a few years before — and had not seen any reason to change things when her niece had unexpectedly arrived. "No," I said, with a slight shake of my head, "there's only just the two of us." I looked around at the vast emptiness of the hallway. There was little in the way of furniture, and our voices echoed as we moved across the marble-tiled floor. "We wouldn't know what to do with this much space."

Lucy, I thought, looked vaguely disappointed at my words. I waited, then, for her to say something about the place she had grown up in, but she remained silent.

"Look at this," she exclaimed. She crouched so that she sat half-hunched, balancing on the balls of her feet, only inches from the object of her excitement: two stone lions that sat side by side in the large, and apparently unused, fireplace. Reaching out her hand, she let it rest on the carving's head.

I felt uneasy, in the quiet of the house, conscious that we were not meant to be there but rather, should be dining with the other girls from our house.

"Don't, Lucy," I pleaded, looking around me, as if expecting someone to materialize and tell us off for not following the rules. "We're not supposed to even be in here."

She looked up, a smile forming in the corner of her lips. "Relax, Alice. Nothing will happen." But her hand remained on the lion, and I was struck by the conviction that this strange little demonstration of defiance was for my benefit — to prove that she was a girl who could not be told what to do, that *she* was not afraid.

A shiver passed through me, and I clutched my cardigan tightly to my body. Without the heat of the sun, the sweat that had slipped down my back only moments earlier had grown cold, and my skin rose in goose pimples as I fought to keep warm.

Lucy stood. "You should have said that you were cold," she said, pulling me closer, enveloping me in a strange embrace.

My aunt Maude was not one for affection, and during my time with her, my life had turned into something solitary and cold. I had missed it at first, those small displays of intimacy, so that even when a stranger would walk by and accidentally brush against me, it was enough so that I could feel their touch for the remainder of the day, burning me, marking me, where we had collided. But now I struggled to relax, and when Lucy finally moved away, I could feel the space where she had just been, humming, vibrating, there in the air before me.

She looked down at the lions. "It's odd, but they remind me of a pet I once had as a child. A dog named Tippy." The smile left her face then. "He was a complete surprise, especially if you knew my mother. She detested animals. She used to cringe at the idea of actually owning one. But then, one day, there he was. I guess a neighbor's dog had had puppies and he was the final one, the runt they couldn't manage to sell, let alone give away for free. He was small. White and tan. Not really a puppy any longer, since they had been trying for so long to get rid of him." She stopped, taking a breath. Her eyes remained fixed on the statue, refusing to meet my own. "I remember taking him in my arms, promising to take care of him. My mother just watched from the corner." A small laugh. "You should have seen her face."

"When did he die?" I asked, my voice little more than a whisper.

"Not long after we first got him."

Something in the distance crashed, and I jumped. I looked back toward Lucy, but if she had heard the noise, she did not betray it. She remained still, implacable, staring at the lion, at the empty fire grate. "What happened?" I asked.

"He was hit by a car," she replied. "No one knows exactly how he got out, but suddenly he was off, running toward the main street." She paused. "The impact should have killed him instantly, but it didn't."

I shuddered, imagining the injured dog, suspended somewhere between life and death, imagining the pain. "Didn't you take him somewhere? For help, I mean?" My voice, I knew, was pleading, but in that moment, standing in the cold, drafty mansion, I felt suddenly that I needed nothing so much as for Lucy to tell me that they had, that, yes, the dog had been saved, that it had lived, that it was still living, and that everything was fine.

I knew, of course, that she wouldn't.

"My mother couldn't drive," she said.

"But what about the neighbors? Wasn't there someone you could call?" I felt frantic then, wanting to shake her, to wreck that stoic attitude, her shield and protection, I had already begun to suspect, from everyone around her. If nothing else, I wanted her to tell me that she had done everything that she could, that she had tried to save the life of this improbable dog that was never meant to be hers — that she had loved him fiercely enough for that.

Finally, she turned her face to mine, her black eyes searching. She smiled, a strange, unnerving expression that sent my heart stammering, anxious to be away from her, from this place. She opened her mouth: "There was no one."

I exhaled, slowly. "So what did you do?"

"We sat and waited for him to die." She stopped, seeming to weigh her next words. "And he did, eventually. But it was slow. And he was in terrible pain. And so my mother went out into the garden and found a rock. It would be quicker, she said. And kinder. And because he was mine, it was my responsibility and no one else's." She shook her head, turning away. "It was horrible, Alice," she concluded, her tone steely and hard.

I did not believe her. Raising my hand to my mouth — in shock, in doubt, I didn't know — I could not help but be struck by the thought that the story, her story, I reminded myself, had seemed strangely distant, as if it had happened to another person entirely. Her words had been slow and measured, she hadn't paused to catch her breath, to wipe away the tears from her eyes. It was as if the story had been cauterized, so that it no longer belonged to her at all, so that I did not believe her when she said it was horrible, did not believe her about any of it.

I thought of the way that she had spoken of her parents, of that detached expression I had envied. In that moment, it was no longer something that I was as eager to covet.

I stepped backward. "Let's go, Lucy."

Her eyes seemed to flash at the sound of her name, as if remembering where she was and who she was with. As if everything that had come before had been spoken in some sort of trance and only then had she awakened from it. "Not yet," she said, reaching for my hand. "There's one more thing I want to show you." Ignoring my protests, she turned us to the grand staircase, moving quickly, so that I had to increase my pace to keep up with her. "Hurry," she called back, as if reading my thoughts.

We continued to race upward until my breath came in short, ragged gasps, and my lungs began to burn. "Lucy," I panted, knowing that I would soon be unable to match her in speed.

"Just a little farther," she promised, not bothering to look back, still firmly holding my hand.

When she stopped — so abruptly that I nearly crashed into her — we stood in front of a window, wide and curved in a half circle. From our new vantage point, I could see that she had led us up to the mansion's top floor. Lucy moved her face closer to the window, her fingertips splayed out on either side of her, pressed firmly into the glass.

"The other girls say it's haunted. That a family died here," she whispered.

I frowned. "What family?"

"The Jenningses, the ones who first owned the house. They say the wife killed herself, that she threw herself out of this window, just here. And then the husband, out of grief, hung himself from one of the trees."

"That doesn't sound true," I replied, though I whispered the words. "I heard that the family donated this building to the college."

Lucy ignored my remark. "There was a student too, a few years ago. She threw herself from this same window, just like Mrs. Jennings."

I turned to look out the window, at the imprints of her fingertips, their individual etchings, pressed against the glass. I thought of the stories, of the women who had supposedly ended their lives here, one generation after another. And then all at once I felt it — something watching me, from somewhere within the dark recesses of the house. I turned to the left and then to the right, knowing that I had seen something, just out of reach of my vision. I thought at first that it might have been Lucy, but then I realized that she was gone. I was standing by the window alone, empty hallways stretching on either side of me, a half-dozen or so doorways down each corridor. I thought of the shadows, certain they were there, somewhere, lying in wait, so that I had the urge to fling open each and every door in order to prove there was nothing behind them.

And then I remembered. About what Lucy had told me, only moments before: how her parents died when she was five years old. I frowned. It didn't make her story impossible. Perhaps she truly did remember that horrible story from so young an age, and yet — *what*, I asked myself, what was it that had bothered me? I thought again of her detached manner, as if she were reciting a story that she had heard from someone else. I shook my head, feeling another breeze, a draft, I supposed, as it moved through the building. There was no reason for her to lie.

I heard something in the distance again, and my heart began to race. I could feel the familiarity of it, beginning in my fingertips. A nervous condition, the doctors had said, most likely brought on by the stress of my parents' death. It was a pressure, a grip, one that felt as though it would strangle me, for surely it possessed enough strength, enough power. Part of me had imagined, naively, I realized, that leaving England behind might mean leaving that all behind as well, that distance was all that was needed to dispel the ghosts of my past. I had been a fool, I thought, angry at myself, at my ignorance. It would follow me, always, no matter where or how far I went.

But then, standing just a few paces away on the staircase, so that I towered over her, and not the other way around, stood Lucy. She watched me, with those strange, inquisitive eyes, and then she smiled and said, "There's nothing to be afraid of, Alice."

Her voice was so certain, so sure.

Lucy extended her hand toward me. "Come on, let's go get supper."

All at once I felt the darkness that had threatened me only a second before begin to lift until it no longer felt like I was some Gothic heroine trapped in a haunted castle, a patriarchal labyrinth that was impossible to ever escape. Instead I was simply Alice and she was Lucy, and there was nothing to be afraid of any longer. I felt her hand searching for mine, her fingers interlacing with my own. I grasped it and together we fled the darkened mansion, leaving behind all the ghosts it held within, both real and imagined.

There was a commotion outside the bar, and then something louder: an explosion of sorts, which brought me hurtling back to the present. I thought at first it was gunfire, thought I could feel the hot bite of it against my skin. I thought of the riots, of the violence that had been erupting throughout Morocco, that had touched Tangier only recently, proving that even she was not immune. John had spoken of it only briefly, making it sound as though it had been amusing that day when the locals had decided to take to the streets, hurtling bottles at the foreign-owned stores and later, when the police responded with gunfire, anything they could use to defend themselves. And when news came out that several lives had been claimed in the skirmish, and almost all of them locals, John had only shrugged, had told me it was nothing to worry about, that these minor rebellions would be squashed eventually. His faith had been absolute. It seemed that not even he, with his professed love for Tangier, had been able to foresee the determination of its people to reclaim their independence, to reclaim their Tangier, had refused to acknowledge, to recognize just how important, how absolutely necessary it was to their life, to their survival.

I turned to look over my shoulder and saw a flash of lights, just beyond the din of the bar. No one was shouting or running away. There was only laughter, and the sounds of celebration. Fireworks, then, I noted. Locals celebrating their approaching independence. The idea caused something to prickle, just there, at the back of my mind. I moved and knocked over the glass in front of me, sending it onto the floor, splintering into sharp, nearly invisible pieces, the gin and tonic soaking my dress.

Letting out a sharp exclamation, I stood quickly, the suddenness of my movement causing the dog beneath the table to let out a yelp of dismay, scrambling from his safe hold — though not before his teeth found purchase, my unexpected movement causing him to sink his teeth into my leg. I looked down to see a trail of blood slipping down my now-tattered stocking. The sight made me strangely dizzy. "He didn't mean it," I whispered to no one, watching as the dog disappeared from the bar. My head still felt light as I moved to help pick up the broken glass — the bartender now heading toward the mess that I had made — and I felt myself blush with embarrassment. I thought, then, of John and his angry scowl that evening. Of Lucy, and her penetrating gaze, always looking, always searching, I worried, for something that was not there. And then I thought I saw him — *John* — at the bar, though he wasn't alone, wasn't with Charlie, as he'd promised. And there was Lucy, just behind him, watching, watching, watching.

76

And then I felt the hard sticky floor of the bar beneath me as I fainted, falling slowly at first, and then faster, without anyone at all to catch me.

# CHAPTER
# FOUR

## LUCY

I found the souks electrifying. The labyrinthine curve of them: dark and packed, with vendors that stood behind stalls or sat on the floor, their bags and buckets of wares splayed out before them. At first, I had been nearly swept up in its fast-moving current, but then I had slowed my gait — walking steadily, with purpose. I stopped at one stall, and then another, purchasing a few grams of bright green olives at one, a stack of hot, sweating *msemmen* at another. I inspected the hanging carcasses of chickens, not recoiling at the smell the way most tourists I observed did, but considering and haggling, as if I intended to purchase one. I paused in front of the brightly dressed Rif women, opting for a handful of broad beans instead, and then a wheel of white cheese, the kind I had seen locals eat, the sides covered with intricately braided green leaves.

I had given up on my day dresses. Although it appeared that there were a number of expat women who still favored them, I found the fitted bodice too restrictive in the heat, and the skirt prone to catching against the jagged edges of the city. Instead I had liberated several pairs of capris from my suitcase, ones that I had not yet mustered the courage to wear back home, and a couple of monochrome blouses that seemed more prepared to handle the climate.

I had tried to convince Alice to come, but she had refused, shaking her head, waving her hands around the cluttered apartment to indicate all the work she should do before John arrived home — work that never seemed to be completed but that went on and on. *Go, she had said, enjoy your holiday.* I had frowned and pleaded, but it soon became apparent that she did not intend to give in. The vehemence with which she shook her head when I had pressed the issue, the thin white of her lips as she moved them together, gave the impression that her reluctance to show a friend around the city was something much more serious than just her need to attend to the laundry.

I thought of her as I walked — Alice, her lovely lily-white skin that had obviously not seen sun for quite some time, locked up within the walls of their flat. I remembered the paleness of her face from the night before, after that wretched beast had bitten her, after she had fainted and fallen onto the ground. She had grown quiet — quieter still — as we had been forced to find a doctor in the hours afterward, a frantic search for a vaccination and a check for any possible concussion. And in the ensuing chaos, I had been forced to push aside what I had seen, what I had witnessed, in the moments before Alice had been bitten.

It had happened shortly after John disappeared from the table.

I had looked up, away from Alice, away from my drink, and into the mirror fastened on the wall before me. I had seen him, his image distorted by the divots in the glass, standing at the bar. Only, he had not been alone, had not been with anyone named Charlie. Instead a woman stood beside him, her face half obscured by a mane of long dark hair. *A local*, I thought, watching as his fingers trailed the upper part of her thigh, pushing at the material of her dress.

I had glanced at Alice, but it didn't seem like she had noticed, and I cast a hurried glance back to the mirror, appraising the angle at which it hung, uncertain whether she would be able to see them at all, even if she did look up. Part of me wanted to show her, to point out the reflection, the truth displayed brazenly before us. But something stayed me. Something whispered that it was not the time, that I should wait before revealing this bit of information to her, this girl I had once known as well as myself and who looked at me now with an expression I couldn't quite understand, couldn't quite manage to breach.

I wound my way through the medina and over to the Grand Socco, where a pleasant sort of plaza greeted me. Green spaces filled with flowers, couples, groups of men, and expat pensioners enjoying a leisurely stroll in the afternoon heat, and several feet away a large, imposing building that towered over the rest. CINEMA RIF, the sign read, its facade dim and grimy. What had once no doubt consisted of brilliant reds, blues, and yellows had faded under the thick application of dust that had since settled. Housed within the cinema was a small café, a scattering of chairs arranged just inside the building, the doors thrown open to the sun, with a few leftover tables and chairs scattered on the sidewalk outside.

I moved quickly to take a seat: a small round table intended for two, pushed up against the building's rough wall, underneath a poster advertisement for a French film I had never heard of before that pictured a young boy standing beneath a red balloon. Several moments passed before the waitress appeared: a short, squat woman whose face was lined with wrinkles. I was relieved to find she spoke French, and although I knew only a scattering of words, it was enough to successfully place an order, as within minutes she returned, a tall glass filled with hot Moroccan mint tea clutched between her fingers. Her severe face broke into a grin as she placed it in front of me.

"*Merci,*" I murmured, moving to adjust the glass. I instantly recoiled, hissing with surprise. I glanced down at my fingers — the tips of which had turned a bright pink.

"*Attention*" — the woman laughed — "*il est chaud.*"

I blushed. "*Oui, merci.*" While all of the guidebooks had extolled the virtues of drinking mint tea in Morocco, they had failed to advise on just how treacherous the endeavor could be. I was used to the thick porcelain of New England diners, not thin glass that seemed to threaten to melt one's fingers. There were no handles and I wondered how on earth one was supposed to drink the concoction.

"*Lentement,* mademoiselle."

I looked over my shoulder to see who had spoken.

"Slowly. You must have patience." He was standing at the opening of the café, neither inside nor outside and without food or drink in hand, leaning with confidence against the wall of the building. I could see right away that it was the same man from the day before, the one who had been watching me in the medina.

I smiled but turned back, hesitant to be drawn into conversation with him.

To the left of where he stood, a shoe shiner was busy at work, moving swiftly between his client's right and left foot — though his own shoes, I noticed, appeared to be placed on backward. After a few moments of closer inspection, I could see that the man appeared to be missing his feet altogether, and that he had placed the shoes backward upon the stumps of his legs only in order to steady himself. I continued to watch him work, falling into an near trancelike state as he first applied shiner and then, withdrawing a rag from his belt, began to swipe with long, vigorous strokes, repeating this movement with sustained intensity before moving on to the next shoe.

I took a sip of my mint tea — no longer scalding — and felt the rush of the syrup as the sweetness exploded on my tongue.

The man was still watching. I could feel his eyes boring, examining, trying to pick me apart from across the way. There was a shift then, a change in the air, so that it seemed rife — with danger, with possibility, though I didn't yet know which. And so I waited, breath held in expectation, already wondering whether

I wanted him to leave me in peace, or whether I would be disappointed if he did.

"I am Joseph," he said, the decision made, moving toward me and extending his hand. He did not wear the traditional djellaba, I noted, though he was most certainly Moroccan. Instead he wore a pair of charcoal-gray trousers, a light button-up shirt that was rolled to the elbows. A thin scarf was thrown across his neck, and a tan fedora hat — adorned with a purple ribbon once again and which I suspected bore the stains of being worn in such unforgiving heat — sat on his head, tilted to the left. There was something dapper about his outfit, despite its thriftiness, or perhaps it was the way he wore it, with a jauntiness that was out of place among the other Moroccan men I had observed and who appeared, in comparison, solemn and grave.

I hesitated at his introduction only for a second — and then the word slipped from my mouth easily, as though it were true: "Alice."

"Welcome to Tangier, mademoiselle." He paused. "And where are you staying during your holiday, Alice?" He said the name so that the last part came out sounding like a hiss: *Al-iss*. He asked the question, his eyes averted, staring down and back into the medina. His tone was casual: deliberately so, as if he had rehearsed the question before it was asked.

"With friends," I replied, trying to make my voice sound light, effortless — as though I were used to answering such questions from strangers, as though my life were spent moving from one place to the next, from Paris to Cairo and on to the Orient. I let the idea settle, the one that Alice and I had given birth to so many years ago now and that remained trapped, just beneath the surface, simmering, it seemed, waiting to be released. There were times when I could feel it — the desperation of wanting, wanting to watch the sun set over the pyramids, wanting to taste the salty egg and sweet cardamom noodles of Arabia. Wanting to be anywhere and everywhere but the depressing tiny shared bedroom of a boardinghouse and knowing that it was impossible.

"And you are not afraid to explore the city, on your own?" he questioned.

I peered up at him, wondering what it was that he intended.

"Should I be?" I asked.

He gave an exaggerated shrug. "Only last year we had a madman running around the city with a butcher's knife."

I eyed the streets in front of us, assessing. "And was anyone injured?"

"Yes, of course," he answered easily. "The man killed five people and injured nearly half a dozen more." He must have seen the hard look that I affixed on my face, for his expression lost some of its seriousness and he broke into a large grin — one that I found somehow more disconcerting than his formerly somber mask. "Relax," he advised, pausing to bring a cigarette to his lips. "I was only teasing, Miss Alice."

I let out a breath I hadn't realized I was holding, wondering still at the motivation behind his words. "So that didn't happen?"

His smile disappeared. "Oh no, it most definitely happened. The man was shot in the stomach before he was taken to Malabata prison. But you are quite safe here — that is the part I was teasing about. There is nothing to worry about now, Miss Alice," he assured me. "Where are you from?"

"Chicago," I lied.

"Chicago!" he exclaimed, frowning. "This is the most dangerous place of them all. I have a cousin who went to Chicago. It was very horrible, he said. Too many murders. You do not have to worry about such things here." He paused. "But if you are looking for a place that makes sense, I feel I must provide this warning — you will be disappointed." He let out a small laugh. "This is Africa, after all." He grinned, his smile stretching across his gaunt, tanned face. "Many forget that, they think we are somewhere different entirely. This might be true, but it is also false. Tangier is still Africa. One need only consult a map to know this." He turned back toward me, eyes boring into my own. "And where do your friends live?"

"In a flat," I replied.

He smiled, thinly. "Yes, but where is this flat?"

I searched for an answer, unsure whether I wanted to part with such information. There was something about him that whispered he was harmless, another mosquito that could easily be flicked away, but still, the answer hung heavily on my tongue. I was not afraid of him or afraid for my safety. Men like him, I knew, were not the ones to fear. I was simply unsure — of what I had to offer him, of what he could offer me, of the potential usefulness that we might offer each other. "Beyond the medina, somewhere," I finally answered. "I'm afraid I can't offer any more specifics. I've only just arrived and I'm not too familiar with the city yet."

Lies, we both knew. I could tell by the glint in his eye, the slight curve of his lip. The only question was how he would react to it. He tilted his head from side to side, as if weighing my answer, my betrayal. "This is good," he finally observed. "It is better to be in a flat than a hotel. Unless you are only staying for a few days, then a hotel is always best." He looked at me, waiting for a response.

"I'm staying for quite some time, I hope."

He nodded, apparently pleased. "So you are a tourist?"

I nodded. "Yes, I suppose I am."

"Not a traveler, then?" He laughed.

I puzzled over the difference in words — between *tourist* and *traveler*. I had never really been many places, had never really seen much, so I supposed myself a tourist rather than a traveler. But there was something in the way he had pronounced the words, a disdain for the former that suggested it was the latter that I should strive for — whether or not it was true. I began to place my coins on the table, my tea now empty. "Is there a distinction?"

"Yes, of course."

I could see then, instantly, that I'd said the wrong thing — but that this was also what he wanted. To be able to shake his head and laugh at the naïveté of the young American woman in front of him. To lean in,

86

with a conspirator's grin, beckoning me to come closer, closer and closer still.

"You are unfamiliar with Bowles, I see. You must read him, if you wish to understand this place," he instructed.

"Is he Moroccan?" I asked, unfamiliar with the name.

He laughed. "He is not Moroccan, no, but he spends a good deal of time here. We see one another often and wave. He is familiar, a neighbor. Not simply a famous writer."

*Bowles.* I placed the name somewhere in my mind, making a mental note to check whether John had any of his work scattered among the unread books that lined the flat. For while I considered myself something of an expert in classical literature — particularly anything British — I was the first to admit my deficiencies in more contemporary work, as it had never managed to hold my attention in the same manner. Give me the wilds of an English moor, or the gritty urban streets of Victorian London, and I would feel, if nothing else, at home. But as to the latest stream of authors sweeping the country, I was essentially a novice.

Perhaps this is what the man offered — a guide to the country that Alice now called home, however reluctantly. Perhaps there was worth to be found there, I thought.

"I promise to read him, the very first chance I have," I said.

"Good. Then you will learn the difference between a tourist and a traveler. And we shall see which one you are." He leaned over, offering a cigarette. "Here."

I paused — Alice did not smoke. The distinction seemed important to uphold, so I shook my head demurely. He shrugged and pulled an expression, as if to indicate it was my loss. And I did regret my decision — almost instantly. I inhaled the fragrant smoke: heavy and perfume-like. French, most likely. Gauloises. One didn't smell many of them around Tangier, I had already noticed. I wondered if I could change my mind, but then, that would reveal a part of me to this stranger that I wasn't yet sure I could trust. Better to remain behind the veneer a bit longer.

"I have a studio by the ocean, where I paint," he said, after a few moments' consideration. "This is where you must come."

"By the ocean?" I repeated. After several days in Tangier, despite the fact that it was a port city, I had seen very little of the water. It was strange, I thought, the way the city was able to swallow you up so completely.

"Yes, it is next to Café Hafa. Do you know it?"

I shook my head.

"Ah," he exclaimed, "this is the place you must go. It is where all the artists are. They also have the best mint tea," he said, gesturing to my empty glass. "And the view — it is much better than this. Just the ocean, nothing else."

"It sounds beautiful."

"It is." He smiled, nodding his head. He peered at me through the smoke. "So, Miss Alice, tell me. Do you want to see the real Tangier?"

I hesitated, assuming he meant to offer himself as a guide and wondering, at the same time, at the advisability of such an idea — disappearing into a city I knew little about, with a man about whom I knew even less. But then I thought of Alice, stagnated by fear, stuck inside the dark confines of her flat day after day, waiting for John to return from work. *Waiting*, both of us, *always waiting*. I shook my head, as if to shake the word from my mind, as if I could somehow physically dislodge it from my vocabulary. I had spent a good deal of my life waiting. Too much time. I nodded — a sharp, pointed gesture that conveyed my acceptance of his offer.

"Morocco is your home." He said the words slowly, watching my face closely as he spoke. "Yes, it is yours. You are a Tangerine now."

He pronounced it *tangerine*, like the fruit. I smiled, letting the thought settle. Morocco was mine. And it could be, I reasoned. After all, what did I have to return to? A damp, shared room on the wrong side of New York. Endless days spent typing up other writers' manuscripts. Here I could finally write something of my own, put pen to paper as I had always dreamed of during college — as Alice and I had dreamed, together. And if that meant making Morocco my own, I was prepared to do just that.

I was a Tangerine now, after all.

# CHAPTER
# FIVE

## ALICE

I did not ask her where she had spent her day, or whom she had spent it with. I did not ask what she was doing in Tangier, why she was here, what she wanted — still too afraid of the answers I might receive. Instead, I smiled, the gesture feeling odd and forced, and told her to sit, told her I would make drinks again — the nights already beginning to take on the shape of those we had spent at Bennington.

I wondered at the ease of it, of how quickly we had slipped back into our roles, how comfortable already it had begun to feel. And I resented it, the feeling that I had tried to clasp onto at the bar suddenly mine, strong and fierce, until I could think of nothing else but the way that she had so carefully reinserted herself back into my life without a mention of the past, of her part in what had unfolded between us, the tragedy that had ensconced us. I didn't know what I expected her to say, not exactly, but there was neither a word nor a glance, not anything at all that seemed to indicate she recalled those last few weeks we had spent together and the tension that had grown between us.

I could feel my anger growing, and I forced myself to concentrate on the task at hand, peeling the zest from the lemon that I had bought at the market two weeks past, the skin of the fruit now dried, withered.

I called from the kitchen: "It's like this most nights, I'm afraid. John is always off to one dinner party or another."

"And what about you? Don't you ever go with him?" she called back.

"No, not anymore." I thought of the faces I had been introduced to those first few months — appraising and cold. "I did at first, but well, it turned out they weren't for me. Tangier seems to attract a certain type, and I'm afraid that I don't generally fit the description."

I found her perched beside the window, gazing out. At my entrance she turned, frowning. "Do you like it at all, Alice? Tangier, I mean?"

My face burned a fiercer shade of red. "Oh, I don't know. I suppose I haven't really given it a chance. Or at least, that's what John always says."

I did not add that I often doubted whether there was any truth in what John said, wondered instead whether the truth wasn't something much simpler: Tangier and I were not suited for one another, that we never would be, no matter how many chances I gave it. From the little I knew of it already, I had realized what a hard place it could be. It was not a place where one simply arrived and belonged — no, I imagined that it was a process, a trial, even an initiation of sorts, one that only the bravest survived. It was a place that inspired rebellion, a place that demanded it, of its people, its citizens. A place where everyone had to constantly adapt, struggle, fight for what they wanted. I looked up at the woman in front of me. It was a place for someone like Lucy.

"I made a friend today," Lucy said, bringing me back to the present. "A Moroccan man. Rather strange, I suppose, though he was quite kind. I was sitting outside of Cinema Rif. Do you know it?" When I nodded, she continued: "I was having a tea and he happened to notice I was sitting there alone. He offered to show me around Tangier, in fact. He mentioned something about being an artist. A painter, I think."

I felt myself flush at her words, felt it spread throughout my body. My dress, despite the pink blush fabric, was severe and unyielding in the evening heat. There was something strangely unsettling about Lucy's piece of information, about the fact that she had already made an acquaintance, a friend, and suddenly I could feel it, a tinge of envy, of jealousy, growing hot in the pit of my stomach. I could feel a sheen of sweat break across my forehead. "Here," I said, handing her the drink I still held clutched between my fingers. I moved toward the sofa, hoping she would follow, that she would forget what it was that she had just been discussing. "Try this," I instructed, worried as she sat down beside me that she would feel it, the heat that now seemed to radiate from my body.

"What is it?" she asked, shifting closer.

"Just my own creation." I let out a nervous laugh, raising the glass to meet my lips. "It helps to pass the time."

She took a cautious sip and I knew what she was tasting — a sweetness, like cherries. "That's the grenadine," I said. "There's a brand that I love in France. I make sure John always brings back a bottle or two whenever he travels to the Continent."

"And you? Do you go home often?" she asked, peering at me over her drink.

"To England?" I shook my head, trying not to think of it, of the smell that was London, fragrant and stale, rich and musty. I pushed it aside, and in its absence something else occurred to me, in the silence of the room. "That sounds like Youssef," I said.

She frowned. "What does?"

"The man you were just describing. I was wondering if it might be Youssef."

"Joseph, you mean?"

I shook my head. "No, Youssef. He's notorious for preying on unsuspecting tourists. Everyone here knows him, if not directly, well, at least about him."

"Perhaps this was someone different," she ventured, her voice sharper than it had been a moment before.

I could see that the information had unnerved her, that the idea that she might somehow have been taken in sat poorly. It was, after all, something that I would have expected of myself — I trusted too easily, too often, I knew. And then, there it was again — that awful feeling, tinged with green, that stirred in my belly and made me strangely glad to see that it was Lucy who had done something wrong, that it was Lucy who had been taken in by another's kind word. I found myself unable to stop. "Fedora with a purple ribbon?"

She frowned and nodded.

"That's him, then. John says he lures tourists back to his house, then demands money for all sorts of useless junk. I think he once had a girl involved, pretending to be his daughter." I shrugged. "The locals never say anything to the tourists. In fact, they find it all rather amusing, I'm afraid."

Before I could say anything more, the front door opened, and John's voice rang throughout the apartment: "I'm not home for good. I just need to grab a few things before heading back out. Ignore me."

I placed my palm to my cheek, willing the coldness of my hand to stop the flush that had spread across my face over the last few minutes, emboldened, it seemed, by Lucy's misstep. "I was just telling Lucy about Youssef," I said, calling out, recalling the litany of amusing stories that John had on the subject. I thought of the other night, of the spectacle John had made of himself, of us, and I wanted him to show her, then, what it was that I had seen in him, to prove that he was not altogether horrible, that I had not made a complete and utter mess of my life when I had agreed to marry him in the tiny register office that rainy summer day.

John murmured something, but it was impossible to tell whether it was just an acknowledgment of having heard or an indication of his interest, a prompt for me to continue. I paused briefly, my hands stilled in front of me, a smile frozen across my features. "You know, the man with the purple ribbon on his hat?" I continued.

At this, John emerged, his face shiny with sweat. He moved to the bar, filling his glass with a generous serving of gin, followed by a small splash of tonic. I noted that he had not bothered to remove his hat.

"I've told her to be careful, that he's a grafter of sorts," I continued.

"A grifter, honey."

"Yes, that," I said, flushing worse. "I'm always mixing up words," I explained, turning back to Lucy. "John is always having to correct me. I'm afraid I can't keep anything straight."

Lucy smiled, though it seemed tight, her demeanor, I had already noticed, shifting in John's presence. I turned away quickly. "Tell her," I implored him — begging, I could not help thinking, the way a child did a parent, or a puppy its master. "About what you heard. From your friends at work."

John nodded and turned back to the bar. He poured a second drink, neat, and only then did he commence his story. "It's typical in Tangier, you'll find. One of the guys at the office knew a couple, some young Americans on holiday, when they happened to run into Youssef. They got to talking, thought he was harmless enough. In fact, they thought he might even be someone to know, or someone in the know, if you catch my meaning. They thought it might be beneficial to tag along with him, see where the night took them." He paused, as if for dramatic effect. "Well, Youssef led them back to what he said was his place — some out-of-the-way dive on the wrong side of the Kasbah. The couple now has no idea where they are, only that they've been walking for quite some time and have lost all sense of direction. Then, before they know it, they're standing in front of a garbage heap of sorts. It's pitch-black and there's no one around except them and Youssef.

"He asks for money, of course. Demands they pay him in order to show them the way back to their hotel. Well, the Americans are outraged. They refuse flat out to pay him. They start walking around, trying to figure a way back into the Kasbah, back into the medina, but they can't. It's late, the wife is getting worried, so eventually they just give in and pay him. He takes them back, but only far enough so that they recognize their way, not to the hotel itself. The Americans say fine, thank you, leave us alone now. They're happy to get on their way. They start walking and then —"

"This is the best bit," I broke in, smiling.

John paused. "Alice, do you want to tell the story yourself?" He let out a short laugh and attempting, it seemed, to lighten his tone, though his words were still short and clipped, said, "I don't know why you even bothered to call me in here, it doesn't seem as if you need my assistance."

"No, no," I replied, affecting something like a pout, though I did not mean to, and sinking back into the couch. "You tell it. It's always better when you do."

John let out an exaggerated sigh, as if to further demonstrate how unreasonable I was being, his silly little wife. I nearly expected him to turn toward Lucy with a shake of his head and a roll of his eyes, followed by a commiseration on the more irritating points of the

96

Alice they had in common. Instead, he looked at neither of us but began his tale once more, picking up where he had left off and diving into the story as though no interruption had ever occurred. "So, they start walking, and about fifteen minutes later, who should show up again but Youssef. He's back for more money — and you'll never guess why."

The silence indicated that this was where Lucy and I, the captive audience members, were expected to join in. "Why?" I asked, at Lucy's silence.

"He says that they should pay him for agreeing to leave them alone." John leaned back and laughed, the liquid in his cup moving dangerously from side to side. "Can you believe the nerve of the man? You have to give him credit, I suppose. He certainly is inventive."

"Yes, I suppose so," Lucy replied, though her eyes were narrowed.

"Why are you so curious about Youssef, anyhow?" John glanced in my direction, a grin breaking across his face. "What? Did she happen to fall for one of his tricks?" he teased.

"No, it's nothing like that," I said, shooting Lucy a nervous glance.

"I happened to mention that I met him today," she said, trying, I could see, to dispel the coldness from her voice. "He seemed friendly enough," she concluded.

"Friendly?" John laughed.

"Yes, well, what's wrong with that?" I demanded, embarrassed by John's cavalier attitude. I had only wanted a chance to change Lucy's mind, to show her that John wasn't entirely awful, that he could be good fun, when he felt like it. Only it had all gone wrong again — John had been cruel, Lucy had been offended. There was nothing, I suspected then, that I would be able to do to convince the other that they were worth knowing. But then, of course, it shouldn't have surprised me, not really. Lucy and I had always functioned as a twosome, held separate and apart from the rest. Distinct.

"Honey," John said, shaking his head. "Friendly is the grift."

I realized then, watching Lucy as she glared at John, as he, in turn, eyed her with something like distaste, derision, there was nothing to be done. Nothing at all.

Everything had changed during our junior year at Bennington College.

I had been away for the holidays, visiting my aunt on one of her trips to the East Coast — a formal dinner in whatever hotel she had been staying fast becoming our holiday ritual — and though she had offered to hire a driver to take me back to Bennington, I had insisted on catching the bus. I had left later that day, already looking forward to returning to my room, to Lucy, to what had fast become the definition of home. But as the bus pulled up at the station, several hours later, I had felt my stomach drop. We were still in Massachusetts, had not yet crossed the border, and while I knew that my ticket included a connection to Vermont, looking out of the window, my nose pressed against the cold glass, I could see that the bus station was completely dark.

*The bus will be here*, the driver assured me when I questioned him. "But the station," I said, casting a nervous glance toward the darkened structure. "It doesn't look open."

"Closes at six o'clock," he replied. "You'll have to wait outside."

I looked out of the bus, into the darkness beyond. The temperature was already hovering somewhere in the thirties, with snowfall forecasted for later that evening.

"But they didn't say," I began.

"There isn't anything I can do, miss," he cut in. "I have another pickup scheduled and I can't wait around." The other passengers had already disembarked, and he pointed toward the steps, indicating that I should do the same.

I nodded, dulled by the realization.

"Be safe," he called, the doors closing behind me.

Afterward, I stood in front of the closed station, holding my suitcase between my hands, hesitant to set it down on the damp, snowy ground. A single streetlight illuminated the area in which I stood, so that while my own person was aglow, only a few steps away there was nothing, only blackness. I struggled to remain calm, my breath erupting before me in great, billowy clouds, the dampness clinging to the scarf knotted around my throat.

"Hey you," a voice called out.

I peered into the darkness, uncertain whether the deep voice had been aimed in my direction. I could see nothing except the snow on the streets sparkling, or so it seemed, under the light.

"Yeah, you," the voice came again.

A figure stepped into my small circle of light. He was young — surely no more than a few years older than myself — his tall, athletic build tightly bundled in a military green jacket, with worn leather patches at the elbows. A single suitcase dangled from his hand.

"Do you need a lift?"

"I'm waiting for a bus," I answered. When he looked around, as if to indicate his doubt that such a thing existed, I hastened to explain, "It's not due for another two hours."

He frowned. "I think the station is closed for the day."

"But the bus driver said —" I let the words die on my lips. I looked around at my surroundings, looked at the boy in front of me.

He glanced over his shoulder. "A few of us are splitting a cab back to Williams College."

I squinted through the darkness, but if there were any others, I couldn't see them. "I'm trying to get to Bennington," I replied. "I go to the college there."

"Bennington?" he asked, a grin spreading across his features. "I've heard some interesting stories about the girls there."

I frowned, wondering whether I should be offended or not.

"I'm just teasing," he said hastily, as if he had read my thoughts. "And besides" — he grinned — "I sort of go there myself."

"What do you mean?" I frowned. "It's an all girls' school." My voice was sharp, guarded. I wondered whether he was laughing at me or something else.

"I know." He laughed. "So as you can see, I don't really fit in, which is why I do most of my coursework at Williams College. But I'm actually part of the theater project at the school. At Bennington, I mean."

"Oh," I responded, taken aback by the response. I was aware, as were most of the girls at Bennington, of the strange loophole that allowed local boys to attend the college, at least on a part-time basis. The school had made the decision back in the 1930s, after realizing the need for a male population in order to widen the scope of stage productions they were able to produce. It was a source of endless gossip for those girls who took part in the college's theater department, a chance to fraternize with the enemy, as it were. But the world of theater was one that rarely touched upon my own, and though I was now into my third year at Bennington, this was the first boy I had met who actually took part in the program.

"You know, I think I've seen you before," he said then, with that same grin.

I shook my head, embarrassed at the idea that someone might have been watching me. "I don't think so."

He nodded. "Yeah, you and this other girl, you're always together."

I paused. "Lucy."

He smiled. "It's nice to meet you, Lucy."

I blushed, realizing the mistake — his mistake or mine, I wasn't sure — and I hastened to explain. "No, sorry, that isn't my name. What I meant was, that it must have been my roommate, Lucy, that you saw me with."

"Oh." He nodded, sounding disappointed by this piece of information. He shrugged. "Look, why don't you come along with us? You can't stay out here on your own. Not in this weather," he said, though I suspected it was the late hour rather than the temperature that unsettled him. "I have a car, back on campus. I could give you a lift to Bennington."

I hesitated a moment, maybe longer, before considering the hour and the darkness and that steady feeling of fear that had slowly begun to encroach upon me before he had appeared, my savior, or so it seemed. And so I followed him, out of my circle of light — of safety, I could not help but think — wondering what it was that I had traded in the process, one unknown for the other. But then, only several feet away, stood the promised group of friends, huddled around a taxi. Packing in together, our bodies pressed tightly against one another, with one of the girls forced to sit on the lap of one of the boys, I listened as they laughed and joked with one another, this group of friends that I had been so hesitant to join at first. There was Sally, an art history major at a college in New York, who was planning to spend the summer in Venice, and Andrew, who wanted to follow his father's footsteps and become an English professor. There was another girl whose

**102**

name I couldn't remember but who was all smiles and laughter, mainly aimed in Andrew's direction.

And then there was the boy I had met first, and whose name was Thomas, Tom for short, and who was the most reserved now, in his circle of friends, though he smiled and listened to them as they spoke. I felt a sudden ache as we pulled away from the station, watching the friendship that existed among those in the group, evident in the easy, casual way they had with one another. It was so different from my own strange little twosome that I had formed with Lucy, which all at once seemed odd and lonely in comparison.

I had found our closeness thrilling at first, but as the years had begun to pass, I had come to feel that for everything I told Lucy, she somehow managed to absorb the information without ever giving back any of her own. Initially I had put it down to shyness, convinced that she, like me, was simply unused to living so closely with another person. Confidences would come eventually, I told myself, in the beginning. I would only have to be patient. But then, it was the holidays, and we were off for home and then back again, and away once more for the summer, and still, I had learned so little about the girl who was closer to me than anyone else I had ever known, who knew all my secrets: each and every little one.

But then, no, I corrected myself: *girl* wasn't the right word. Lucy was a woman — she dressed liked one, acted like one, she even walked like one. Secretly, I had always believed it was down to the loss of one's virginity, as if the act of copulation would somehow bestow upon one a sudden sense of maturity, as if that one act had the power to dispel the insecurities and worries that plagued most girls from the start of puberty. It was nonsense, of course. I was convinced that Lucy had never so much as kissed another human being, and yet she dressed, acted like, and walked the way I wanted to — with confidence, with control, as if she were entirely certain of who she was.

*Covet.* It was a peculiar word. One I tended to associate with long, dull lectures on Hawthorne and other early American writers from the Puritan age. I had to look it up once, as part of an essay I had been forced to write in school. What I found was: *to desire wrongfully, inordinately, or without due regard for the rights of others.* There were other definitions. More words, different words, although all of them meant the same thing. But it was that first part that had stayed with me: *to desire wrongfully.*

It struck me as strangely beautiful and yet frighteningly accurate.

The feelings I felt toward Lucy, I often thought, were something like this — something sharper than a normal friendship, something that I felt threatened to overwhelm and, quite possibly, destroy. There were moments when I had thought that I did not so much want her as wanted to be her. The two feelings were so strong and so opposite, yet they continued to merge and mingle until I was no longer able to tell one from the other. I coveted the easy way she had, and I desired that: her way of being. I wanted it for my own. And there were days when I almost felt it — when, emboldened by her nonchalance at the world that, already, even in my young years, seemed so cruel, I was able to withstand the shadows, the anxiety that so often plagued me. And so there were days when I never wanted to part from her, when I felt that my whole being depended upon my close connection with her. And there were days when I hated her, resenting myself, resenting her, for this reliance, this symbiotic relationship that we had formed — though on the darkest days I wondered whether it really was, whether there was anything that I had to offer her, and whether what she offered me wasn't more a crutch than a benefit. Lately I had struggled more with the strangeness of our relationship, as I was never able to explain it fully, not even to myself, and sitting in the back of that taxi, surrounded by this easy, carefree group of friends, I was struck once more by the need to be able to, to understand it all before it threatened to overwhelm me, totally and completely.

Piled into the promised car, Tom's friends reluctant to abandon him to the back roads of Vermont, we made the final leg of the journey in silence.

Once at Bennington, it was with something near regret that I eventually left them, dismayed to find that the thought of returning to my room, to Lucy, had since grown terribly dim.

"Wait."

I turned and found the boy with the leather elbow patches, Tom, I reminded myself, running toward me. He leaned over, taking the suitcase from my grasp. "Let

**105**

me carry it for you." And so he walked me back to my room, made sure that I was able to get in safely, setting my suitcase beside my bed as he gazed around the space. I wondered what it was that he saw reflected there: in the hopelessly childish duvet that adorned my bed, a ghastly shade of pink and white that my aunt had purchased in a misguided attempt to welcome her new ward into an adult home, at the embarrassing effort that I had made to decorate my side of the room, various sketches tacked to the wall. He paused at the map on Lucy's side of the room, studying, or so it seemed, the numerous pins that we had once placed there. A silly game we played with some intensity our first year, when the newness of our relationship had made anything seem possible.

And then he moved to the row of photographs that I had taped above my dresser.

I had signed up for a design class on a lark that fall, and the instructor, a working photographer who spent a few days out of the week in Vermont and the rest in New York City, had been encouraged by several photography enthusiasts in the class to erect a makeshift darkroom on campus. My mother's old camera had been among the few things I had brought with me to Vermont, though I had never really thought to learn how to use the thing. Soon, however, I began spending hours in the darkroom, happy to lose myself in the process of developing and printing, feeling as though I had found something of my own at last. Something separate and distinct from the Alice I was with Lucy. It was a strange experience, one that began to unfurl within the folds of my stomach, so that there were days when I felt filled up by it, as if this new knowledge — of what I might be capable of — was nourishment enough.

I felt my heart beat faster, waiting for him to speak — but then the door opened and Lucy rushed in. "You're home." She breathed. "I was worried, I just checked the bus and it said —" She stopped then, and turned.

Tom smiled, nodded his head.

"Lucy," I began, "this is Tom. He was my knight in shining armor today," I said, before relaying the whole tale for her, anxiously, nervously, so that both of them looked slightly embarrassed, slightly aghast by the time I had run out of breath. A frown had crept across Lucy's face at the story, and she remained silent once I had finished.

We stood there, the three of us, the knowledge that something had changed, that something had shifted, coursing through the room. But then, later, I wondered whether Tom had even noticed, or whether it wasn't something that Lucy and I had felt alone, another example of our strange duo that defied explanation, that defied normalcy.

And one that I, for the first time, felt myself suddenly anxious to shed.

Suddenly, it was no longer Lucy and me.

It was both of us, and Tom too, a strange little threesome that I soon learned refused to fit together. At first, I had made a concerted effort. When I was given an assignment by my professor to learn how to use a view camera — the weight of the piece requiring more than one set of hands — I invited Lucy to join Tom and me as we hauled the equipment around campus, Tom joking he was both subject and subjected. Lucy accompanied us only the once, when we spent nearly an hour lugging it to the edge of campus, to what we laughingly christened the End of the Universe, that stretch of land at the entrance to Bennington, and which dipped, low and jagged, as dangerous and threatening as the End of the World was not.

"I pity the man unfortunate enough to drive off into that," Tom had said, smiling back at us as he leaned against the rail, waiting for me to set up the camera and begin.

Lucy had stood, tersely, staring out into the woods, and even though I had begged her to let me take her photograph as well, she had remained silent, so I wondered, in the end, whether she had heard me at all.

Later, as we walked back to campus, Tom had tried to talk with her, about literature, about what she was working on in her courses. "I'm jealous you've got Professor Hyman here," he said. "I would love the opportunity to take a class with him. Have you signed up for any of his yet?"

She had turned to him, her gaze steely and hard. "No. But then, I suppose I'd rather take a class with his better half."

Tom was silent after that.

I tried to talk about it with her once, not long afterward — to try to dispel the strangeness that had stolen over us, between us. But she had only turned

**108**

away, her face closed, guarded. I suspected she meant to punish me — for my relationship with Tom, a closeness that not only did not involve her, but which, oftentimes, left her alone. And though I felt guilty, I was confused by her odd behavior, knowing that if the situation were reversed, I would not have been so cold.

"There's something not right about her," Tom said one evening late into the spring as we lay, hidden from the Commons Lawn, just beneath the End of the World, waiting for the sun to begin setting.

"Oh, don't be cruel," I had protested, pushing against his shoulder — protective, even still, of my odd roommate. It was true that I did not condone her behavior, that I was just as embarrassed as Tom was likely offended by it. And yet, I could not help but pity her too — for those long afternoons she now spent alone, trapped in the library, for those nights we passed, silent and held apart from each other.

"I'm not," he said, pulling me closer with a laugh. "I promise." He grew quiet then, and as I leaned up against him I could feel the rise and fall of him, could smell the scent that was uniquely his — something like sun and sand and bit like laundry that had been left out for an afternoon. I moved closer. "It's just," he began, "it's just the way she looks at you."

I frowned. "What do you mean?" When he did not respond, I turned to look up at him. "How does she look at me?" I demanded.

He looked away, as if embarrassed, as if he were hesitant to say the words aloud. "I don't know. I mean, I don't know how to explain it."

**109**

"Try," I said, desperate to have the answer.

But he only remained silent.

I turned, feeling a shudder run through me. I was quiet then, pressed up against his warmth, feeling as though I would never be warm. Together, we watched the sun set in front of us.

One month after I met Tom, things began to disappear.

It was little items at first. A tube of lipstick that I couldn't locate. A necklace that went missing for a few days, only to turn up in a spot I knew I had already checked. A scarf that I could not remember wearing and that appeared in the laundry bin, ready to be washed. I thought nothing of it at first, and later, when I realized it must be Lucy, I only assumed that it was how sisters lived — borrowing things from one another without asking, the mutability of their wardrobe and accessories an unwritten law between them.

But then one day in early May, I walked into our room and found her standing in front of the mirror, wearing my clothes. I blinked. It wasn't simply one item — a scarf or a sweater — it was everything, from head to toe. I recognized my ivory dress with the eyelet fabric and Peter Pan collar, a smart beaded cloche that my aunt had purchased for me the previous winter. Lucy was standing, her head tilted to the side, watching herself in the mirror as she pulled at the waistline in an attempt to adjust the fit, but the dress hit strangely on her body, as if she were trying on clothes that had once been worn by her younger self.

It took a few moments before her eyes met mine — before she realized that she was no longer in the room alone. "I'm sorry," she said, quickly removing the hat. Her face had turned a deep crimson.

"No, don't apologize." I smiled, trying, and failing I suspected, to dispel the strangeness of the moment. We had not spent much time together lately — I was either in the darkroom or with Tom — and the moment seemed rendered somehow more strange, more unsettling, by our distance. "You're free to borrow it whenever you like," I finished quickly.

Despite my words, she hurried to remove the clothing. She placed the hat on my bed, looking more angry than embarrassed, I thought. The dress she lifted from her body, quickly and with such force that I worried she might tear the seams. It was all over in a matter of seconds, and once more Lucy stood before me in one of her own outfits, her face blazing with an emotion I could not quite interpret.

In the end, I thought it best to ignore the incident, turning from her and taking a seat behind my desk, arranging and rearranging my books until the tension in the room settled and then passed, as if nothing had happened at all.

But then, two weeks later, as Lucy readied herself for the morning, I found myself startled by the item she had clasped around her wrist: my mother's charm bracelet, that thin piece of once-gleaming silver that had now worked itself to a tarnished gray. It was nothing valuable, of course, and yet, I still counted it among my most prized possessions — a fact that Lucy well knew. I had spent hours, after my mother's death, studying the charms. A small couple, the girl in red, the boy in blue, preparing to ski. A bubble gum machine, with tiny little colored beads serving as the candy. A violin. I knew each and every one by heart, had memorized all their intricate details, particularly in those moments when the weight of the truth, the reality of never seeing my mother wear it again, sat heavily on my chest.

As I watched it dangle from Lucy's wrist, my heart began to pound, and I saw spots in my vision — like little twinkling stars, bright lights that crowded and fought for space in front of my eyes. I blinked. I told myself that she did not mean anything by it, that surely she had just forgotten about what I had told her, about just how special the bracelet was to me. But then I paused, trying to recall — a conversation, a brief mention, anything I had said or done throughout the years we had lived together, only to find that it was all becoming too blurred, too confused in my mind.

"I'd be grateful if next time you could ask." The words left my mouth and I tasted something bitter and hurried to swallow.

Lucy stopped. She held a notebook in one hand, the other — the one with the bracelet — hung limply at her side. She was silent for a moment. "Ask about what, Alice?"

I turned to face her, chiding myself for feeling nervous. After all, the bracelet was mine, had once belonged to my mother, and was one of the few things that I had left of her. There was nothing wrong with asking Lucy to get permission before taking it from my jewelry box, I told myself. "It's nothing, really," I said, feeling the heat as it burned my cheeks. "It's just, the bracelet. I don't mind, honest, it's just, if you could ask next time."

Lucy continued to peer at me with that same queer expression. Her hand had moved to the doorknob but it froze then, as if she couldn't decide whether to respond to my request or leave the room without deigning to answer at all. Finally she dropped her hand and said, "I don't understand."

"My bracelet," I replied, stammering over the first word. I pointed to her wrist.

A small laugh escaped from her then. "Alice," she said, "don't be silly."

She was staring at me, her dark eyes boring into mine. I squirmed under their gaze, feeling as though I were the one who had done something wrong, as though the stolen object dangled from my wrist and not her own.

"What do you mean?" I asked.

Lucy held up her arm, so that her wrist appeared to me sideways, a portion of the charms hidden from my sight. "This bracelet?"

"Yes."

She frowned. "Alice, this isn't your bracelet."

I stopped. "What are you talking about, Lucy?"

She dropped her arm. "I mean that this is my bracelet." She turned, so that her words came to me, distorted by the distance. "It was *my mother's* bracelet, in fact."

I opened my mouth, then shut it. I didn't know what to say. I didn't understand. I wanted to say: *No, it was my mother's bracelet* — and perhaps I did — though the words sounded thick and far away, as if someone other than I was speaking. Lucy continued to stare at me with that strange look, so that I was unsure of whether she had heard me, or if, in fact, I had actually spoken the words at all.

She took a step toward me. "Alice, are you feeling well? I could get the school nurse if something is wrong."

I felt a rising tide of panic, suddenly overwhelmed by it all — her strange behavior over the last few weeks, the incident with the clothes, and now this. I wanted to shout at her. To race forward and rip the bracelet from her arm. But would they believe me? I wondered — simultaneously questioning who *they* even referred to. After all, who could I go to with such a problem, who would not turn away, laughing? It all sounded so absurd, of course I realized that. The idea that two girls would claim the same story about a bracelet — that their respective dead mothers had gifted it to them — it was so unlikely, how could it ever sound anything but absolutely ludicrous?

*That was what she wanted.*

The thought came to me quickly. It seemed absurd, hard to believe — and yet, I told myself, it had to be true. It had to be true for no other reason than that *there was no other reason.* Why else would she claim the bracelet had been her mother's if not for that outcome — she wanted to drive me mad.

**114**

She knew about my past. I had told her once, in those early months of friendship, about the time after my parents' deaths, about the darkness and shadows that had hovered above me so that my aunt Maude had wanted to send me away, to commit me to a place where I would never see the sun again. About how they still came, so that at times I questioned the accuracy of my mind, of my memories.

I would be lying if I did not admit that for the briefest of moments it had passed my mind, that I had wondered if the bracelet did not in fact belong to Lucy and I had somehow confused it as being my own. One dead mother's bracelet for another.

But no, I told myself, looking up at her, watching her confusion with suspicion.

It was mine, I knew it.

I could feel my face burning, but this time it was not in embarrassment or nervousness. "Please, Lucy," I implored.

She let out a sigh. I thought at first she meant to relent, to admit to it all, to claim it as some sort of cruel prank. But then her expression changed: her eyes narrowed and her face looked suddenly small and mean. "We'll have to sort this out later, I'm afraid. I have a class now." And with those words, she was gone.

Lucy didn't return home that night.

It was the first time I had slept alone in our room, and I found the sudden absence, the total quiet, to be unnerving. Shadows that I had never before noticed danced across the length of the walls. A shrill noise awoke me in the middle of the night, and it was only some time later that I realized it was simply the sound of two trees rubbing together. By then, my heart had begun to pound and I could hear a strange roaring, loud enough that it blocked out the other sounds that had frightened me only seconds before.

*Stop it*, I chided myself. *You're a grown woman. You can certainly manage to spend one night on your own.* The truth was, it was the first time I had slept alone at all. Someone else had always been in the house with me — my parents, and then later, my aunt. And yes, I knew that there were other girls just a door away, but somehow the house seemed empty, as if it were possible that I was the sole occupant. I worried for a moment that this might somehow be true. Perhaps there had been an emergency drill that I had missed. I peered out the window, wondering whether I would see a row of girls there, huddled together in the night air. There was no one. Still, I could not quite manage to convince myself that I was not somehow totally and completely alone within the walls of our clapboard house. My ears strained for sounds of the other girls. For anything other than the eerie shrieking the two trees continued to produce.

There was nothing.

Or was there?

At some point in the night, I began to feel a presence. My heart stammered, the blood rushed to my face. Where before Lucy had acted as a barrier, a shield, between me and everything else — for nothing would ever happen while she was there, I had reasoned

— at that moment I was alone, defenseless. I pushed myself to the edge of the bed, so that my back aligned with the cold glass surface of the window. I closed my eyes and held my breath — certain that, as I did, the sound of breathing continued. *It's not real*, I told myself, although the words did little to comfort, to dispel the feeling that I was being watched. That I was no longer alone in the bedroom.

I slept little that night. In novels, the heroines always tossed and turned, exclaiming that they were unable to remain still and pass the night in a peaceful sleep. I did not toss and turn. Instead, I remained entirely still, *rigid*, I thought, as if the preservation of my life depended upon the immobility of my body. After several hours of this, I began to sweat from the exertion. Passing in and out of sleep quickly enough that I could no longer tell how much time had passed, my body bathed in dampness, I could pass a hand across my chest and feel the wetness clinging to my palm. The terror abated only at the first bit of sun peeking through the curtains. Instead of waiting for the day to start, I swept aside the sheets, as if this movement would somehow hasten the arrival of dawn. I had had enough of night. And yet still I lingered, unsure where to go and what to do without Lucy's presence to guide me, to help mark the time. She was always the first to rise, and I waited until she had retreated to the toilet to do the same. Without her, I stalled, lying, waiting.

Sleep-deprived from my night alone, I drifted off, despite my intention to stay awake. Instead my eyelids began to droop, my breathing becoming slow and heavy. I could feel myself falling asleep and yet I could do nothing at all to resist its soft, insistent call.

I awoke, heart pounding.

At first, I wasn't sure what had woken me, but then I became aware of her presence. I watched, my eyes still half-closed in pretense of sleep, as she lifted her blouse over her head, so that she stood in just her bra and underwear, a garter belt, rather than a girdle, holding up her stockings. My aunt had insisted I purchase the latter, despite my protests. *You may be naturally thin now,* she had said, *but just wait until you're married and have had a few babies — you'll be happy for it then.* I realized that I had never seen Lucy this unclothed before. It seemed strange that after years of living together, I had yet to see her without clothes, though I knew I had done much the same to avoid such a situation — changing when she was out of the room, or rushing to the bathroom to hastily throw on my outfit for the day. I was struck by the sheer whiteness of her skin. She was pale, I knew that already from her complexion, but there was something different seeing it stretched out along the rest of her body. She seemed to glow, so that I was convinced that even if it was completely dark in the room, I would still be able to find her.

I was suddenly conscious of just how naked she was. Both her bra and underwear were white, though not the same shade, and typical of the fashion — plain, with a simple trim of lace on the top, which fitted just below her navel. Her bra also had few adornments, just a

**118**

single white flower between her breasts. My eyes rested there for a moment, wondering at her generous proportions, ones that seemed ample compared to my own, and how she managed to hide them underneath her clothing. I tore my gaze away and back to her face. "Lucy," I said, sitting up, the word sounding like a whisper, too soft for what I had intended. "Lucy, where is it?" I asked, working to make my voice strong, sturdy.

Lucy looked over at me and frowned. "What?"

I let out a deep breath. "The bracelet."

"What bracelet?" she asked, shaking her head.

"My mother's bracelet," I pressed.

She shrugged. "I'm sure it's here somewhere. I haven't seen it since you last wore it. About a week ago?"

The words that I meant to speak, that I had prepared and memorized over the hours since we had last parted, evaporated then, disappearing into a vaporous trail before I could make them concrete. I struggled to understand what was happening. It was as if the past day, our past conversation, had not happened at all, as if — I stopped, shuddered — as if I had only imagined it. I looked up at my roommate, searching for something — anything — that could be considered as proof, evidence, of what she had done, of what she was still doing. There was nothing. She looked sincere, had sounded sincere, as if she truly didn't understand what it was that I was talking about, as if she were genuinely worried for me.

*I don't believe you.*

I was surprised by the vehemence behind my thoughts and worried, for one moment, that I had spoken them aloud. I shook my head. I held firm, resolute, reminding myself that I knew the truth. She had taken the bracelet, angry at me for Tom, for not spending as much time with her. But then — the idea was too strange, too unsettling. I wondered why I had even thought of it in the first place.

"I don't — I don't know," I finally said. They were the only words that I could think of as my brain stuttered and failed to keep up with what was happening, the only truth I could arrive at. I didn't know.

Lucy frowned. "Don't worry, Alice." She gave a brief smile. "We'll look for it together, I promise."

She enveloped me then, a more intimate gesture than the others we had previously shared, and not simply because she was standing in her underwear. For it wasn't my roommate who was exposed, who was laid bare — it was me, and all of my shortcomings, the fragility of my mind silently splayed between us. I did not like to think of it, of that period after my parents' death — but now it seemed to burst forth between us, undeniable, so that there was no other choice but to take it out and look at it once more.

I remained frozen, still unsure in that moment what to believe. But then, eventually, my arms left my side and I grasped her tightly — too tightly, I knew, but I was suddenly afraid to let her go, this person who knew each and every one of my secrets and had never judged me.

And so I clung to her, afraid to break from our strange embrace.

# CHAPTER
# SIX

# LUCY

I met Youssef at Cafe Tingis, several days later, at the agreed-upon time. He stood, leaning against the wall. "Ready?" he asked with a grin.

I smiled in return, ready to set out, to toss aside the words and warnings of others. For there was something about Youssef, I had decided, that felt infinitely more familiar than the Johns of the world. We were, both of us, on the outside, the periphery — myself by birth, Youssef by circumstance. There was something, if not quite as strong as the affinity I shared with Alice, at the very least an understanding, which I felt ran between us. I was still wary, of course, still cautious, but I trusted the otherness that marked us to form a connective thread that would keep us tied to each other, in spite of, or perhaps because of, the world around us. We left the medina behind, the confined and chaotic streets giving way to long, wide stretches. Fewer people dotted the path. We walked in a companionable silence, and though I was content to let my mind wander, I found myself turning to him and asking, "So is it Youssef, or Joseph?" I had been thinking about it in the hours since we had last met, ruminating over the difference. *Joseph. Youssef.* Were they the same, only derivations of one another? I wasn't sure. In fact, I was no longer entirely certain which one he had first introduced himself as, and which one Alice had used when referring to him. In my mind he was already Youssef, but that was possibly my projection alone, trying to instill upon him a particular brand of *foreignness* that appealed to my own sensibilities.

He shrugged. He had lit a cigarette as we began walking, and he reached for it now, taking a long pull, his calloused, darkened fingers apparently untroubled by the still-hot ash that spilled over them. "Does it matter?"

I frowned. *Did it?* I found I was no longer sure as I turned the question over in my mind. "It's your name," I protested.

"We, all of us, have many names," he responded.

I squinted. "How do you mean?"

"Husband. Father. Brother."

"Those are titles, not names," I countered.

He shrugged again, apparently unconcerned with the distinction. "Tangier has many names. First, she was Tingis." He paused and reached again for his cigarette. "In French, she is Tanger. In Spanish, she is Tánger. In Arabic, she is Tanjah. So you see, she has had many different names. Or titles. It is all the same."

I was quiet a moment more. "And so you go by either Youssef or Joseph, without any preference one way or another? Like her, I mean."

He smiled at this. "Yes, like her."

I moved toward the cliff's edge, looking down below. There were a few other couples, scattered here and there, to either side of us. Some sat, staring out at the ocean. Others unwrapped bundles of food. I saw bread and cheese, a few pieces of fruit. There were women in niqabs, women in Western dress. It seemed that this was a place for both locals and outsiders alike. Although where *here* was, I had yet to learn. I turned toward my companion, waiting for an explanation.

"This," he began at last, "is where the Mediterranean meets the Atlantic."

"Another layering," I observed ruefully.

"Yes, Alice." Again, he smiled, as if he were pleased, as if my answer had satisfied him and I had passed a test to which only he held the questions and answers. "It is a layering of history." He pointed to his feet, and I shifted my gaze to take in the white formation below us. "These are tombs. Phoenician. From the ancient city of Tingis."

I knew Tangier had been repetitively conquered throughout its existence, so it was always absorbing culture after culture until it had become an accumulation of everyone and everything that had passed through its gates over the centuries. I wondered whether anyone could still trace their lineage from this moment back to the very start without discovering at least one interruption, one interference from the outside world. I looked at my companion and wondered whether he had ever tried, wondered what his blood, what his heart would say, if it murmured as mine did. Whether his words would also be indecipherable or whether the message would be clearer, stronger — succeeding where I had failed.

"Come," Youssef called. "The café is just this way."

We moved onto a narrow pathway, one that was quickly ensconced by gleaming white walls set on either side of us. There was something different about life set high above the medina — quieter, cleaner perhaps, somehow apart from the frenzy that marked the streets below. It seemed only natural that this quiet, this stillness, should be reflected in the very stone. I placed my hand out. It was cool to the touch, and I let my fingers graze over its surface as we walked, my hand trailing languidly at my side. Soon the entrance appeared before us, the title formed by a grouping of rocks affixed to the white wall. CAFÉ HAFA. FONDÉ 1921. I reached out and swept my hand over the now-smooth pebbles, just a slightly darker shade than the stark white walls they were placed upon, wondering how many other hands had done the same in the years since they were first set there. I thought I could feel it then — *history*, heavy and weighted, as if the knowledge that great writers and painters and musicians had similarly passed through this entranceway provided a gravity missing from every other place before it.

Tangier, I decided then, was a ghost town in many ways. Only instead of being dead, empty, barren — it was alive. It was thriving and bursting with the remembrance of those great minds who had walked its alleyways, who had thought and sipped tea and been inspired here. It was a testimony, a tomb, to those who had come before. But there was not a sense that it was over, done with. There was something still here, churning, thriving, waiting to be discovered or released. I could feel it, tingling in my hands. I wondered if Alice felt it as well. In the days since my arrival, I had already found myself thinking that it was as if I had been waiting for Tangier my entire life. As if everything that I had done, every thought and action, had brought me here, specifically for the purpose of finding her once more, and the life we could have. It was perfect, I wanted to tell her, desperately wanting her to see it as well — how wonderfully perfect it all was: Tangier, her, the two of us together in this foreign city.

I turned the corner, my eyes quickly taking in the terrace-style seating that faced the ocean, the blue of the water offset by the dazzling white of the teahouse. "It's beautiful," I whispered, conscious of the words even before I uttered them.

Youssef did not seem to hear. Instead he moved slowly down the terraces, one by one, until selecting the very last. "So you can lean over and look out," he said, settling into a chair.

I nodded, knowing the moment had come. For I had another reason for agreeing to meet with him — something more important, more urgent than sightseeing, the knowledge of what Youssef had to offer now beating steadily within my chest. I sat next to him, trying to stop myself from imagining what he might be able to give me — a magic key, a secret incantation, something, anything, that was more definitive, more concrete than a glimpse caught in the reflection of a mirror.

I removed a photograph from my purse and placed it onto the table. "There is an Englishman," I said, but then, before I could continue, a young boy appeared, asking for our order. "Tea, please," I replied, and turning to Youssef, assured him, "It's my treat."

Money was an issue we had not broached before, but the look in his eyes as I glanced toward him warned me never to make the same offer again. I shifted in my seat, remaining silent, waiting. Although the words I wished to speak, the questions I wanted to ask — about John, about the local woman I had seen him with — burned, begging to be released, I could see that Youssef would have to set the tone, the pace of the conversation, after the misstep I had just taken.

"This is him?" he asked, after a few minutes of silence had elapsed, the tea delivered. He did not move to pick up the photograph, only let his fingers — clenched around a cigarette — linger above it. I worried for a moment that the ash would fall and leave a burn mark. I had removed the photograph earlier that morning from one of the frames in Alice's sitting room, my fingers working quietly, afraid that Alice would walk in and find me stealing a photograph of her husband. If caught, I hadn't a clue as to what I would say. I flinched now, watching as the ash from Youssef's cigarette grew, forming a leaning tower that burned, white and hot. If it fell, there would be no way to explain its presence — Alice would know.

I breathed a quick sigh of relief when Youssef moved his hand away, the ash tumbling to the ground.

"Yes." I hesitated, still waiting. In my mind, Youssef seemed to exist on some border, halfway between official and unofficial, between light and dark. In my imagining of how this conversation would proceed, I had assumed he would direct the ebb and flow of our words, that he would know how and where this was supposed to move. "There is also a woman," I said, casting a quick, hurried glance in his direction.

His eyebrows raised. "Not his wife, I presume?"

I shook my head. "No. But I wonder . . ."

He looked over at me. "What do you wonder, Alice?"

I held his gaze. "Who she is."

"Will it help?" he asked, tilting his head to the side. "To know this answer?"

I nodded, trying not to betray my eagerness. "Yes, I think so."

He paused and then said: "She is French." He tilted his head, apparently reconsidering his previous statement. "Well, half. Half this, half Moroccan." He gave a short laugh. "Not so uncommon as one might suppose."

I was about to sip my tea, but at his words, I stopped. "You know her?" I asked, surprised. "And do you know him?" I pointed to the photograph. I had figured that after our conversation Youssef might ask around, perhaps look into the matter himself — I had not considered that he might already possess the answers.

He shrugged. "Do you want to know?"

"Yes," I said, eagerly, adding *please* only as an afterthought.

He paused, as if he did not wish to continue, as if to emphasize that he was doing so only as a favor to me, and I wondered then what he would ask for in return, for I was certain that he would, that nothing he did was ever done without consideration of what could be gained. There was, I knew, a difference between refusing charity and giving something away for free.

"She is a Frenchwoman. An artist. That is how I know her." He paused. "She also works at a nightclub."

I let the word settle. A nightclub. We both knew what he actually meant. Despite the pretense, the nightclubs in the city were little more than a gathering place for prostitutes, geared toward Westerners. They were scattered throughout Tangier, most of them run by Frenchwomen who had decided to leave behind a life of selling their own bodies in order to sell another's.

"And her name?" I pressed.

"Sabine." He turned to look at me. "Her name is Sabine."

I leaned forward, all pretense at disinterest gone. At this information, at the power it provided me, my ears began to roar, my hands shake. I had not thought it would be this easy, and up until that moment, I had not wanted to admit to myself just how much I needed the answers. "And how long has this been going on? Between *them*, I mean."

He looked as though the question did not interest him. Instead he shifted in his seat, tossing his cigarette to the ground, and said lazily, "I would advise you not to be that girl."

At the word, I felt myself retreat, and though I could not explain my reaction, the sound and shape of it, the implication behind his use, set my heart racing. I silently chastised myself — it was only a word, after all. It did not mean anything. But no, I knew that was not true. It did mean something — everything. "What girl?" I demanded.

He looked at me pointedly. "*That* girl."

He was not talking about me, of course. I knew that he had wrongly assumed that it was my husband in the picture — and since I was supposed to be Alice in that moment, I supposed it technically was — and yet, though his words were not aimed at me, I was livid. Angry at him on behalf of Alice, and angry at something else, something I couldn't quite define.

I grabbed my purse and began to walk away. It was only several minutes later when I realized he had not shouted for me to come back, had not chased after me in order to apologize. No matter. I continued walking, out of Café Hafa, back to the spot above the tombs. If Youssef would not help, I decided that I would find a way on my own. I paused, looking out at the blue merging of the Atlantic and the Mediterranean, and I wondered if there was a word for it, a name, a title, to indicate this strange layering that seemed to be commonplace in Tangier, where everything was something else first, and nothing was ever entirely one thing. I thought of Alice again. She was something else in Tangier too, something completely different.

**129**

Hardened, distant, tired. A new Alice had been layered upon an old one, subsuming the original. But I had not given up hope. She was not simply Alice, John's wife. She had been her own person once, she had existed without him. What I needed to discover was how to get her back, how to move from Tangier to Tingis — and whether such a Herculean feat was even possible.

I had been walking in the Place de la Kasbah, alongside the fortified walls, stopping every now and then to scribble something in my notebook, trying to shake off my strange conversation with Youssef. I stopped at Bab Bhar, one of the gates that opened and broke up the monotony of the stone, so that there was nothing before me but the sea and the sky. Youssef had told me a story about the place, though I struggled, under the heat of the sun, to recall the exact words. Something about a beautiful female spirit who supposedly haunted the area, tempting men to their fate. I smiled at the idea.

And it was then that I saw him.

I was standing just outside the *bab*, hidden from his line of vision. At first, I thought he was alone, but then I saw him pull the woman beside him toward the wall — *the same woman from the bar*, I quickly realized, and my breath caught in my throat.

I noted first the confidence in the way the woman held herself, so unlike Alice: shoulders back, chest out, her body accentuated by the dress she was wearing, despite the loose shape of it. Her hair was piled on top of her head, her arms weighed down with heavy bracelets, both silver and gold, which clinked together as she moved.

I could see, under the light of the day, that she was most precisely as Youssef had described — a little Moroccan, a little French, the combination resulting in something that arrested one's attention, that seemed to clamor and fight for it, in fact. Her skin was golden, her eyes dark. I thought about John's love of Tangier and decided it all made sense — that his lust should find itself manifested in this creature, this woman who placed her foreignness on display in a way that was suited, designed, to attract a foreigner's eye. I pitied the girl — for that was, I could now see as well, all that she was. No more than seventeen years old, I guessed.

Moving closer behind my hiding space, feeling the hot bite of the wall behind me, I watched as John's fingers — his hands freckled and sun-kissed — splayed themselves across her tiny waist, his desire so evident, so easy. I stood, mesmerized by his hands, by their quick, insistent movements under the hot, unforgiving sun. My face burned, though not from the heat of the day, and ashamed then at the ache I felt watching them together, I moved quickly to turn away.

Later I would wonder at the calmness of my reaction, for I supposed that I should have felt something like outrage, upon seeing John there, his betrayal displayed so brazenly under the hot, brilliant sun of Morocco. He must have reasoned that Alice would never find out, as she rarely left the apartment and knew no one else in the city. He had, it seemed, decided to take full advantage of that fact.

But now, she had me.

It was something that must have occurred to him as well, when he turned and saw me standing there, underneath the arch. His face visibly paled beneath his tan and he started toward me, his arms still wrapped around the woman, *entangled*, I thought, and not in any way that could be explained away — particularly not if I had witnessed what had come before. I could see him thinking, calculating, wondering how long I had been there and just how much I had seen. At last his hands dropped away and he started toward me.

But I was quicker.

I moved from my perch into the crowd — tourists crowding the *bab* for a perfect photo, locals trailing behind, trying desperately to unload their jewelry, their hats, whatever piece of merchandise was on sale. It was easy to become lost, to let myself be swept up in the tide. I surrendered to its chaos, to the ebb and flow that grasped me in its clutches and refused to release me. I let it carry me farther and farther away until I felt brave enough to glance over my shoulder. I could barely make out his person. He was simply a small speck of color against a brightly decorated canvas.

My face was flushed from the exertion of my escape, my breath coming in small, sharp gasps. I wondered then whether John would confront me, whether I would return to the flat only to find him waiting, demanding to know what I had seen and whether or not I would tell Alice. A part of me hoped that he would, that his figure would be the one to greet me — I could feel the promise of it rush through me, could feel my fingers begin to tingle, my toes curl in anticipation. Walking back to the apartment — for I could no longer imagine pursuing my earlier wanderings — I noticed that I had managed to drop my notebook somewhere during my escape. And yet the realization seemed dulled somehow — far away and altogether foreign, as if it, what I had been doing earlier, could not possibly belong to the person I was in that moment, a person who burned and raged and did not wish to be silent. I headed for the flat, walking for what seemed like hours, though it could not have been more than a handful of minutes. I watched as the shadows around me began to lengthen, felt the heat of the day begin to dissipate. My heartbeat began to slow, my breath return to normal. By the time I reached the Quartier du Marshan, the emotions that had earlier coursed through me seemed to evaporate, leaking out of my skin, my pores, until there was nothing left but pure and utter exhaustion.

I let out a small sigh and continued inside.

# CHAPTER
# SEVEN

## ALICE

'It's so hot."

Lucy paused at my words, waiting for me to catch my breath as we made our way to Café Hafa. The day was too thick, the sun too hot — but she had been determined, earlier that morning, that I accompany her to the café. I could feel my face, already red and sticky with sweat.

"I can't believe you've never been," she said, trying, I suspected, to distract me from the heat, though the comment only sat poorly with me.

I could feel my face grow more crimson still, my breathing ragged.

I placed one foot in front of the other, the sun burning the back of my neck, warming the top of my head, so that I looked with envy at the turban that Lucy had wrapped her own hair underneath that morning. She had traded, it seemed, her usual hat — an awful design made of black straw — for a pale wrap she had no doubt found in one of the shops frequented by expats. Earlier I had stared rather hard at the sight of it, just as we were leaving. *It's the fashion now*, she had assured me, though I had continued to watch her with

**134**

unease. It was not the design itself that had stopped me — but rather, the realization of just how well Lucy blended in with the rest of the expatriates that flooded the streets of Tangier. I had been here for months already, while her feet had barely touched soil for a week, and already it looked as though she was the one who lived here, as though I was only the visitor. It was with embarrassment that I had then reached for my own hat — a rather small white pillbox that fit oddly on top my hair.

"It's supposed to have breathtaking views," Lucy said.

I peered at her, curious. "How did you hear about it?"

"Some friends at the bookshop. The Librairie des Colonnes," she replied.

I nodded, wondering when she had managed to sneak in a visit there as well.

"You sound almost like a local now," I said, my voice, I knew, tinged with something that made me uneasy.

After that day when she had first told me about Youssef, she had continued to return to the flat late each night, ready to regale me with further tales of her adventures, and I had listened with that same envy, the little knot growing into something large and not so easily managed. Instead I had tried to reshape it, had tried to see Tangier though her eyes, her enthusiasm, similar to John's, describing a world I could never manage to catch a glimpse of, though all three of us walked upon the same cobblestones. And so when she had demanded, at the end of her first week, that I

**135**

accompany her, I agreed, anxious to discover what it was that I had been missing, that my eyes refused to see.

"You should come with me next time," she offered now. "To the bookstore."

I did not respond.

We walked for a few more minutes in silence until at last we came to stand upon a strange white surface, just a few feet, I could see, from the edge of a cliff. "It's beautiful, isn't it?" she ventured, looking over at me. She waited for a reply so that I could feel her, reaching out. *It is, of course it is*, I wanted to say, but something stopped the words, something stilled me. There were still too many questions and answers obscured by the fog, but which shone, nevertheless, red and bright and warning.

"It's bluer than anything at home," I conceded, continuing to stare out at the ocean, working to make my face unreadable.

"These are tombs, just below us," she continued.

We stood close together, staring at the rectangular formations, at the strange dips and curves and the puddles of water that pocketed the white rock. "Where? Directly below us?"

She nodded. "The tombs are nearly two thousand years old. From when the city was called Tingis."

"Tingis?" I asked, with a small smile.

"That was the name of the ancient Phoenician city, before Tangier ever existed." She removed her sunglasses, squinting against the sun. "Tangier has had a lot of different names, apparently. Tingis is only one of them."

"What were the others?" I asked, feeling my voice become lazy under the heat of the sun.

"There's Tingis, of course. Tingi, Titgam, Tánger, Tangiers, Tangier — I guess it depends who you ask and how they pronounce it."

I turned to her. "How do you pronounce it?"

She liked the question, I could see — that it mattered to me what she thought. She seemed to consider for a moment, as if weighing the answer. "I suppose I'll always say Tangier. But I like the idea of Tingis. Of what it was originally, before it was changed by all the various invaders."

"There is a sort of romance," I admitted.

"It's a country steeped in mythology," she replied. "Do you know it's thought that even Ulysses must have passed Tangier during his travels?"

She looked so proud, standing on top of the Phoenician tombs, as if she had made the discovery herself. I tried to picture it — Lucy as some great explorer or conqueror, and I found the idea suited her. Her excitement was so palpable that I could almost feel it, transferring from her body into my own. The heat pulsed around us, the sun pressing down, and yet still, as we moved away from the view, I could sense that we were both reluctant to leave it behind. It was calm here, as if some sort of magic spell divided it from the rest of the city. While down below there was shouting and bartering, the scent of thousands of perspiring bodies pressed up against one another, dirty and unwavering

— up here, there was only silence. Only the warm, inviting blue that stretched out and rushed into the currents of the Atlantic, only the smell of the ocean, clean and fresh. I might have imagined it, but I felt as though our feet dragged as we turned away, as we began to close the short distance between us and the café.

We sat on one of the lower terraces, under a few scraggly trees. The relief was immediate and I could breathe again. Up until that moment, I had not realized just how warm I had become, standing in the open field before the ocean, without a single tree for protection.

At our entrance, one of the workers ran over, balancing a swinging contraption that allowed him to carry several glasses of tea at once, its metallic coating glinting off the bright sun. Lucy ordered two, and thanked him: *Choukran*.

I mused briefly over the fact that "thank you" and "no thank you" were so closely related — the difference of a word added to the latter. It was, I realized, the type of inane observation that Lucy would probably enjoy. I closed my eyes and sighed. Wasps swarmed the blossoms on the trees above but for the most part ignored us, even our tall glasses of sugary, hot tea. It should have been peaceful, I should have felt relaxed — but anxiety gnawed at me, refusing to be ignored.

Her arrival had set something in motion. I could feel it already — churning, refusing to remain dormant. And yet, I could feel us both stalled, waiting for that something to happen, as if we had been waiting for it ever since that day she had stepped off the boat. I had the sudden irresistible urge to set it in motion then, to push us, together, over the cliff — to ask her everything that I had been wondering, puzzling over, ever since she had arrived in Tangier, ever since I had first met her at Bennington. All the things that eluded me, slipping through my fingers, the strange wisps of a girl I seemed to have conjured out of my misery but who had never seemed to materialize into something real, something concrete.

I was angry, the heat turning my mood. I could feel it, simmering around me, those things that I did not understand, the places and people that remained a mystery to me, that refused to yield no matter how often I puzzled over them. Tangier and Lucy were the same, I thought. Both unsolvable riddles that refused to leave me in peace. And I had tired of it — of the not knowing, of always feeling as though I were on the outside of things, just on the periphery.

"Are you all right, Alice?" Lucy asked.

"I'm fine," I replied, though I knew there was an unmistakable edge to my voice as I pushed my sunglasses farther up the bridge of my nose. They had begun to slip from the sweat. I sipped my tea and then thrust it away in frustration. I was silent for a time, and then, only when I was certain that she did not intend to break the silence herself, I began, my eyes squinting in the sun. "I'll never understand it."

Lucy turned to me. "What?"

"This." I indicated the mint tea. "How on earth anyone can drink hot tea in weather like this."

"You can get used to anything eventually," she surmised. "It all starts to seem normal after a while."

"Not to me," I said, rubbing at my fingertips, angry that I had held on to the glass for a moment too long, so that the hot surface had burned my skin, angrier still that Lucy had not rushed to agree with me, with my inane complaint. "Not this. I don't think I'll ever be able to drink this in such hot weather. I don't think I'll ever *want* to drink it in any weather, to be honest."

She took a sip from her own tall glass. "Don't you enjoy it?"

I shot her a look then — *hysterical*, I thought — though I quickly swept it away. "I would quite literally murder someone for a cup of builder's tea at this point," I told her.

A few heads turned our way, and I realized that my tone was wavering somewhere between lighthearted and serious, skirting the liminal boundaries between laughing and crying. Lucy extended her hand to me, but I did not take it. "Are you all right?" she asked again.

I considered, tired already of the question — of what I suspected was the truth.

"In New England," Lucy began, abruptly, "my father had the most ingenious way of keeping us all cool during the heat waves."

"And what was that?" I asked, the question curt, irritated by this shift, this change in conversation.

But if Lucy noticed, she only carried on, and I wondered then if it was *because* she could sense my flaring temper that she had introduced the topic — an attempt at distraction. "He used to bring out the garden hose — you have those in England, don't you?"

I nodded but remained silent.

"Well, he used to take the hose and then walk around the house, watering the bricks."

I frowned. "The bricks?"

"Yes, the bricks of the house."

"Why on earth would he do that?" I questioned.

She smiled. "That's where all the heat is — the bricks trap it all in. So, very carefully, my father would circle the house, spraying the water onto every inch, until the bricks steamed from the combination of hot and cold." She stopped, and in her silence I imagined it, conjuring up the image of a tiny brick house, a father who cared for his daughter enough that he lingered on the bricks surrounding her bedroom window, making sure they were properly glistening before moving on.

"Did it really help?" I asked, my voice softer than it had been. I looked at Lucy and I wondered what she was thinking — if she was also imagining that small house in the middle of nowhere New England, or if she was thinking of somewhere else altogether.

"It did," Lucy said, in a tone that I suspected was meant to assure me, to calm me. "I remember lying on my bed, listening to the water as it sprayed against my bedroom wall. And I could feel it. As I lay there, my eyes closed, the curtains drawn to keep out the sun, so the room was entirely lost in darkness, I could feel the moment the water hit, the instant relief it provided. As if someone had turned on a fan and placed it directly in front of me. Sometimes I would get goose bumps, it was so cold."

I was quiet for a moment, thinking, imagining the cool breeze on my skin. I felt strangely calm, surrounded by the love of a father for his daughter, by the cool draft he had sweated and worked to provide for her. Something tugged at my memory. I remembered that day in Jennings Hall, all those years ago, and turning to Lucy, I lowered my sunglasses and said, "I thought you didn't remember your father."

A moment passed by, and another still, so that I wondered if she would ignore my words altogether. And then, she did not turn to me, did not take off her own sunglasses; instead she remained facing the ocean, her face as sturdy as the stone we had just stood upon. "I remember *that*," she said, her tone a warning, a threat.

I turned away from her and remained silent.

It had been snowing heavily that night. Of course, it was the Green Mountains, and in the heart of winter it seemed like it was always either snowing or threatening to snow, a blanket of ghostly white providing a permanent coat on the ground. But that night had been different. The snow stuck not only to the pavement but also to the lights, to one's own person, so that everything passed by in a swirl as you fought and struggled to make your way through it.

Lucy and I had been fighting.

I had returned, earlier in the day, before the snow began, from a trip to New York. I had told everyone that it was an assignment for my photography class, but really it had been a chance for escape, a respite from the suffocating unease that had steadily crept between Lucy and me over the last year, so that it was suddenly all that existed between us. My aunt had not even been in town that weekend. I had arranged to stay at a boardinghouse in the city, one that I had passed numerous times and had deemed safe enough. I had thought, for a moment, of inviting Tom to join me, to make it a mini break rather than an escape, but in the end, I knew what I needed most was to be alone, from both of them, from the constant back-and-forth that I had begun to experience each and every day. As if I could actually feel it — my bones, my skin, being pulled between them, taut and threatening to break.

In New York, unlike Vermont, the air was neither clean nor crisp.

Instead it was heavy, laden with dust and grease and smoke. It seemed to hang, damp and thick, clinging to my skin. Stepping off the bus and into the city, I had smiled in relief. I spent the next two days roaming the streets, taking pictures. I finished all the rolls of film I had brought with me and ended up stopping into a camera shop to buy half a dozen more. Those, I finished too. There was something relaxing about being alone — finally alone — among a sea of people that I did not know and who did not know me. I lost myself in the facelessness of it all, thrilled to find myself surrounded by strangers. I sat on park benches, listening to the conversations that took place around me. I explored the stainless steel diners of the city, sitting at the counters, eating grilled cheese and sipping burned coffee, enjoying the weighty feel of the porcelain mug in my hand. And while rations were now a thing of the past, the notices still hung, fading and colored with grease — DO NOT ASK FOR BUTTER TODAY. NO HAMBURGERS, IT'S TUESDAY — an enduring reminder.

Returning to campus Sunday evening, I went straight to the darkroom to begin developing, not yet ready to shed the feeling of calm, of peace, that I had managed to summon amid the chaos of the city. I hummed quietly to myself as I removed the film in the darkened room, my hands moving with quick, memorized movements as I wound it around the spool, feeling for that little groove where the film would catch. I placed each one, gingerly, inside the canister, and once developed, hung them carefully on the line. Almost an hour later, the chemicals returned to the correct shelves, the negatives dry, I made a contact sheet of each, eager to see whether I had managed to capture anything worthwhile during my short stay.

It was then that I noticed her.

At first I thought it was only my imagination, or a trick of the light. Perhaps my eyes were simply tired. I told myself that there was any number of explanations for what I was seeing, that it was not real. That the evidence of her — the back of her coat, the profile of her face — could not in fact belong to her.

But then I found it: the one photograph where she hadn't managed to step completely out of the way, where not only a glimpse of her could be seen but also the entirety of her face. It was her. It was Lucy. And she

144

was there, following me — *stalking* me — present in each and every frame I had taken in New York.

It was easy to miss, if I hadn't been familiar with her long, tangled hair, if I hadn't seen her peacoat draped over the chair in our room, day after day. Perhaps then I wouldn't have noticed it. She was only in the background, after all, only in the corner of the photograph. She was never the focus, never in the forefront.

But then, there was the one where she had not managed to avoid my lens, where her face stared up at me, her eyes large and unblinking. Watching me, always watching.

I clasped the photograph in my hand, which was now trembling, and left the darkroom, not bothering to clean up, not bothering to switch off the lights, but walking out into the dark, out into the snow, the steady throb of it making even the short walk between the darkroom and our house nearly impossible. I kept the photograph, the evidence, hidden inside my coat. An effort to keep it protected from the elements, so that when I produced it, when I placed it in front of her at last, there would only be a streak here or there where it had been distorted by the snow.

She had been sitting at her desk, head bent over a book, and made no move to rise at my abrupt entrance. She was silent for a moment, looking down at the photograph, a strange stillness to her movements as she raised her eyes and asked, "What is this?" Her face closed and unreadable.

"Look," I said, my hand shaking as I pushed the photograph closer to her. When I was met with the same stony silence, I thrust my finger toward the figure displayed before us. "I know it's you, Lucy," I said, doing my best to make my voice hard. "The photograph may be a bit grainy, but I know it's you."

She did not speak, and in the absence of words, my eyes traveled to the photograph. I was struck, then, by just *how* grainy the photograph actually was. I scanned it again. Everything was just as I remembered, but it was as if the focus was off, just a tiny amount, so that the distinct lines of each face — *her* face, in particular — were blurry rather than sharp. Shadows.

She frowned, standing now. "You saw me in New York?"

No, that wasn't what I had meant. I shook my head. "No, in the picture," I said, fumbling for words. "You were there, I know you were."

"Alice, I've been here the entire weekend."

Her hands were on my shoulders, her fingers pressing into my skin. It was meant as a gesture of comfort, of concern, I knew, but instead I felt as though her fingertips were burning into my flesh.

I had to get out.

My heart had begun to beat, fast and unsteady. My throat felt as though it were closing up, and each breath was a struggle, a strain. I felt my skin begin to flush, and I wrenched myself free, desperate to put space between us, to remove myself from her touch. "You're lying," I said, heading toward the door, the words strangled in my throat.

In the hallway, I found the pay phone and called Tom. Afterward, I struggled to recall what it was that I had told him, my voice low and urgent, words tumbling from my mouth before I could consider them. But I remembered, always, what he had said in return — that he would come, that it didn't matter about the blizzard. That he would come and get me, that he wouldn't leave me alone, he promised.

I headed outside, into the freezing cold, the snow falling to the ground at a faster rate than I had seen in all my years in the Green Mountains, and Lucy followed, at first placating, then arguing and then begging — for me to stay, for me to forget the photograph. I did not relent, only stood, waiting until Tom eventually arrived, his face distorted from the melting ice on the car. I had turned to go then, when a hand, hard and unyielding, forced me to pause.

"Don't get in the car, Alice."

"Let me go, Lucy," I commanded, wrenching free of her grasp.

"Alice," she said, her voice desperate now, I thought. "You can't just go."

I spun around. "Why not?" I didn't need a response, I could have simply gotten in the car and left, but I wanted to know, in that instance, what she would say, what words she would find to extract herself from this as well. She was silent, and I shook my head. "I want you to leave me alone," I shouted then, the wind burning my cheeks, stealing my words. "I want you to disappear and never come back."

Then I turned and got into the car.

★　★　★

Tom was quiet as we drove away, perhaps sensing that I did not want to speak, that I did not want to discuss what had happened. I thought instead about where we would go — town, perhaps, to our favorite little diner, on US Route 7. We would sit and drink good, strong coffee and it would steady my hands, which now trembled in my lap. I shook my head, trying to dislodge whatever was left of Lucy there. No more, I promised myself. Instead I would concentrate on the future, on Tom. And once we reached that diner, perhaps I would finally tell him what I had once told Lucy, about the months after my parents' death, the shadows, the asylum — and then, even those things I had not.

I would tell him, I had decided, about the real reason for the bouts of anxiety — about the accident that had killed my parents and how I worried, still, even then, that I was the one to blame. After all, I had been the last one to use that wretched paraffin heater. I could still picture it in my mind: the little black contraption my father had brought home one day. He had been so proud, showing me how to carefully lift the lid in order to fill it with the paraffin, and from there, how to press the wick into the liquid on one end and light it on the other. It would keep us warm during the winter, he had promised. And what was better, it would save money, since the heater was portable and could be picked up and carried from room to room. But *you must always be careful*, he had warned me, *the paraffin is highly inflammable*. I still remembered my childish response: *Inflammable? Does that mean it won't catch fire?* He had laughed at that, at his *silly little Alice in*

**148**

*Wonderland*. He had pulled me into a tight embrace — the last I could ever remember receiving from him.

That was what I had been thinking about — the ghosts of my past that I could never quite manage to dispel, along with the simple nagging question: had it been my fault, had I been the last one to use the heater that claimed my parents' lives? — when it happened.

We had reached the top of the hill and begun the descent down the drive, on the long twisting road that would lead us out of the college's property and into the town, when Tom turned to me, panic flooding his eyes, and said, "They aren't working."

"What aren't working?" I asked, my voice lazy as I peered out of the car and into the darkness. It wasn't yet six o'clock, but already the winter darkness had fallen, making it nearly impossible to see anything within a few feet without a light. I lifted my hand in front of me, wondering whether I would be able to make out all of its features. I exhaled, watching my breath emerge in a tiny cloud before dissipating into the air.

"The brakes."

I dropped my hand. I took in Tom's stricken face, which I could still make out, even in the darkness. That was what struck me first, in that strange little moment. But then I heard his foot, pumping away at the useless pedal and something inside me stilled. "What do you mean?" I whispered.

"I mean they won't work," he said, his voice rising in panic.

The car had nearly reached the end of the drive by then, that point at which the private pathway of Bennington's road connected with the public one. In front of us, I watched as one car passed by, and then another, each one half-hidden, it seemed, by the darkness. I closed my eyes, held my breath. But I knew that even if we somehow managed not to crash into another car, there was still the problem of the road — which stretched immediately to the left and right, but not directly ahead. Instead, there was a flimsy barricade and beyond that — I swallowed nervously — our self-christened End of the Universe. My gaze quickly took in the sugar maples beyond the railing, standing in sinister formation.

I turned then. Twisting around, peering back at the darkness behind us, knowing that I would not be able to see anything — that I would not be able to see *her*, even though I could feel her still, watching. I thought of her words, of her insistence that I not get into the automobile, and I felt my stomach lurch — though whether from the movement of the car or the realization of something greater, something darker, I was never entirely certain.

And then Tom shouted, telling me to jump, so that my shaking hands reached for the cold handle. There was nothing then. Only the strange sensation of my body being lifted into the air, weightless and suspended. Afterward, there was blood and fire, broken bones and bruises, but I did not feel any of it. Only the snow underneath my face, the cold, biting pain of it against my cheek.

**150**

And Lucy.

Somewhere in the distance, looking at me — her eyes wide, watching — *alive*.

It was the last thing that I remembered from that night.

Aunt Maude arrived in the days afterward. I was never sure how many had passed before she swept in, her stern, frowning face serving as a source of comfort, a return to normalcy in the swirling chaos that had surrounded me ever since I had woken. I had scarcely been left alone during that time, so it seemed there was always someone beside me, in the room, outside the room, peering in. And yet, not one of them ever spoke to me, with me — only around me, at me, instructions and directions, orders, but no information, nothing that told me what had happened, how it had happened, and perhaps most important, why.

"Maude," I whispered, my lips parched and cracked.

She moved quickly beside me, though she did not take my hand. "Quiet, dear," she said.

I closed my eyes at the sound of her voice, at her familiar accent, so similar to my own. Her face, though decidedly feminine, still held something of my father, her brother, in it as well, such that I felt her reassurance wash over me, blanket me. My body sagged, and for the first time in days, I felt the adrenaline begin to seep from my pores, so that all at once I felt comforted, and I felt pain, the bruises and cuts I had ignored, that I had refused to feel, creeping upon me so that they could no longer be denied. I felt wetness against my cheeks and realized that I had begun to cry.

"Lucy," I whispered. "Where is Lucy?" But I was uncertain whether she could understand my words, distorted as they were by my increasing sobs. "You have to speak with her, to ask her about what happened."

"There, there," Maude whispered, lowering herself into the seat beside me. She still did not move to touch me, though in that moment I wished that she would. "You're overwrought, Alice, confused. But everything will be all right, my dear. I will take care of it, you have my word."

A week later, I was out of the hospital and on my way back to England. No one spoke of Tom, of his funeral, of an invitation I knew would not come. Only once was Lucy mentioned, when the police, bullied and cowed by Maude, were permitted to ask a few questions, under her direct supervision. My answers were short, clipped. They raised their eyebrows when I asked about Lucy Mason, about whether they had spoken to her — but then a sharp look from Maude silenced any further questions. "She's confused, Officers, you must excuse her." She turned to me and smiled. "You're confused, Alice, dear."

At first, I had frowned at her words, but soon I had begun to wonder whether perhaps she was right. That night already seemed distant, the details lost to me, so the only thing remaining was the conviction that Lucy was somehow the key to it all, the answer to the question that I could not quite figure out. I searched my memory but could find nothing more definitive than the injured feelings of a girl that had been abandoned by her best friend, or the look she had given me that night as I had walked away, had crawled into the car, choosing another over her, severing whatever bond it was that had connected us. I pushed the image from my mind.

Perhaps Maude was right.

"You're confused, Alice," she whispered again, the crinkles around her eyes deepening. "Your grief is causing you to imagine things. But you must not allow it to — you must put them out of your mind." She attempted a smile. "Do not worry, my dear. I will take care of everything."

I had nodded dully, still lost in a cocoon of my own grief. If Aunt Maude said that Lucy did not hold the answers, then I would trust her, completely. I thought back to when my parents had died, how lost in grief I had been, how the shadows had stolen across my vision and I had howled for her to make them go away. And she had. She had fixed me, just as she had promised, if not completely, at least the best she could, gluing and taping back the pieces of me that had fallen apart in the aftermath of my parents' death. And so now, now I would trust her again, to put me back together, just like the old nursery rhyme, to make things right. I found comfort in the thought, in the ability to let it go — my anger, my hatred, my conviction. There was a peace in letting it slip between my fingers, no longer a mass that I was forced to grasp, to cling to, with all my might. After all, Tom was gone, nothing else mattered. Not Lucy, not what had happened to her in those days afterward, her side of the room empty and still, not even the strange words that my aunt had spoken.

And so, I did not ask her what they meant.

In the quiet, I could feel it again — the anger, just like that night — beginning to grow. I was tired of the elusive answers, of the bits of information that Lucy fed me only when it suited her. I still did not know why she was in Tangier, not really, or how long she planned to stay. I did not even know how she spent her days, only the stories she told me each night. I could feel my face start to flush, feel my hands start to tremble. I willed myself to remain calm, to instead focus on my mint tea, which had grown cold and thick, but I found I couldn't concentrate. I was tired of the pretense and I could not continue, even if she could. I felt my emotions begin to well, begin to creep inside, to the hollow of my bones, the accusation sitting on the edge of my tongue.

The truth was that nothing had felt right since the night of the accident. And between us, between Lucy and me, things had started to sour long before then, so that the time since we had been close was so long ago now that I struggled to remember. There were moments when I would catch pieces of it, glimmering in the distance, when I could feel that same pull toward her, strong and insistent — but then there was something else there as well, something hard and unyielding, so that I still did not entirely trust her, felt that I could never trust her, after everything that had happened, not even if I had wanted to.

154

I knew, of course, that she was not responsible for what happened, not in the sense that I had first suspected, that dark, cold night when I had turned around in the car, eyes blazing, certain she was the one. In my mind, I made her into something profane, something monstrous — one of my shadows that lurked in the darkness, waiting, always waiting, to lay hold of me. The truth was much more simple. The truth was that, had it not been for her, I would not have made that telephone call, would not have crawled inside his automobile the night of the blizzard. If it had not been for her jealousy, her strangeness, it would never have happened. That was the truth, or at least part of it. It was the real reason why I had stopped and stuttered at her presence the morning she had arrived in Tangier, for in her I would always be reminded of him, of what had happened, of what she had made happen.

But there was something more too.

I turned to her now, lowering my black sunglasses once more, so that my eyes peered out at her, wide and unflinching. I opened my mouth to tell her, to accuse her, finally, but instead, what I said was "You left." I had meant the words as a question, but they fell, heavy and dull, and I wondered then whether that wasn't the real reason why I had spent so long blaming her — for abandoning me when I needed her most. "After the accident, after Tom," I said, giving voice to what I had long since puzzled over, of what I had read as evidence of her guilt, of her admittance. "You left."

She looked up at me, squinting. "You told me to, Alice."

155

Her words were simple, but true. I had told her to go that night, had told her other things that I could no longer remember but that I felt in the pit of my stomach on those rare occasions when I let the memories find their way in. I had wished for awful things in those moments and they had come true — only it hadn't been to her that they had happened. They had happened to me, to Tom.

And it was my fault, not hers, that they had.

It began to slip away then — the wall that I had placed between us since her arrival, since that night of the blizzard. I felt it give way in that moment, the resistance that I had worked so hard to cultivate, its mass no longer something that was tangible, solid, so that my fingers grasped, unable to hold on to it any longer.

"I haven't felt like myself since we arrived, not really," I said then, pausing a moment, letting the confession settle between us. "It all feels too much sometimes, don't you think? Sometimes I feel as though I can't breathe. I'm filled with so much dread at the thought of walking out my front door on my own. I know it's ridiculous, but I can't help it. I just don't feel myself here." I stopped, staring into space, my breath heavy and ragged. "I know it's all down to me — isn't it? I chose to come here." A laugh escaped from me. "Although what other choice did I have, really."

Lucy waited the space of a few moments before speaking: "Is it really as bad as all that, Alice?"

I wanted to flinch then, under the intensity of her gaze, but I didn't. I could see from her face — could

**156**

tell from the sound of her voice — that she didn't understand, that she couldn't. I thought of what she had said earlier, about the different names that Tangier had had over the course of history. In some ways, I felt like it was appropriate to the moment — we were both of us in the same place, but in two very different versions of Tangier, and I could not imagine hers, a place of excitement, a place to start anew. Mine held only fear and isolation. "Of course not," I murmured, my voice barely above a whisper. But then, because I could not stop, not when the words were finally pouring from me, I asked, "Do you ever regret going to Bennington?"

Lucy frowned, startled it seemed by my words. "Regret it?"

My voice wavered as I spoke. "Yes. Sometimes I feel like I do, regret it, I mean, almost horribly so. I feel like they lied to us, in a way. Making us feel like we could go off into the world and be equal to them — to men, I mean. But it's all lies, isn't it? They lied to us. We thought we were learning a vocation, but really, they're just a finishing school in disguise. Preparing us with hobbies to pass the time once we marry. It makes it all so much more difficult."

"But, Alice," Lucy began, "it doesn't have to be like that."

A laugh escaped me, one that sounded more akin to a sob than anything else. I rushed to cover it. "Don't mind me, Lucy. It's the heat, I think. I never was very good with it. There's something about a hot, sunny day that puts my teeth on edge. I always feel as though I'm

**157**

teetering on the precipice of something." I paused. "It will pass."

But in that moment I knew that I didn't want it to pass. I wanted — oh, I didn't know what. For her to take my hand, like she had in the old days, to tell me that if I wanted to get away from Tangier, she would be that for me — my way out. The words swelled on my lips — everything, the whole mess: how distant John had grown over the months, how I had become convinced that I had made the wrong decision when I had agreed to marry him, to come to this wretched place. I longed to speak then, to confide, to tell Lucy everything. But the words would not come.

I stood, fumbling in my purse for francs, looking around for the boy who had served us our tea, anxious to leave, though to go where, I didn't know. I felt stuck, trapped, and the realization that there was no way out, no place that I could escape to, threatened to overwhelm me. In response, Lucy stood, placing a few coins on the table, her movements anticipating my own once more, I noted.

We were halfway up the aisle of the terraced settings when I felt Lucy's body press against my own, when I heard a crash sound, directly below. I jumped, startled by the noise but certain, in that moment, that it had been one of the waiters, perhaps the boy who had served us our tea, having dropped one of those swinging contraptions from his hands. But then I glanced backward and saw her — a woman, vaguely familiar, though I couldn't quite manage to place her — lying at the bottom of the stairs, the broken glass surrounding her an intricate mosaic that shimmered underneath the afternoon sun.

My hand flew to my mouth, aghast. "Lucy?" I heard myself whisper.

The café erupted in pandemonium then. The waiters rushed down to assist the woman, who was, I saw with a relieved sigh, sitting up, slowly. Customers rose from their seats, a few even leaving their belongings unattended as they rushed to offer aid. I could see that the woman's arms and legs had been badly scraped up — by the fall, by the glass, I didn't know. She stood, testing her ankle, as though hesitant to place any weight on it.

And then she looked up, to where Lucy and I stood, her eyes dark and shining.

I felt my stomach turn, felt the taste of the mint from the tea go sour in my mouth. Something like fear ran through me then, so that I reached out my hand, clamping onto Lucy's wrist. "Can we go?" I asked, my voice broken, shattered. My fingers, I knew, were digging into her skin, but I could not stop, could not pause the strange rising tide of panic. For in that moment, despite everything, despite all my uneasiness and suspicions, and everything that had occurred between us over the years, I was certain of the one thing I had always known about Lucy: that she loved me, that she would do anything to help me. And so I turned to her now, my voice pleading, and said, "Oh, please, Lucy, can't we go?"

I wasn't sure exactly what I meant by those words. I knew only that I had to get away — from the café, from the woman's insistent gaze, from the truth of my relationship with John. I could not look at it, could not take it out into the sun and examine it — not just yet. In that moment, I only wanted to be away from it, from him.

From Tangier.

# II

# CHAPTER
# EIGHT

## LUCY

"We should go to chefchaouen."

I made the pronouncement over breakfast as Alice and I sat silently over our tea and bread, voicing the words before thinking them through, before worrying about whether her answer would be yes or no. I knew only that after the incident at Café Hafa, I was desperate for more traces of Alice — of the original, ancient Alice who had once spent late nights with me in the local diner, laughing over coffee and maple syrup pancakes, the one I had sat next to during winter, watching as the fire rose and fell before us. I realized now that Morocco threatened to burn those memories away — burn the both of us to ash. We needed a break — from the heat, from the city, from Tangier.

"We could hire a grand taxi to drive us," I explained. "It's not that expensive and it's fairly easy. I could go now and find one and be back in no time at all. You wouldn't have to do a thing but pack a bag. And it's supposed to be beautiful, Alice." I spoke hastily, as if a torrent of words would be enough to protect me from her protestations, her probable refusal.

Alice nodded, her teacup held tightly between her two hands, her knuckles white. "All right, then." The words slipped out quickly, as if she needed to expunge them from her body before she had time to consider — to reconsider. "All right, Lucy. Let's go."

She smiled, and in it I could see a glimmer of hope, a glimmer of *her*.

I knew that it was time then. To tell her what I had seen, first at the bar and later in the streets of Tangier. That now was the time to relay all my hopes and dreams for the future, for us, so that the two of us could move forward together, just like we had always planned. But first we needed to get away — from John, from Tangier, where the past would remain steadfastly behind and the present could no longer touch us.

We arrived three hours later. The ride was supposed to take only two, but Alice had pleaded for the driver to pull the taxi over so that she could hop out and take photographs of the scenery — of the Rif women, of the rolling green mountains that looked entirely out of place in Morocco. At first the driver had not understood. The poor man had, in fact, looked fairly frightened when Alice had begun exclaiming wildly for him to stop and then, failing to make her point with words, began vigorously tapping him on the shoulder.

It was the first time I had seen her produce the camera that had once belonged to her mother. The casing surrounding the lens had been chipped — *my mother's fault*, Alice had once insisted — and there was a jagged line that appeared in the lens when you looked

**164**

through it, though for some reason it did not appear on any of the printed photographs. Alice had explained it once, but I had forgotten. The world of photography and science in general made little sense to me. It was full of numbers and absolutes, something I had never been very good at. But I had always loved to watch her work, watching from the doorway as she poured and measured the required chemicals, stirring and shaking until they were just right, until the negatives had become something real and tangible and she at last pinned up her contact sheets to the rack.

I had wondered, over those first few days in Tangier, if she had left the camera behind in England along with the other traces of her former life that she had seemed to relinquish. Once, while she was in the bath, I had even gone looking for it, though a search of her room had produced nothing but dresses I did not recognize, tiny perfume bottles that did not smell quite as I remembered her, and a strange emptiness that seemed to pervade the room, as if it were not quite real, as if it were all for show.

I cast a glance out of the back window of the car, watching the trail of dust that we left in our wake, watching as Tangier disappeared behind us, imagining that I could already feel the change, the difference, its hold, its grip, suddenly less.

The camera, I thought, was proof.

In Chefchaouen, we moved slowly through the medina. "Can you believe how blue it is?" Alice murmured, repeating the words over and over again until it seemed that she was no longer speaking them, expecting a response, but as if they were an incantation necessary to reassure herself that it was real.

At times she disappeared from my sight, but I was able to locate her by the clatter of metal, as it echoed against the silent walls. I could turn the corner, I knew, and she would be there. So I slowed my pace, allowing her to run off as she pleased, knowing that I would be able to find her when needed. There was a calm to the city that was immediately at odds with Tangier. No one rushed to sell us anything, no one beckoned from restaurants or cafés. There was an eerie quiet after all the noise and bustle of Tangier. I wasn't sure I entirely enjoyed it. I was, I had always been, I felt, made for cities — for the dark and dingy alleyways, for the twenty-four-hour cacophony of noise, for the overbearing and often cloying smells and the tightly packed familiarity of strangers. Chefchaouen was the opposite. It was light, where Tangier was dark. It was airy, where Tangier was stifling. It was soothing, where Tangier refused to let anyone within its grasp exhale or take a breath. I did not belong here, I felt it instinctively, but I could see that Alice did. This place was made for her — and for that reason, I decided it was perfect.

We continued on like this — an ebb and flow, I thought — for nearly an hour, at the end of which Alice turned to me, her arms hung limply by her side. "I'm exhausted, Lucy." She sighed. "And in desperate need of a cup of tea."

"It's likely to be mint," I warned her, with a hesitant smile, wondering if it was still too soon to laugh about yesterday, her anxiety, her frustration, boiling under the Tangier sun.

She took a deep breath, her lungs exhaling for what seemed like the first time. "I don't care," she said, looking around us, the smile on her face deepening. "Tonight, I don't care about any of it."

After that, we hurried to find a place in the medina to spend the night. "Look there, a bed-and-breakfast," I observed, pointing at the first establishment, for though its sign was a bit tattered, a bit worn, it seemed promising all the same.

Alice laughed and swiftly corrected me: "A *riad*. See, there are still some things you don't know about Morocco," she said, her tone light and teasing.

We entered, arms linked, happy to exchange the requested francs for a room key.

"Roommates once more," Alice whispered while we waited. "It will be just like Bennington again."

I nodded but did not mention that at Bennington we each had our own bed, while our current accommodation contained only one. The knowledge that we would soon share such a small space together, the possibility of this closeness, made my skin hum, as if every nerve was alive with anticipation, with the promise of what that night might make possible.

"Tea," Alice quipped over my shoulder as I paid, lest I forget to make the request.

"Yes, tea, please," I echoed.

The man behind the desk looked momentarily confused.

"*Thé?*" I tried again.

**167**

His face lightened. "*Ah, bien, thé à la menthe.*"

We both suppressed a smile. "*Oui, merci.*"

With our tea, we ordered a couscous and tagine, although, in the end, we did not manage to finish either, our stomachs unused to the heaviness of the dishes. Still, the act of eating, of gorging, seemed somehow necessary. A release for everything that we had seemed to hold in and away from each other. Sitting on the floor of our rented room, we pushed aside the utensils, attacking the dishes the way the locals did, with our hands. The juices dripped down our fingers, but we didn't bother wiping them away. Instead, we licked at them, delighting in the foreignness. A piece of what we suspected was lamb. An apricot. A raisin. Not typical fruits we associated with savory meals, but there, in the fading light of Morocco, they made a perfect kind of sense. Grease shimmered on our lips by the time we finished, both of us leaning back with a slight laugh of embarrassment as we observed the other.

"We look absolutely frightful," Alice declared but laughed as she did so.

I looked at her once-white dress, now covered with blotches — dirt from our travels, stains from our meal. I wasn't much better, I suspected. For although my own capris and blouse stood in stark contrast to Alice's white dress, they were of a similarly light hue and had also suffered from our hasty meal. "No point in saving these, I suppose." I grasped the collar of my shirt, pulling so that I could fully inspect the damage.

"Of course we save them!" Alice exclaimed. "They're souvenirs now. A remembrance of our trip."

I looked at her: smiling and unencumbered, her face smeared with grease, her dress askew. Part of me wanted to seize her then, to grasp her fragile shoulders and demand to know *why* — why had she locked herself away with a man who was so obviously unworthy of her love? But that meant mentioning him, and his unfaithfulness, and I couldn't, not in that moment. It was not a day for John, not a day for Tangier. We had shed our layers at last, and Alice had returned — old, original, ancient Alice whom I had fallen in love with. I was not ready to see her buried once more, weighted down by both the present and the future — not yet.

"Oh, but I can't wear this back to Tangier," she said, looking down at herself, taking in the full measure of her clothing and the mess she had made. "I didn't pack a second dress, Lucy," she said, looking up at me. "Only nightclothes. I suppose that was rather silly, but I guess I was caught up in it all."

I could see the frown beginning to form. "Don't worry," I said, anxious to dispel the oncoming storm. "I brought an extra blouse and trousers. You can wear those."

She wrinkled her nose while still managing to look pleased at the same time. "Do you think so, Lucy? Trousers?" She leaned forward, as if to inspect the ones I was currently wearing. "I've never worn trousers before."

"Here," I said, reaching for my rucksack, a recent purchase from the souks. I could still smell the newness of it, the leather a mixture of something dark and earthy. Manure, perhaps. Most of the tourists wrinkled their noses at the scent, but I found comfort in it. There was something familiar, something real. As if the smell itself assured me of its authenticity, that its material and construction were indeed a product of Tangier, of Morocco, and not some sanitized re-creation that had been shipped overseas and marked up in price, specifically for the tourists who wanted that version of Morocco. I retrieved the two garments, already wrinkled from our journey, I noted with some dismay, and handed them to her. "Try them on."

"What, now?"

"Yes, now."

She looked down. "But I'm a mess. I haven't even had a bath yet."

"It doesn't matter, just do it quickly to see how they look."

I could see the idea pleased her, and so I pressed until she relented, smiling at her retreating figure as she ran to the bathroom to make the change. The door stood slightly ajar and I watched as she removed her dress, letting it fall unceremoniously to the floor, the fabric pooling out around her feet. She kicked it aside. I noticed then that she no longer wore the girdle she had in college, so that though her figure was still slender, it was no longer bound and constricted by that stiff garment she had once insisted on wearing. Instead she stood in only a bra and underwear, a simple garter belt holding up her stockings. Its absence made her look older. Not in a regrettable way that made me long for the past, but one that put our years of living together in perspective. I was suddenly aware of just how much time had passed since that first day I had seen her and all the things that had fallen between us since then.

"Well, what do you think?"

She stood before me, wearing my white linen blouse and tan trousers. I had never before seen her outside of her youthful dresses, her childish frills. I had long come to regard them as an extension of herself, so that when I conjured up an image of Alice, the two were inexorably linked. Stripped of such adornments, even her makeup and hair a pared-down version of the usual, she looked entirely different, so that I felt, oddly, that I did not know her at all. The change left me momentarily speechless.

At my silence, her face collapsed in fear. "Is it that bad?" she asked.

"No," I said trying to reassure her. "No, you look wonderful. I almost suspect that if I passed you on the streets, I wouldn't recognize you," I said, meaning it.

Alice smiled and did a little movement like a curtsy before disappearing back into the bathroom. I heard the start of the bath, the water pounding against the bottom of its enameled surface. She appeared in the doorway, still dressed, though the top button of the blouse was undone. "This was exactly what I needed, Lucy." She closed the distance between us, swiftly, reaching across and grabbing my hand. "Thank you."

I smiled. I could still feel her hand's warmth, even after she removed it.

I did not sleep that night. Instead I remained awake, long past the hour when the sun had set and the sky had begun to darken. Without warning, rain started to fall against the sloped roof of our *riad*. I had first heard it as I lay in bed, watching as Alice frowned and sputtered in her sleep, murmuring words I could not decipher. Minutes had gone by, maybe hours. Eventually I rose, winding my thin dressing gown around me and exiting our room, slowly and quietly, so as not to wake her.

I turned my face upward, watching as the rain fell on the glass and then began to slide down, away from our building.

In the common room, the temperature had shifted. I passed the tables where tomorrow our breakfast would be served — fresh cheese, olives, and bread. A bit of oil, or butter, if we were lucky. I walked, without purpose, without aim, past the floor cushions that served as sofas, the decorative coverings hiding the dilapidated state of the frame. I noticed a forgotten pack of cigarettes, nearly full, sitting on the table, and although I already had some in my handbag, I reached for them. Extracting one and placing it in my mouth, I palmed the rest of the packet, tucking it into the pocket on my nightdress. The cigarette was harsh and it burned my throat. I tried to remember the last time I had had one of this poor quality. Senior year, I recalled. When Alice and I had snuck into the dance studio one night. Of course, it wasn't really sneaking in, since none of the buildings were ever locked. I had always thought that Bennington inspired a peculiar brand of rebellion in its students — particularly, when the idea of breaking *into* a school, rather than *out*, was our definition of amusement.

*Martha Graham used to teach here, you know,* Alice had said as we made our way into one of the dance studios. The floors, even in the dark, had shone with a fresh coating of wax. Three sides of the room were covered with mirrors, while the fourth was glass, looking out across the campus, although the view was blanketed in darkness. There, I could see our reflections: thin, long hair, one a bit taller than the other. There was nothing remarkable about either of us, not at first glance. But I had thought then, staring at our reflections, that we could have passed for sisters. There was something so similar in the way that we held ourselves, in the way that we moved, one motion made in reaction to another.

*Did you hear? What I said before?* Alice had moved over to the mirrors, where a long, sturdy-looking rope hung from the ceiling. She was holding it between her hands. *About Martha Graham?*

Yes, I replied, smiling. I didn't know who Martha Graham was, but I didn't say so, eager to have the night go well. Things had been strange between us, with Alice spending most of her time with Tom, or tucked away in the darkroom on her own. Paris, and all the plans we had once made, seemed far away — promises made by two girls I could no longer remember.

She motioned me over to where she stood. *Here,* she said, thrusting the rope between my hands.

I stared at it, doubtfully. *What am I supposed to do? Swing.*

I continued to look at her in confusion until she sighed and took the rope back from me. *Watch,* she instructed. Alice pulled the rope to the far corner of the room. Stepping onto the thick knot at the bottom of the rope with one foot, she folded her body, so that her arms and one leg wound themselves around the roping. She jumped, pushing her leg back and up, the force propelling her forward. The rope swung across the space of the room, and I stepped back to watch. Alice's hair flung first forward and then back, so that her face was obscured, her laughter echoing throughout the small room as she swung back and forth, a human pendulum.

A clap of thunder sounded overhead, and I was brought back to Chefchaouen. I turned toward the window, although all I could see was blackness and my own lonely reflection. I continued to stare, realizing how much had changed between my memory of that dance studio and Chefchaouen. It was not just Alice who had altered. Without her, my own sense of self had wavered. I had tried, in the days after the accident, to accept that I would never see her again, that whatever had existed between Alice and me had been ravaged, had been burned up inside that raging inferno until there was nothing left but cinder, the remains of something that once was. And I felt it, this loss. A physical pain, a knot in my stomach, that churned, acidic and angry. There had been moments in New York when I had wandered the streets, unable to sleep, unable to stop thinking of her. I had walked until my feet cracked and bled, and then walked farther still, unable to stop. I had been lost, adrift.

There was that same swooshing noise in my ear, as normal to me by now as it had once been strange. Carefully, I examined it. There was still no pain, no sign of infection — just that unusual feeling of fullness. But then, there *was* something. I looked at my finger, now covered with grit. It didn't matter how much I had washed in the bath, Tangier refused to let me go. But where only a few days before I would have relished this notion, I thought of it now with something like panic. Morocco was becoming too dangerous, not just for the expats who remained, but also for Alice, the city threatening to hold her captive. Both of us needed to get back to our original selves, I realized, and not just for twenty-four hours.

I stood by the window, though the view outside was obscured in the darkness. Alice would have to know. There could be no more stalling, no more waiting. I would have to tell her about what I had seen, about the fast-ticking clock that was sounding behind us, everywhere we went. I knew that John would not wait forever.

*Ticktock. Ticktock.*

And then, Alice was standing behind me, as if she had simply materialized, as if a part of my brain had somehow managed to conjure her. I looked at our reflections in the glass, but we no longer looked like sisters. I wasn't sure exactly what had changed. It was true that we had different hairstyles now — mine was still long and old-fashioned, whereas Alice had cut hers into something that resembled a bob. I wondered if she had done it before or after her move to Tangier, if it had been in response to the heat or in anticipation of it. There was something else too, something in the way our expressions settled upon our respective faces. They were no longer interchangeable. Gone were the shared gestures, the intertextuality that had once existed between us. We were simply two women — close, once, but different. No longer the same at all.

"We need to leave, Alice." The words came out hoarsely, as if they had caught in my throat.

A slow, sleepy grin settled on her face. "I know. Although part of me wishes that we could stay longer. Forever, even."

She thought we were speaking of Chefchaouen. "No, Alice," I said, with a slight shake of my head. "I mean we need to leave Tangier."

Suddenly awake, her body tensed. She took a step backward, away from me.

"You can't stay here anymore. It's not safe," I continued.

"No?"

"No." I cleared my throat. "John knows that I know — about Sabine."

She looked at me then, confusion crowding her features. But something else was there as well, a peculiar expression that pinched her face and told me what I had already begun to suspect: *Alice knew.*

**176**

Perhaps not her name, and perhaps not even with any real certainty, but she knew that John was involved with another woman. Somewhere, however deeply she may have buried it, she knew.

Alice blinked and asked, "Who?"

I shook my head, ignoring her feigned expression. There could be no more hiding, I told myself, no more pretending. My voice was stronger, sharper as I told her, "You know who she is, Alice."

She looked taken aback, but whether at my tone or my words, I was uncertain.

"I don't know," she protested.

I leaned forward. "You do."

"No," she said, continuing to back away. "I don't know. I don't want to know." She looked up at me, her expression pleading. "I don't want to know, Lucy."

"Alice." She began to shake her head then, with such force that I moved toward her, worried. "Alice," I murmured, trying to keep my voice low and steady.

Her face was red, her cheeks streaked with tears. "I know," she said, the words, sounding like a gasp, hanging in the air between us. "I know, Lucy. It's all so horribly embarrassing, but of course, I do."

I exhaled — certain in the knowledge that I had been right, that I could still read her, that I still knew her, just as I once had. "What do you think he'll do, Alice?" I continued. "When he finds out that you know. When he realizes that the money will stop." She remained silent, her eyes wide. "You know what we have to do, then?" I pressed. "We have to leave, before he realizes."

"Realizes what?" she whispered.

"That you know as well." She was silent, and so I whispered: "There isn't any other way."

I was no longer certain if she was listening. She was shivering violently, though it was still warm, the humidity evident in the trail of mist on the glass windows. She wrapped her arms around her body, as if to protect herself against the cold, and I felt myself shiver, as if in response.

"We'll go back to Tangier tomorrow. We'll tell him together. And then we'll leave," I whispered, my voice steady, calm.

"Yes," she whispered, turning toward the window.

"Isn't that what you wanted, Alice?" I asked her. "To leave Tangier? To go back home?"

"Yes. Yes, of course," she replied.

I felt my heart flutter, felt the realization that now was the time to move, to declare. I leaned forward so that I was only inches from her, my face hovering above her tear-stained skin. And then I kissed her.

Before *him*, we had been inseparable.

But that year, our fourth at Bennington, something changed. Alice began to spend less time in our room, always making her way to and from the photography lab, or into town, arranging to see Tom whenever she had the opportunity. I would often catch sight of her as she bounded across the open lawn and toward the parking lot, headed to the warm interior of Tom's waiting Skylark. It was easy to spot. A deep red that gleamed in the sun, its outline shimmering against the pale, more conservative cars of the faculty. It was a wonder that anyone as young as Tom could afford such an indulgent vehicle, since most auto shops were still clinging to wartime rules, requiring several months' down payment before anything could be driven off the lot. I felt the resentment begin to prickle, hot and sharp.

Tom Stowell. He was, I soon learned, from an old family in Maine — not the side filled with fishermen and carpenters, but the one full of Colonial houses and lobster bakes every summer Sunday evening. One built on old money, which meant that what little of it still existed was tied up in the house, or whatever they could borrow based on their last name. As a legacy, he had received a full scholarship at Williams College — without it, there was no hope of the Stowell name being represented within the walls of any respected educational system in New England.

Some of this information I had gleaned from Alice herself — though she was surprisingly secretive when it came to Tom — and I'd gathered the rest in various ways, including from other students at Bennington. It turned out that the girls knew everything about the boys at the next college over — had made it their business to know their future husbands. For although the girls majored in literature and mathematics, a few even claiming pre-med, the vast majority of them, it seemed, had already realized their only profession was destined to be wife and mother.

It became my business to know everything there was about Tom Stowell — what classes he took, the other boys he counted as friends. I received such information eagerly, as if I were dying of thirst, as if their whispers and rumors were the only water in the world that would quench it. The car, I soon learned, had been a sixteenth birthday present from his grandfather, the stoic patriarch. My studies began to suffer, but I didn't mind. Tom was my major now — and my life, my happiness, depended on knowing everything about him.

In the absence of Alice, I retreated to my old haunts, spending afternoons in the library, convinced that she would soon tire of him, that one day she would simply return, walking through the hardwood doors, smiling, her arms stacked with books. The previous months would fall away then, dissipating as if they had never happened. I watched and I waited, patiently, knowing that Tom's time was running out.

And when, at the end of each day, she failed to appear, I would head home, shivering, winter falling fast and quick, wondering if I would ever feel warm again.

To keep her near, I began to borrow pieces of her wardrobe. A scarf, a pair of stockings. Each and every one of them seemed to carry something of her scent, a mix of spice and floral, as distinctive as any perfume. I had once pulled on one of her outfits, the fabric stretching and straining, refusing to be malleable, to my initial disappointment. I reminded myself, then, that Alice and I were not the same. We were each of us separate and distinct, only whole when placed together. Dressed in her clothing, her scent reminded me of this, and worked to still my mind, if only for a brief moment.

**180**

But then she had walked in.

I'd felt my cheeks burn with shame, so that I had hastily clawed at the dress, feeling the seams as they pulled and gave way. And on her face, I could see the astonishment — and something else, horror, I realized — at finding me like that, dressed in her clothing. And though she reassured me that it was fine, that I could borrow them anytime I wanted, I only sagged beneath her words. She had not understood, had carelessly attributed my actions to vanity alone, not thinking, not realizing that it was all only in order to be closer to *her*. Afterward, I had felt the need to be cruel, to punish her, consumed by the desire for her to know what it was like to be lower, inferior, to be held at the whim of others. She had done it to me time and again without so much as a second thought, and I wanted, in that moment, for her to know what it felt like.

And then one day Alice reappeared in our room, held out her hand to me, and everything else fell away. A small rose gold band with a minuscule diamond gleamed back. I looked up at her and asked, "So, it's all been decided then?" My voice distant, so that I was convinced that I could hear it echoing throughout the room.

"Almost," she said, smiling. "There's nothing official yet, but we plan to have the ceremony sometime after graduation. After that, Tom's going to take me abroad."

There would be no Paris, no Budapest, no Cairo.

Not for us.

I had shaken my head then, had told myself no, I would not be made to go back, to return to my dull little life, a life of obscurity, of mediocrity. She was the one who had dragged me forth from the shadows of the library, from my own mind, and I, in turn, had helped her to dispel the shadows, helped her to move on from the anxiety that had gripped her since the death of her parents. It was all so plainly obvious, but somehow her vision was obscured. She could not see that Tom Stowell could not care for her as I would, that he did not understand her. She needed, I realized then, to be reminded.

And so, I smiled and offered my congratulations.

And I started to plan.

I pressed my lips against Alice's own, the movement so familiar from the hours I had spent thinking of it — at times convinced that it would never come — and I waited: for a response, for an indication, for anything that told me what she was thinking, feeling. And then — yes, I was certain — I felt Alice respond, felt her body shift and her lips open just slightly. Closing my eyes tighter, I worked to put everything into that one gesture — all the longing and dreaming that I had done in the years since we had first met, the pain of our year-long separation, and the hope I now had for the future.

Later, in our bedroom, I turned to her and smiled. "It's fate, don't you see? After everything we've been through together," I said, my voice dropping to a whisper. "That night with Tom and the accident —" I saw her flinch, but I pressed on, knowing that this too was something she could no longer ignore. "I thought you would never survive, not when the brakes had been cut, and then I saw you and I was certain that you were dead, I was sure of it — but then you weren't and —" I stopped, noticing her face. She had gone pale, her eyes boring into my own. I watched her, waiting for her to speak, but she only remained silent. I glanced at the window, the traces of humidity obscuring most of what was once there. I could no longer see Alice reflected back, only my own strange face as it peered at itself.

# CHAPTER
# NINE

## ALICE

She had nearly fooled me.

In her presence, I had allowed myself to forget about the horrible past, the tedium of the present, and the depressing future that any fortune-teller worth a grain of salt would be able to read in my sad, shattered palm. I had closed my eyes in the back of that beaten-up taxi, allowing my body to be flung one way and then another as we bounded over the dips and around the curves of Morocco, letting the wind and the sand whip across our faces and forgetting that it all existed. I worked my way back to that place, before everything had gone so spectacularly wrong, when all I had felt was determination and hope and the knowledge that the future would be whatever I made out of it.

And it had almost worked. For a few, heart-clenching wonderful hours — so absolutely pure and beautiful that I felt at times that I could not breathe for the joy of it — I had managed it all. I dug out my camera, taking photographs. I smiled into the faces of strangers, I laughed at the kindness of children. I stood face-to-face with the unknown and I only wanted more. And so I ate and I drank until I thought I would burst from it. I laughed until my muscles ached, until my limbs grew heavy. And then — and then the facade came shattering down around me, breaking and splintering around my bare feet, and I knew that it could never be put back together again.

She had whispered to me about John's infidelities, reminding me of knowledge I already had possessed, though I had worked to bury it, deep. She had convinced me that I must leave Tangier, that *we* must leave Tangier. In secret, under the cover of night, because she also knew about the money, about the allowances passed from Maude to me and on to John, knew about what he would really lose with my absence, and I did not question how, knowing only that she must, in that way that she always knew everything. It had all made a perfect sort of sense, and so I nodded and agreed. Tangier was not mine, I had never laid claim to it, nor it to me. I knew that I could leave and not be too bothered.

But then she had mentioned the accident. She had said the word — *Tom* — magic in its incantation, dispelling everything all at once, bringing it to light so that I had no choice but to look at it again, once more. I had not wanted her to say his name, I had not wanted us to be forced to confront, to remember. I had wanted to continue as we were — if only for a little while longer. But then she had said his name, and the spell had broken. She had said the next words, ones that were never mentioned in any newspapers, by any police officer, not even by Maude, because I had never mentioned it, had never told them — what had happened in the span of those last minutes, tucking it away and keeping the information to myself, knowing that voicing it aloud would not change anything, could not change anything. Aunt Maude had told me, weeks later, when I started to come out of the shock, when at last I could sit and listen and eat again once more, that there was little left of the wreckage, just burned-up bits and pieces that the police had done their best to sift through, though they had never arrived at any official answers.

In the taxi ride home the next day, something pulled at my memory and I struggled to bring it to the forefront. I thought of the few stories she had told me about her family, her father — about the garage that he had worked in — and I felt as though the air had been ripped out of me, as if my lungs no longer worked. I struggled to breathe, the space between Chefchaouen and Tangier fragmented and blurred, so that I remembered nothing, nothing at all except what she had said, what she had whispered, lying in bed, the rain slanting down the rooftop, loud and insistent, so that for a moment I thought I was mistaken, had hoped that I was.

But I wasn't, I knew. I had heard her correctly, had heard what it was that she had said, her breath hot and moist against my cheek as she had smiled and sighed and leaning toward me whispered his name, whispered about that night.

Whispered about the brakes.

★　★　★

When John greeted us upon our return, watching from the threshold of the doorway as Lucy and I made our way, one slow step at a time, back up and into the flat, I did my best to rearrange my face, to inhabit some semblance of the person I had been before we left. I mounted the steps with something like dread, the knowledge of what I had learned pressing against me so that I could no longer foresee the future, could no longer, in fact, see past one step and then another.

As we came into view, John called out to me, "What on earth are you wearing?"

I looked down, tugging self-consciously at the blouse and running my hands nervously over the pleats of the trousers, eager to be rid of them both. "I borrowed them from Lucy," I said, blushing as I said her name, as if that night was something etched into my face, as if John would only have to look in order to read everything that had happened, that had transpired between us.

His face rearranged itself into a frown. "What happened to your own clothes?"

"They got dirty." I knew my voice sounded short, curt, but there was nothing that I could do to change it — I felt as though all the energy had been leaked from my very bones, that the effort I had made, all these months, to smile and nod my head, to act as though I had not made an enormous mistake in coming to Tangier, with him, had suddenly left me.

It was no longer possible.

"Dirty?" He laughed. "What on earth from?"

I heaved a loud sigh. "Does it matter?"

**187**

John looked momentarily taken aback. Finally he said: "No, I suppose it doesn't." He gave a shake of his head and stepped aside to allow us into the apartment, followed by a quick gibe about his surprise at finding my note, although it was clear that what he really meant was displeasure. Running his fingers through his hair, he attempted a lighthearted laugh, but I could feel his eyes searching out mine: wondering, speculating, puzzling over whether Lucy had managed to pass along his little secret. He did not realize that I had already known — that he was not the only one who could keep things hidden.

"Maybe you should take a bath," he said, his voice hollow. "You're covered in dust." He laughed again. "And in those clothes, people will start to wonder."

I looked at him, eyes narrowed. "Wonder what, John?" A dare, just there, beneath my words.

"I don't know," he said, with a touch of defiance. "But not anything good, I suspect."

I wanted to respond, to snap, but the words stuck in my throat and then the moment was gone, along with the insinuation. In the silence came John's insistence that he didn't mean anything by it, that he was just on edge, worried by my absence. And there did seem to be a truth to it — his eyes were red and swollen, as though he hadn't slept the night before. I felt ashamed then, for snapping, for being angry at him for something he knew nothing about. I began to tell him this, but he had already moved on, suggesting drinks, suggesting that we go out, visit a jazz club, that promise he had made the first night — and which now seemed like ages ago —

his enthusiasm for the outing, I suspected, built upon the prospect of keeping an eye on us, of monitoring what was and wasn't said. I wondered why he even cared, now that he had someone else. Or perhaps he meant to try and keep us both — *Sabine*, that was what Lucy had called her. It would not have surprised me. I felt Lucy's gaze — hard and insistent, as always — demanding me to speak, to set our plan, no, *her plan*, I reminded myself, into motion. I stood, feeling the intensity of both their gazes upon me and I felt for a moment that I might burst, shatter into a million pieces, right in front of them. The idea filled me with something like pleasure. I ground my fingernails into my palms. "I'll just take that bath first," I said, trying to make my words light, though they seemed to resound throughout the room, heavy and dull. John had been right. After our long drive home, Lucy and I were both filthy, covered in dirt and sunburned, our bodies peeling and flaking with each move.

I moved quickly from them, feeling their eyes on my back.

Once I was behind the closed bathroom door, a long, heavy sigh escaped me, and I wondered if they could hear me, wondered whether they, both of them, were listening from the other side of the door. I ran the water, sitting on the edge of the tub's ceramic shell, letting it develop into a scorching heat, not caring, but rather welcoming it — the moment my sunburned skin would turn an angrier shade of red.

I lowered myself under the water, grateful that it muffled the sound of my scream. And when I resurfaced, when I at last felt the air enter my lungs, burning, I coughed and sputtered and feared that I might retch from the force of it.

She had done it. And I had always known.

That was what the fog had hidden from me — but I remembered now, remembered how, in the days afterward, I had been convinced that she had been the one responsible. But when I had tried to say it, first at the hospital, and later in England, Aunt Maude had brushed aside my accusations, had told me instead to be quiet and still. And because I was not entirely certain, because I was never entirely certain when it came to Lucy, when it came to the dark recesses of my own mind, I had listened, closing my eyes to the possibility.

I thought of Chefchaouen, of everything it had stirred within me, both good and bad and frightening, and I was furious with Lucy, with myself. I turned the water spigot farther to the left, willing the scorching heat to burn away the thoughts circulating in my head.

I would tell her that I knew what she had done, and then I would make her leave.

I shut my eyes and willed myself to be brave enough, smart enough this time, to ensure that she left, and not just Tangier, but my life as well. There could be no more reappearances, no more unexpected knocks on the door. I needed to cast her out, to purge her from my life, once and for all.

I had done my best to forget it, to bury it, to move past it. I had married John, I had moved to another continent, hundreds and thousands of miles away from the place that reminded me of him, of Tom. But now, I knew — that the past was never truly past, and that I could not outrun it forever, that the fog would not always protect me. I felt it begin to resurface then, every painful detail of that time, so that I could no longer feel the heat of the water, of Tangier, pressing against my skin.

I shivered, suddenly feeling as though I would never be warm again.

# CHAPTER
# TEN

## LUCY

We walked through the Ville Nouvelle district in silence. As we moved, I felt almost instinctively that the space was somehow outside of my jurisdiction, as if those other places in the city — the medina, the Kasbah, and all the twists and turns that existed between them — belonged to me entirely, while these streets continued to remain unknown, refusing to yield their secrets. Instead I felt as if I was on John's territory. And there was something else too — an uneasiness as a result of Alice's silence, so that Chefchaouen seemed all at once far away, and I found myself unable to read her, to understand why she had not told John about our plan, why, instead, we were following him through the streets of Morocco, an unsettling scavenger hunt where none of us knew the prize.

"One other stop first," John said, turning down a darkened alley that I did not recognize.

"Oh, John," Alice began. I could tell Chefchaouen had taken its toll on her. Dark circles had appeared under her eyes, and although she had spent time in the bath before we departed, it looked as though some of the sand and peeling skin still clung to her, as if she had made no real attempt to scrub them away at all. "Maybe another night."

"Don't be like that," he said, laughing. He tugged at Alice's arms playfully, though there was something urgent in his movement, something insistent and desperate. I was reminded of Alice that first night, the way she had smiled and laughed, the falseness behind it, and the sinking feeling that it would inevitably all come crashing down around us, the shards splintering onto the ground. John had that same manic look in his eyes, I thought. But where I had felt concern for Alice, I felt only unease under John's wavering temper. He turned from us then, increasing his speed, so that he walked in front, rather than next to us. "Hurry up, we're almost there!" he called, the singsong lilt in his voice making it seem like we were playing a game, as if this were all in jest. I thought of the Pied Piper, leading the children out of the town and into the forest. And although I knew the fairy-tale version that children were told, I was reminded of the much darker telling, where the man, in an act of revenge, led the unsuspecting children to their deaths.

But instead of directing us out of town, John ushered us into one of the city's many anonymous bars. It was stained and weathered, the inside intentionally dark so that it hid whatever refuse the light may have illuminated. I wondered aloud why John had chosen to bring us here, but he only ignored me, walking farther into the belly of the place until at last it seemed we had come to the end and were going to continue out the

**193**

exit. John came to a halt, sending us both crashing into him.

"Here," he said, indicating the floor. "Take off your shoes and leave them."

I frowned, looking over at Alice — but if she was startled by John's game of follow the leader, she did not show it. Instead she bent down, undoing the ankle straps on her kitten heels and letting them fall onto the grime-covered floor. I watched her in surprise and then, realizing there was nothing to do but push on, I undid my own, placing them in the corner, hoping that they would not get trampled in my absence.

"Good." John beamed at us, looking over his shoulder. "Now, follow me."

I was the last to enter the back room, and it took a few moments of rapid blinking to adjust to the dim light, so that by the time I took in our surroundings — a floor mat of some sort, not quite bamboo, but not quite wood; walls so deeply stained with tobacco that in the dim light I could not make out the color; and finally, a few low tables, around which a handful of men in traditional djellabas sat, smoking from pipes — John and Alice had already claimed one of the low tables and were sitting cross-legged beside it. I quickly joined them.

"It took a fair amount of convincing to get you in here," John said, his face serious, though his tone was self-congratulatory. "This is what would amount to an old boys' club here, so strictly no women allowed. You're both in luck that the owner of this joint owes me a favor — still, I promised him no more than fifteen minutes, a half an hour tops."

"And what are we doing here?" I asked, eyeing the other men in the room. Most of them appeared to be well into their fifties, maybe sixties, and though they had turned to us with interest upon our arrival, a majority of them had already looked away, rejoining conversations that had stalled and picking up their slackened pipes.

"This," John said, producing his own pipe, one that had apparently been stashed somewhere within the folds of his suit until then. "You aren't afraid, are you?" he teased, waving the kif pipe nearer to Alice's face. His smile seemed to alter, turning small and mean. Not the Pied Piper after all, I found myself thinking: more like the big bad wolf, tempting us off the path. It felt as though he wanted to poke, to prod — to turn us upside down and see what would fall out. He was nervous, I realized — of what I had told Alice about Sabine, of what, perhaps, had happened between us. I could see it — his suspicions, his paranoia — shimmering in the air around us.

Alice extended her hand and dutifully inhaled the smoking pipe, only to then cough and sputter, much to my amazement and John's apparent delight. I hesitated when it was passed in my direction. While I had always liked cigarettes — from an early age when I had stolen my first pack from the corner shop and ridden my bicycle down by the creek to smoke them — this was something different. I pursed my lips, trying to decide whether or not it suited me, trying to decide what it

**195**

was that was happening, the night already taking on a strange disorder that I could not figure out, could not reassemble into something familiar and known.

John, meanwhile, laughed loudly. "There now," he proclaimed, snatching the pipe back from me. "That wasn't so terrible, was it?"

I tilted my head, not entirely sure who the words had been directed at. And soon it was as if they had never been spoken at all. In fact, it was all becoming rather muddled. The drink we had sipped back at the apartment before heading out, and now the kif — all of it crowded and confused my mind. It began to seem as though we had been sitting there for an eternity, and yet I was certain that very little time had passed at all. I decided then I didn't like it, if only for the way it seemed to swallow time whole. And yet I felt strangely emboldened, sitting in our strange circle of three. I thought of the words I wished to speak, prepared, I thought, to voice them at last if Alice would not. I looked over at her, to ensure that she felt the same, and found her slumped in the corner, her eyes glassy and distant. I wondered whether it was the kif, or whether she had looked like this before and I had somehow failed to notice.

I felt then as though the air had gone out of me. I stood, moving quickly toward the back door, leaning my body out and into the night sky. I inhaled deeply, slowly, grateful that the sun had already set, that some of the humidity had begun to leak out of the day. I grasped my head, willing it to stop spinning, to stop moving so swiftly.

I glanced back at the table. Alice remained still — like stone, I thought, impenetrable. John, sucking determinedly on the pipe, looked up and caught me staring. I tried to read what was there behind his eyes, but then he blinked and rose from his seat, asking, "Shall we go on?"

I heard a general chorus of agreement, though I had not spoken a word. Still, we followed him, Alice and I, traipsing after him once more like schoolchildren. Neither of us asked where we were headed, we only continued to walk, silently and obediently, our heads both bowed as we concentrated on the unleveled road beneath us, careful not to misstep in the darkness.

We had walked for some time in silence when John disappeared through a hidden doorway. It was darker than the place we had just left, so I stumbled a few times before finding a place to sit. Onstage was a group of older men, sitting in a semicircle, though the music they were playing was decidedly not jazz — even my uninitiated ear could distinguish as much. Instead a blend of Arabic and Andalusian music emerged from the instruments held by the men, their voices occasionally adding to the melody. They played often together, as a collective, and then there were moments where one of them paused and the others took over the music, each one seeming to anticipate the rhythm and flow of the other. I watched as one of the old men used this interlude to produce a kif pipe, tucked unceremoniously in his back pocket until then. The old man inhaled, a second or two stretching out into three or four.

I noticed the look of annoyance that passed over John's face. "Wrong night, I suppose?" I asked him, fighting to keep the smirk out of my voice.

He ignored my comment. "So," he proclaimed instead, looking back and forth between the two of us, as if deciding what route to travel down — whether to give in to the desperation or to cling to the illusion, the falsity, that everything was fine, that everything would continue to be fine. I looked away, not knowing which one I hoped for. Despite John's jubilant tone, there was something hard, something rougher than there had been before. "Alice finally left the flat."

The words hung among the three of us, John looking back and forth between us, as if anxious to see who would respond first, who would rise to his bait.

"Don't be absurd," Alice said, reaching for her drink and taking a deep gulp. "I'm not a recluse." Her voice was low, so that I had to lean across the table in order to make out the words. She seemed dulled, harder, so different from the lively creature she had been only the night before. I struggled to understand what had changed.

"Yes, well, I must admit I was surprised. I wondered at first whether you hadn't just headed back to England," John observed, his smile wide, his eyes bright. He let out a laugh. "Oh, my little Alice in Wonderland, what on earth am I going to do with you?"

"Don't call me that," she whispered, though her voice was largely lost in the din of the noise.

**198**

John turned to look at me then, his eyes moving up and down, taking in my appearance. A blouse and trousers once again, my unfashionable long, dark hair pulled back into an equally unfashionable plait. I could read the disappointment on his face. "What on earth should I do with her?" he asked, his gaze locked onto my own.

A million responses flitted through my mind, the very first among them: *let her go*. I didn't say it, though I could feel the words forming on my lips. Instead I turned, breaking his gaze, and reached for my drink, anxious to feel the warming calm of the gin.

There was silence for a moment, and then John said, looking at me, "Say, isn't your little holiday about over by now?" He leaned back in his chair, swirling the ice cubes in his drink. "Surely it's nearly time to return to the real world." He laughed, though I could see the glint in his eye.

He meant it as a slight. I could feel it in his words, his resentment for my relationship with Alice, boiling over the dips and curves of every syllable. I saw her too — the slight flinch, the quick intake of breath. She had heard it as well, had felt it — after all, that was the point. For his words to insult — to cut, to tear, to wound. I would never really fit in, never really be one of them, that was what he was trying to say. Those girls from good families, those effortless girls. The ones who woke up with long, blond shiny hair, pale, nondescript features, an aquiline nose that spoke of wealth and good breeding. Girls who did not have to work for their supper, who only had to look first to Daddy and then to their husband. I was different, marked out. My engagement with work an enduring testament to the differences that separated and, ultimately, divided us. My friendship with Alice was something that John could not understand, but more than that, it was something he did not like. I could see that now clearly. I had tainted her, altered her — or his perception of her, at any rate. Our friendship was a detriment to her character, something that he wished to expunge.

I had not bothered him at first — the strange woman who had turned up at his doorway, independent, alone. Those meant two different things, I knew. One could be alone but entirely dependent, like Alice. She was alone at Bennington, she was alone here. She had always been dependent on someone — her aunt, John, even Tom for a brief period of time. I was another species altogether, one that had not roamed the same circles as John McAllister. He had been intrigued at first, delighted even, by the woman sitting on his couch, drinking gin. Now he was angry, unamused by my continued presence, and perhaps most important, he was threatened.

I smiled, my lips stretching tight against my teeth. For a moment I thought that I tasted blood. "Actually," I said, feeling the full effects of the night, my mind loosening, my words slipping easily from my tongue, "I've no *real* world to return to, as it happens. I've resigned from my position at the publishing company." I noticed how Alice frowned at this piece of information. I hadn't meant to tell her, not until we had left Tangier, but perhaps it was best that such a secret came out beforehand. Yes, I felt like I could see this admission working to my advantage. After all, there was no longer anything tying me to the States, to New York. Together, we would be able to go anywhere.

John nodded, sipped his drink. "So, what, you were hoping to find work here, in Tangier?" He raised his eyebrows as he spoke, as if the notion were ridiculous, as if he had never heard of such an outlandish idea. "I don't think you'll find many publishing companies. Besides, won't your family miss you? So far from home?"

I felt Alice stir. "Lucy hasn't any family, John. I've told you that," she said, a distinct edge evident in her voice.

He nodded. "Sure, I remember now, only" — he stopped, turning to me — "only that's not entirely true, is it?" He gave a quick laugh. "You see, I did a little digging. I know, I know," he said, looking at Alice, who had started to protest, "I shouldn't have, an abuse of power and all that. But I like to know who's living under my roof."

I was still, waiting, wondering what it was that he had managed to unearth, what skeletons he would drag out of the closet and into the light. He paused — waiting, as well — his grin, his laugh, dragged out for full effect, as to emphasize his greatness, his perceived triumph over the woman who had threatened to best him.

And Alice.

Alice was watching me, I could feel it, feel her gaze, burning — hot and accusatory.

She was the one to speak first, her voice small, trembling. "What did you find?"

"Oh, nothing too interesting, in the end. A struggling, lower-class family. A tiny flat above a garage. An absent mother and father. Nothing too unexpected. I suppose that's the better turn of phrase."

"But —" Alice began.

"Do you know, it's strange, I sometimes think," John said, interrupting her.

"What is?" I asked.

"This whole situation. You, here in Tangier. How you showed up, uninvited." His words were coming faster, spit starting to gather in the corners of his lips. The sight made my stomach turn, and I looked away in disgust.

"Alice wanted me here," I said, my voice steely, loath to answer his accusations but anxious to defend myself nonetheless.

"No."

I turned. It was Alice who had spoken. She hadn't shouted, not exactly, but the word was loud and drawn out. It seemed to echo in the space around us, despite the presence of numerous bodies. It was as if we were, the two of us alone, as we had once been, rendering John's presence uncanny.

"No," she said again, quieter this time, as if she could not quite believe in the word itself or what it stood for. "No, I didn't. Lucy. I never invited you." She held my gaze. "I never wanted you here," she whispered, the last word all but lost in the noise around us, so that I was not entirely certain it had actually been spoken.

202

Alice stood, sending our table off balance, so that the drinks we had ordered swayed precariously, threatening to spill. I watched, my eyes riveted to the swaying glasses. In truth, I could not bring myself to look up at her, to see what was written there after what she had said. When I finally did, it was only to see the back of her, disappearing through the front door of the bar. I snuck a quick glance at John, surprised to find that instead of the smirk I had expected to see, he only sat, his face long and drawn. I wondered whether it was confusion or something else reflected there. He did not make any movement to chase after his wife but instead pulled out his kif pipe. I waited for the space of a moment — counting under my breath, one, two, three — and then I stood and followed Alice out the door.

The streets were crowded. Hundreds of locals were singing, waving banners in the air. But this wasn't a protest, that much was apparent. People danced and laughed, clapping one another on the back, as if in congratulations. I could feel it, the pulse of the city, pumping through them, through me. For one wild moment I wanted to crouch down onto the ground, to lay my hands on the road and to feel the murmur, the beat of it, against my skin. It was as if the city knew — things were happening, finally, after all this waiting. I could feel it, tingling in my hands. Watching as the people moved around me — locals, expats, tourists, travelers. I wanted nothing more than to follow, to be swept up in it, to move and continue moving and never stop.

But then I remembered Alice.

A sharp distinctive wail cut through the night — the noise, I knew, that the women in Tangier made in celebration. *Ululation*, I had learned, my mouth delighting in the dips and curves of it. In front of me, I saw Alice, a few paces ahead, her arms wrapped around her waist, just like the night before. And yet the temperatures had not yet abated. The heat, despite the sun's absence, still lingered in the air around us. I could feel the sweat pooling at the base of my throat, in the small of my back.

"What is that?" Alice asked, lips trembling as I approached.

"It's nothing," I said, though I was uncertain whether she could hear me over the noise, whether she would be able to hear me regardless, the look on her face unreachable.

I looked around for John, unsure whether he had followed me out of the bar. The voices were beginning to grow louder, and there was chanting now, though I could not make out the words. Fewer foreigners dotted the streets.

The wail started up again, and I saw Alice shudder. "It's horrible," she cried. "Why won't they stop?"

"It's just to do with the celebration, Alice," I told her.

She looked around, her eyes scanning the crowds. "It sounds like someone is dying."

"They're not, I promise," I said, reaching for her. She let me pull her forward, and together we began to move again, though her steps were heavy, as if she were walking through mud. There was no expression on her face, and yet, somehow, this absence seemed to fill her so completely, so entirely, that it crowded her features. I moved to speak, to ask her about what she had said in the bar only moments before, but something stopped me — a hand on my shoulder — and I turned, my heart racing, expecting it to be John.

Instead Youssef stood, watching.

I shrunk back, wondering how he had managed to find me, how, in fact, he had ever managed to find me in the continued disorder and confusion that was Tangier. I fixed him with a stare, my mind flooding with distrust, and I felt all of it then — the strangeness of the night, the uneasiness, the anger — and I hated him, for intruding, for interrupting my moment with Alice, for jeopardizing my chance to make things right. I cast a weary glance over my shoulder. Alice did not seem to notice Youssef's presence but instead continued to stare blankly ahead — her eyes taking in the chaos that surrounded us. I felt his hand on my shoulder again and I grimaced under its pressure.

"I worried after our last conversation," he said, his voice low and insistent.

I blinked. Our conversation — about John, Sabine — it seemed as though it had happened weeks ago, months even. I thought about how much had changed since then — and how much more everything was about to change again. I remembered what he had said

— *girl* — and how I had reacted. I blushed, the anger slowly seeping from my veins, grateful that the night hid the red creeping up my cheeks. Perhaps I had acted with haste — it certainly seemed so now. And yet, the word sat badly with me still, leaving an acidic taste in my mouth.

"You've been avoiding me," he said.

Something inside me grew still, quiet.

He squinted through the darkness. "I cannot think why, but it is quite clear that you are," he said, moving toward me, closing the distance between us.

I took a step backward.

He sneered, as if reading my thoughts. "You are all the same, in the end. Tangerines. Every Moroccan you see is for personal gain, for sale." He stepped closer. "I wonder, mademoiselle, what exactly you are willing to pay," he said, reaching for my wrist, his fingers clasping my skin, hard, pinching, "and what precisely it is that you are wanting to purchase."

I wrenched my arm away and in the process collided with Alice, so that she fell to the ground, a cry escaping her lips. In that moment, I forgot Youssef and his menacing tone. He was only a mosquito, I told myself. It was time at last to flick him away. I turned my back to him completely and helped Alice to her feet. "Are you hurt?" I asked, brushing at her skirt, her knees — both of which were now caked in grime and filth. "Alice," I started again, but John appeared then, had already started to make his way back to us. His hair, now sweaty and limp, clung to the sides of his face, his hat nowhere to be seen.

206

"I've got to head to the office," he said, standing, his arms hanging limply at his sides, as if the frantic energy that had pushed him forward only moments before had drained away, leaving behind only a shell. He stopped, taking in Alice's disheveled appearance.

"She fell, but she's fine," I said.

John hesitated, then nodded, his eyes taking in the street revelers that flanked us. "It appears Tangier is done. At least as we know it." He wiped the sweat from his brow, and I saw, so clearly, his love for the country, for this strange little stretch of land that belonged to no one and everyone. I saw how much it pained him, the thought of it changing such that he would no longer be the one in charge but rather the outsider, perhaps for the very first time in his life. He felt powerless, trapped, unable to do anything. And though it pained me to think that we could be at all similar, that any sort of connective tissue existed between us, particularly after what he had tried to do that night, I had felt that before too, felt it, in some ways, every day of my life. I tried to take pleasure in the fact that now he would feel it as well, but the thought only hit, hollow and empty. "Has something happened?" I asked, unsettled by the change in his demeanor.

"Everyone is getting anxious." He shrugged, though his face conveyed his worry. "What with all the riots in the past few years. They don't want to be around when things are made official." He shook his head, his expression weary. *Tired*, I thought. "I have to go. I'll be back later, though I've promised Charlie that I'll head to Fez with him later tomorrow," he said, speaking the words to Alice, who still did not appear to be listening. He turned back toward me. "Please get her back to the flat." He hesitated. "And be safe."

And then he was gone, lost in the crowd.

I woke in the middle of the night, gasping for air. At first, I was unsure of what it had been — a nightmare that had snapped me back to life, or a noise from somewhere within the room. My heart beat fast and I felt a sort of confusion cloud my mind as exhaustion made it impossible for me to recall where I was and what had happened. *Tangier*. It came flooding back to me. *I was in Tangier. With Alice.*

And then I saw her, standing at the threshold of my bedroom.

In that moment, there was nothing I wanted more than for her to cross the barrier between us. For her to walk into the room, for her to crawl into the small bed — the same one that she had made up for me and that had smelled like her and now smelled of both of us — for her to allow me to comfort her, to care for her. It was a realization that I had come to years ago, on the very first day I had met her. There was no one who would look out for her, who would love her, who would take care of her better than me.

I had waited for her to realize this over the years we lived together in Vermont, tripping happily through the months, wrapped in a cloud of our domestic bliss. There had been picnics, eaten on the lawn and at the End of the World, on sunny spring days. There had been walks around the campus in fall, crunching leaves under our feet, spending afternoons locked away inside the library. And there had been winter. Her favorite season and mine too, because of how much it made her smile, how much it reminded her of being a child, of being a daughter. We stayed inside by the fire, sipping tea and cocoa. I would always check to make sure the wood had been delivered to our house, and if not, would place a gentle reminder. I knew how much she enjoyed watching the flickering of the flames as the snow fell outside. And that final year, when the stability of the life we had created together was threatened, I had taken care of that too. I had done all of it for her — silently and without complaint. I was happy to do it, I wanted to do it. I did it all, waiting until the day when she would notice. That she would realize.

I remained quiet, patient, waiting for her — as always.

But then she spoke, her words cracking the darkness in half.

"I want you to leave, Lucy."

My heart stopped, my stomach clenched. I thought of all those terrible clichés I'd read in books my entire life and I felt and understood every single wretched one in that moment. I shook my head, trying to shake Alice's words from my mind. This was not how it was supposed to be. This was not what was supposed to happen. I frowned, turning it all over in my mind, trying to make sense of it, how everything could have changed and I had somehow failed to notice, in the space of only a few hours. I felt the anger, hot and sharp, pressing at my throat. She had already agreed to go with me, she had already promised.

"You mean John wants me to leave," I finally managed, my words short, clipped. "That's what you mean to say."

"No, Lucy."

She stood tall and erect, as if her confidence, her resolve was bound up in her posture, so that I wanted nothing so much as to push her to the floor, to dispel whatever it was that was forcing her to say these awful things.

She crossed her arms. "*I* want you to leave."

I sat up in bed, tossing the covers aside. "You don't mean that," I said, my voice, I knew, wavering between placation and harshness. Her words had unnerved me, unmoored me, so that I could no longer figure out what I was supposed to be to her in that moment, could no longer read what she needed me to be. I shook my head. "You can't mean that, Alice."

"I do, Lucy," she said, nodding, the movement sharp and succinct.

"I don't know what else he said to you," I began, "but you can't let him do this to us."

For a moment, she looked confused; then she shook her head again, this time a small smile accompanying the gesture. "No," she said softly, her eyes meeting my own. "No, this isn't John." A laugh, sharp and bitter, escaped her lips. "This is me, Lucy. Entirely me. I'm the one asking you to leave. I'm the one who wants you to go." She stopped. "To go and to never come back. I want you to leave me alone."

My insides crumpled. It wasn't John, she had promised, but I wanted to reach out and shake her and

210

scream, *Of course it is! Of course it's him!* She was too lost, too far under his spell to be able to see it clearly. "Alice —" I began.

She held up her hand, as if to physically impede my words.

"We were going to leave," I argued, moving out of the bed and toward her. "You had said that we were going to leave — him, Tangier. All of it."

"No, Lucy. *You* said. *You* decided." She shook her head.

"Alice." I reached out for her.

"No." She stepped back into the hallway. "I should never have opened that door. I should never have allowed you in." She started toward her bedroom door, then stopped. "I know what you did. At Bennington. I know it was you."

"Alice —" I started.

"Why did you ask me to stay?"

I frowned, startled by the question. "I don't understand."

"That day. That awful day in Vermont," she said, her voice cold and hard. "You told me not to get into the car. Why?"

"Because," I said, looking away, only for a second — but she had noticed. "I didn't want you to leave. I didn't want us to be angry with each other any longer."

"No," she said, shaking her head. "Don't say anything more, Lucy. I won't listen. I won't believe you."

"Alice, you're confused." I stopped, looking at her, imploring. "Do you really think that I would ever do anything to hurt you?"

I saw her hesitate, but then she shook her head, swiftly, as if determined to convince herself. "You need to leave, by tomorrow." She turned, as if to go, but stopped, her words glinting, sparking in the darkness: "And if you don't, I'll telephone the police and tell them exactly what you've done."

She crossed the hallway and closed the door to her bedroom.

The lock turned, loud and resounding.

I did not sleep that night.

Instead I sat, watching as the light broke into the room, casting long shadows across the walls before me, my eyelids feeling heavy, my thoughts scattered and confused. When morning arrived, full and bright, I left the flat.

Once outside I began to walk. I went down narrow paths and tight corners, to familiar places and new territories. I walked until my feet hurt, until they cracked and bled. I discovered the tomb of Ibn Battuta, the explorer. I laid my hand across the rough wall, brushed my fingers across the plaque that had been placed in his honor. And just like him, I refused to stop. I was not tired — thirst and hunger did not exist. I pushed ahead, the knowledge that I had to keep walking, that I must keep walking, buried somewhere deep within me. It was the most important thing. I must not stop, I must not think too hard. At the end of it, I knew, all would be right. Alice would come to her senses, she would tell John what we had decided, and the two of us would leave, head back to England together, maybe stop in Spain for a few months first. I imagined it — the pair of us, in Madrid, then Barcelona. We would drink sherry in one and gin in the other. We would sit outside until the sun faded and night crept in, eating tapas and drinking Rioja. Alice would like that better than gin.

And then I stumbled. A rock I had not seen. A piece of debris sticking out of the ground that had hidden itself. It was a short fall but enough to wrench my ankle so that it smarted when I tried to place my full weight on it. No one had seen. I was alone in an empty alleyway. And yet, despite this knowledge, I felt my cheeks burn with embarrassment, with anger. I had loved this country from the moment I first stepped foot on its shores, and yet *this* was the way it treated me. Placing unforeseen obstacles under my feet, causing me injury in its filthy streets, the ground covered in a litany of bodily fluids that I shuddered to think of, my hands and knees now red with scratches, my ankle useless. I thought of Alice. It was the same, wasn't it? I had done everything for her, loved her, watched out for her, and she had treated me just the same. Hiding things, obscuring my vision. Making me think I was safe. The buzzing in my ear increased. I batted at it, desperate. The effort it required to remain calm seemed impossible, insurmountable. I could feel the anger, the rage, boiling just beneath my skin. Tiny pinpricks emerged along my arms, followed by larger, more sinister red hives. And yet, despite the heat, my skin refused to sweat. It was trapped, somehow, inside my body, refusing to come out. The results were angry red

**213**

welts that rose across my arms and ran up and down my stomach. I could feel them spreading from my neck and onto my face.

A man rounded the corner. I ignored him, willing him to do the same — daring him to do otherwise. He passed by me, silent, and for a moment I felt the anger start to retreat.

Then he turned and spoke: "Smile. Be happy."

I shot him a look, one that boiled with hatred, overflowed with violence. He shrank backward, and I was suddenly anxious to get away from him, from this putrid-smelling alley. No, not anxious, desperate. I was desperate to get away, feeling my cheeks flush red again, hot with newfound anger. I was embarrassed and I was angry that this man was able to make me feel this way, that anyone could make me feel this way. I could feel it, as I had in the past, growing out of control. As it had that day of the accident. I could feel its energy coursing through my body, as if I had been shocked, zapped, brought back to life so that all of me was burning, electric, and the source of energy could no longer be contained. It took everything in my willpower not to lunge at him. I knew, rationally, that my anger had nothing to do with him. That it was directed somewhere else altogether. At the same time, I was powerless to stop. I did not want to. I worried that if I did, I would simply break apart, break down, the anger and power — yes, it felt powerful — seeping out of my pores and leaving me small and pitiless, a figure to be laughed at, one to be derided. I felt the tears begin to well. "Get away from me," I hissed, aware that while he

214

probably would not understand my words, he would by no means miss my tone.

A look of confusion swept across his features.

I almost wished that he would do something — shout, slap, spit — anything, but all he did was slink away down one of the city's countless alleys, disappearing into the labyrinthine maze.

In that moment I felt nothing but contempt — for all of them. I hated John and his confident smirk, I hated the nameless faces that I had to push past in order to find one solitary spot in this sea of strangers, and even, for the briefest of moments, I hated her. Alice. I had done everything for her — traveled halfway across the world in order to find her, to rescue her from the mess that she had made *of our life*. I hated her for her weakness, her spinelessness, for always going back on the decision she had made.

There was only one thing to do now.

I turned quickly, leaving behind the darkened alley and heading back into the heart of the medina, back to the Petit Socco. I slipped into Café Tingis, ordered a coffee, and then asked the waiter to use the telephone.

I dialed the number, hoping he would still be home, hoping he would be the one to answer. I held my breath and waited to hear John's voice.

Alice was not supposed to have been in the car that night.

Tom was not supposed to have died.

But then we had fought, a torrent of angry words and accusations, powerful enough to match the snowstorm raging outside around us. A blizzard, I had later heard it referred to, so that by the time I had realized what was happening — the car pulling up, Alice stepping inside, the storm at its zenith — the roads were covered in a sheen of ice and the accident was far worse than I had ever intended.

I had meant it as a scare, imagining — as I felt for it, underneath the hood of Tom's car, alongside the firewall, moving quickly, my hands working from memory, from experiences I no longer wanted to claim as my own, as I inhaled the deep, unnerving scent of oil that was both home and somewhere else entirely foreign — a broken leg, a lost scholarship, something that would take him far and away from Alice so that she and I would be alone once more. With a pair of pliers I had crimped the line, knowing it would affect the pressure, affect the brakes — but I had not expected it to burst, had not expected the snow and the ice and the mountains and Alice.

I had tried to stop her, to warn her, but she wouldn't listen. I had thought about following, about pushing past, crawling into the car alongside her — but I had stopped, frozen, from both the growing storm around us and the words she had spoken to me, about disappearing, about never wanting to see me again. She had fixed me with a look of such anger, such hatred, that I had been rendered useless by my surprise.

Afterward, I had gone back inside, had stood in our quiet little room, and had realized it was over. That there was no longer a reason for me to stay. And so I had packed my bag, a single suitcase, nothing more,

filled only with the things that I had come there with —
a few dresses, a couple pairs of stockings. The bits I had
acquired along the way — a novel from the town
bookstore, a pressed leaf from the previous autumn —
these I left behind.

At first I had thought to avoid the main road and
what I might find there — but then I had thought of
the woods, of the darkness and the snow, and I had
pushed ahead.

Walking through the blizzard, my hands shaking,
blue and numb, I had paused at the wreckage that my
desires had conjured, had stood, wondering, my blood
thrumming loudly within my ear, what it was all for. I
had found Alice, lying in the snow, a good distance
from the car, her body smeared with red and black,
nearly unrecognizable. And as I stood over the lifeless
body of the girl I had loved, the consequence, I
thought, of my dreaming, of my wanting, I had felt it:
the darkness around me, transforming and moving me,
making me into something that I had not intended, a
monster I had not foreseen.

I had moved to New York, to the city — stopping first
by the garage I had grown up in, which only days
earlier I had been thankful for, for the summers I had
endured, sweating alongside the other men in the
building, casting them murderous glances when their
own lingered too long. From the garage I had taken
what little money was in the register — it was owed, I
thought, for my years of servitude — and purchased a
one-way ticket on Greyhound. Once there, I did not

bother to change my name; the city was big and no one would come looking for me, I knew.

And so I had disappeared. Into a boardinghouse with a dozen or so other girls, running from abusive husbands or neglectful husbands or those just running toward something more. Those first few weeks I had scoured the newspapers, searching for an obituary. There was a tiny newsstand, several blocks away from my rented room, that carried our town's local paper, and I would make the daily trip, my shoulders shaking in the cold morning air, certain that each new day would bring the announcement I was waiting for, was dreading. A week passed before one appeared for Thomas Stowell, the length of the notice a testament, it seemed, to the great and long line of white-collared Stowells he had descended from, as if such lineage demanded that his passing be recognized. I waited for a similar mention of Alice, but there was nothing, and as the days passed, the man behind the newsstand expecting my arrival, paper in hand — comfort, I supposed he wrongly assumed, for a homesick girl in a new city — I began to feel the justice of it all. It was fate, it was punishment, this eternal waiting. My days were marked by it, my anonymous footfalls that took me from boardinghouse to newsstand to work and back again, all that I could hope for now. And for a while I convinced myself that I could do it, that I could continue on, hidden in the cold gray emptiness of the city, the perfect cloak to hide my monstrosity from the world.

But then one day, I had seen her: Alice's guardian, Aunt Maude. I watched her emerge from a taxi not five feet away from where I stood. She wore a smart dress that looked as though it cost more than my entire year's salary, her hair sleek and expensive. And though I had never met her before, I recognized her instantly from the pictures that Alice had kept in our dorm room, and so I moved toward her, needing, in that moment, to be close to someone who had once been close to Alice. I had pulled my threadbare coat closer to my body, hoping that it would hide my even more depressing dress, which had begun to rub in places from so much use that it wasn't impossible to see through the fabric.

"Miss Shipley," I called out.

Alice's aunt had turned, her eyes quickly taking in my form, her lips turned down in displeasure. "Yes?" she asked, her tone curt.

"Miss Shipley," I repeated, fixing my face with a small smile. "I thought it was you." I ignored the slight frown that had settled on her face, as she tried — and failed — to place me in her life. "I went to school with your niece, Alice." It was the first time in months that I had said her name aloud, and the word stuck, caught in my throat.

At the mention of her niece's name, Maude Shipley's face changed — though it did not relax, I noted. "Did you? Well," she said, "I'll make sure to tell her you said hello."

And with that one sentence, that one promise, everything changed.

Later I decided that Aunt Maude's presence was a sign, one that could not be ignored, one that demanded

— no, *begged* — for my attention. And I felt it then — the thread that held Alice and me together begin to pull taut. We were not finished, not yet. Our story was still being written. It was fate, I decided later, as I felt the darkness that had hovered above me throughout my time alone in New York begin to recede, my sad little rain cloud pulling away at last. I had moved closer to Aunt Maude and said, "Actually, it's quite fortunate that I met you here. I've been trying to get an updated address for her — alumnae stuff, you see — and I haven't been able to find it anywhere. I don't suppose she's still at her old address? The one in London?"

Her eyebrows arched, and she asked, "And what did you say your name was, my dear? I don't believe I caught it."

"Oh," I said, my gloved hands moving to my throat, "how silly of me. I'm so sorry, Miss Shipley. I'm Sophie, Sophie Turner," I replied, using the name of a girl who had lived down the hall from us at school, a forgettable figure whom most of the other girls only ever spoke to because of who her parents were, because of what their wealth meant. I had kept up-to-date with a few of them, using my resources at the publishing company and the newspaper to do a bit of digging, reading with envy of their accomplishments, their plans, so I knew Sophie Turner had been a bit of a disappointment. She had married, though not particularly well, and was living out her days deep in the South, in some state I hoped never to cross the border of, in a town that rolled easily off the tongue and out of the mind. I knew from experience that she was a girl no one could ever remember by sight alone, though they knew the name, knew the weight of it. I had reaped the advantage of this for a time, so when drinks were placed on bar tabs or an occasional night stayed in a hotel, it was always with a smile and a nod of the head, no questions asked and no chance of an embarrassing run-in with a girl no one could remember. Then the Turners had experienced some sort of financial crisis — I had never bothered to learn the specifics — and the managers then became more reluctant to book rooms, to serve drinks, without any guaranteed method of payment. Still, I used the name when it suited me, and now, standing in front of a woman who represented all the things the Turner name had once stood for, I found its usefulness once again.

At the sound of the name, Maude smiled — though it was still tight — and told me of Alice's husband, of Tangier. "A part of me regrets introducing them," she had confided, the frown line between her eyes deepening at the words. "But how on earth was I supposed to know that he would whisk her away to Africa?" For, according to Maude, she wasn't at all certain that her niece was happy, wasn't entirely convinced, in fact, that her husband had married her for anything beyond her money. "Can you imagine it," she had demanded, "a girl like her, in a place like that?"

It was those words, more than anything else, that persuaded me, in the end.

Maude took a small metallic notebook from her handbag, its outside a darkly embossed botanical design, the kind one saw in Victorian wallpaper, and using the gilded pen within, wrote the address on a slip of paper. I took it, my hand trembling as I placed it into my pocket.

The very next day, I withdrew my rent money from the bank and stood in line at the ticket office for Cunard, booking a passage across the Atlantic.

We had been walking for nearly fifteen minutes. During that time, neither of us had spoken. At first, I thought maybe the temperature was to blame for his silence — for while the sun had set, there was still a powerful heat that seemed to burn against the back of my bare head. I could feel my blouse cling to my body, smell the scent of my own sweat as the material around my armpits dampened. I wondered if he could feel it too — but he always looked so unbothered by the heat, it was impossible to tell. Perhaps it was just an affectation, like most of his life. Or perhaps he was still upset after last night. I wondered if that was the real reason he looked straight ahead, at the road in front of us, at anyone and anything, it seemed, but me.

Then, at last, he spoke.

"I know you saw us." His voice was neither kind nor threatening. The words were spoken without emotion, as if waiting to see how I would react.

I looked at him. "You and Sabine."

I saw the flash of surprise on John's face. He had not expected me to know her name, and I wondered what he would have said if I had remained quiet, if he would have eventually tried to pass it off as something

222

innocent, a colleague, a wife of a friend — as I suspected he would have that day in the Kasbah.

"I won't ask how you figured that out," he said, that same teasing smile emerging on his face once more, though there was something halfhearted in the gesture, as if he could no long muster up enough energy for such pretense. "I'm surprised, of course, but you seem rather resourceful." He cleared his throat. "Have you told Alice?"

I smiled and said instead: "I'm leaving soon, John. And Alice wants to leave with me."

I noticed the change in his face, the way his eyebrows dipped — not quite a frown, nothing quite so declarative as disapproval. It was confusion, I decided. Was he really so naive as to think that Alice would not leave him following his indiscretion? We continued walking to our destination, and almost instinctively, I moved away, creating a slight gap between us as we continued. I wondered whether it would be violent, his reaction, or whether he might cry and beg me to change her mind. I couldn't decide which one displeased me more. We moved slowly, the night setting in fast. Already it was becoming more difficult to see, the lights of the medina far behind us.

"You've told her, then?" he asked, though his voice sounded neither fearful nor worried. Instead it was almost as though he were amused, as if the notion that I had shared the news of his infidelity with Alice was something trivial, something to be cast aside.

"She didn't need me to tell her, John." I paused. "She already knew. She'd figured it out all on her own."

He was silent for a moment, and he nodded, as if attempting to let the words settle. "Yes, I sometimes supposed she would. She's not dim, that one, is she?" he said, with a short, quick laugh that conveyed his uneasiness.

"No, she's not." I swallowed the bitter taste in my mouth. "So what will you do?"

He looked at me. "About what?"

"About Alice." I stopped. "Surely you don't expect her to stay with you, not after this."

He let out another laugh — this one more real, more authentic, I thought. "And why wouldn't she?" he asked. "All this was her aunt's idea, you know. Both she and my mother had been quite keen to introduce us. And though I suspect I'm not Aunt Maude's favorite nephew-in-law, I think faced with the option of having to care for Alice herself or having someone else take care of her, well."

I turned to him, my step momentarily faltering.

He must have sensed my confusion, even in the night, for he continued, "Alice isn't going anywhere, Lucy. I think you know that. Beyond all the family ties, we're good for each other. We're — what do you call it? Symbiotic. Isn't that one of your fancy terms? We need each other, Alice and I. Haven't you already figured that out? I need her money — well, maybe not *need*, perhaps *appreciate* would be the better word." He laughed. "And she needs me to keep her out of the loony bin."

I stopped. We had arrived. Even in the darkness, I could see him, looking around, trying to familiarize himself with his surroundings. He didn't recognize the place, which told me that he had never been there before. I was glad. It would make things easier.

I had decided, sitting at Café Tingis. John was the problem, the patriarchal head that had to be cut off, the dragon that had to be slain in order to rescue the heroine. I could not compete against John, just as I never could with Tom, not really — for the world told me this was not possible. I was their better in every way but one. I only needed to best them in order to make Alice see this as well. That her future lay not with them, but with me. I could feel the insistence in the air — beating, strongly. The days of suppression, of subjugation, were dwindling for the Moroccans, and I thought, in that instance, that I could feel it, the herald sounding for myself, for Alice as well.

"She will," I said, my voice flat and even. "She will come with me. She will see that it's the right decision."

"Lucy," he said, his voice tinged with something like irritation now. I could feel it, his temper, growing, fanned by my insistence, my determination. "Alice doesn't care about this whole mess with Sabine, not really," he continued, his words rushed. "If she had, don't you think she would have said something, done something by now?"

I struggled to find my voice. "She's afraid of you."

"No, Lucy." He laughed. "She just knows there isn't any better option. Not for a woman like her."

I felt it then — my breath jagged, sharp, so that it hurt to breathe, so that each and every inhale was labored, painful. "This is my favorite place in all of Tangier," I said, pushing the feeling aside. "Those are

**225**

tombs, just below you." I paused, turning to him, my voice wavering with emotion. "Alice *will* come with me, John. She already agreed to it, while we were in Chefchaouen. She's already decided to leave you. You're just not smart enough to have realized it yet."

He lunged then, and surprised, I lost my balance, falling to the hard, dusty ground. "You bitch," he spat. I pushed backward, working to right myself, to keep away from him so that he would not be able to stand over me, towering. I couldn't see his face clearly, not in the darkness, but I imagined it was red, swollen with anger. It seemed absurd that he should be so enraged. He had had Alice and he had let her go, traded her for that other woman. I think that was it — the thought of his betrayal — that convinced me, absolutely, that it was the right thing to do.

The only thing to do, I knew then.

John had subsumed Alice entirely, rendering it impossible for her to survive autonomously. As long as he existed, she could not. There was only one way to free her, to ensure that she would not always belong to him, to this place. I thought then too of how much John loved Tangier, realizing that he was right. Things were changing, shifting, and Tangier — all of us — would never be the same again. I knew that if he could, he would choose to remain there forever, with her — his Tangier — just as she was in that moment of time.

Once I realized that, the rest was surprisingly simple.

# III

# CHAPTER
# ELEVEN

## ALICE

When I woke that morning, for one strange, beautiful moment I was back in New England. I could feel the frozen blast of the winter months, could smell the cold, clean air, so that I moved to bury myself deeper within my bed, reaching for the familiar comfort of down. But then, that feeling of euphoria shifted, tilted, replaced instead by a growing urgency, a sense that something was wrong, the realization pulling me under, further and further, until I could no longer find my way out from under it. My stomach ached, and I kicked and clawed, but it was no use. I was back there again, in Vermont, and it was no longer nostalgic and breathtaking. There was now a darkness, something large and uncontrollable that threatened to hold me within its grasp once more. I saw Tom, then, lying in the snow, the white pristine blanket underneath him bleeding slowly into a deep, startling red. I stepped closer. No, it wasn't Tom at all, I realized. It was John, still and motionless — dead. And suddenly I knew. I knew that —

I sat up abruptly.

Someone was knocking at the door.

My head still slow with dreams, I turned to John, to see if he had heard the knocking as well. I saw his empty side of the bed and remembered. The other night at the bar — the kif, the drinks, his subsequent disappearance to Fez, which I could not blame him for, the need to escape apparently one of the few things we shared between us. After all, I had run to Chefchaouen while he had waited at home — now, it seemed, I would do the same, waiting until he reemerged on the doorstep from Fez, tired and full of the realization that there was no escape from the life we had created with each other.

I took a deep breath, willing my heart to slow, willing the sweat on my skin to dry, but the thought of John, pale and silent, remained before my eyes.

It seemed ages since I had last seen him in front of me.

I had stayed in bed the morning after our night out, nursing a horrendous hangover, so I wasn't even entirely certain what time he had arrived home, whether he had passed the night beside me, in our bed, or out on the sofa. I had woken to the sounds of him in the kitchen, making breakfast. A boiled egg and a slice of *msemmen*, followed by a quick cup of tea. It was always the same. Later, I had heard the phone ring — Charlie, I presumed, remembering what he had mentioned about Fez — and the closing of the front door not long after that.

I had listened, after, for sounds of Lucy. For any indication that she was packing, leaving — but there had only been silence. A few hours later, tiptoeing past her door — sometime in the late afternoon, judging by the way the light fell against the walls, insistent, as if clinging to life — I chanced a quick look into her room. It was empty. I had exhaled, feeling something like relief as I returned to my own bedroom and crawled back between the sheets, content to let the day slip by from the comfort of my bed, certain that everything was at last working its way back to how it had been before. And there was a comfort in that, in the realization that Lucy was gone and John was off with Charlie — that I was, once again, alone.

Toward nightfall I had woken and, unable to sleep, passed an hour or two by the window, looking out at Tangier, at the city that had somehow become my home. In the quiet, I allowed myself to wonder whether I could ever love it, wondered whether I could ever really be happy if I was to remain, with John. Our life was already so different from the way I had imagined it, and now that Lucy was gone, now that it was done with at last, I did not know what that would mean, for John and me, whether we would be able to slip back into the normalcy that we had created together — whether that was something that either of us even wanted. I had retired to bed early then, anxious to still the swirling thoughts in my mind, if only for a moment or two longer.

The knocking grew louder.

I pulled my dressing gown tighter and hurried down the hallway. "Coming," I called, my footsteps sounding against the cool tiles. I reached down and touched the brass knob, already convinced I would find John on the other side, back from gallivanting with Charlie, sulking, most likely, having misplaced his keys somewhere during his adventure and ready for a hot bath and a cup of tea. I smiled at the familiarity, eager to dispel the image of the John from my dreams, and opened the door.

It wasn't him.

Instead a man I did not recognize stood before me, a hat clutched between his hands. He was tall, his stature filling the doorway, his body, it seemed, expanding on each inhale. A scar, I noted, cut through his eyebrow, such that a patch was missing, and the smooth sheen of it, stark white against his skin, seemed to be illuminated in the darkness.

I frowned, peering through the dim light into the corridor, trying to place the man in front of me.

"Pardon the early hour, Alice," he began, his accent indicating he was a fellow countryman.

I started at the sound of my name. "Yes?" I asked, regretting how small, how tentative I knew my voice sounded.

"I'm looking for your husband. He wasn't in the office yesterday. Or today, in fact." He paused, looking over my shoulder, into the flat. "As you can probably imagine, we're a bit concerned at his absence."

"Oh," I said, feeling, as I did, the relief that surged through my body at the realization it was only a concerned colleague from work that stood on my doorstep, not a policeman out of uniform, carrying with him bad news that would transform my morning nightmare into something real. "He isn't here. In

Tangier, I mean. He went with his friend Charlie to Fez," I said, giving him a tentative smile.

The man frowned. "When was the last time you saw him?"

"He left yesterday afternoon, after breakfast," I said, ignoring the tiny pinpricks starting in the tips of my fingers. "Can I ask what this is about?"

"But you saw him?" he asked, ignoring my question. "Yesterday, I mean, before he left."

"No," I admitted, the word leaving my mouth slowly. "We had a bit of a night out and I'm afraid I slept rather late the next morning, so I didn't see him off." It seemed important, somehow, to explain how it was that I could be so unsure of my husband's movements, to this stranger who stood before me, assessing.

The man looked behind me again. "But he was here with you, afterward?"

I frowned. "I was asleep when he arrived home."

"Then how do you know he did? Arrive home, I mean?"

"I heard him," I said, defensive. But I wondered then what it was that I had in fact heard, whether it had been John after all, making breakfast the previous morning. I felt my stomach contract and worried, for a moment, that I might be ill. "It was him."

The man smiled, but there was something about the expression that made my insides clench further still, made me shrink backward, into the apartment. I thought about all of John's allusions to his cloak-and-dagger work. I had often scoffed at his stories, believing them to be exaggerations built on insecurity and pride, the result of having nothing but his name to cling to, but now I was seized with the thought that there might be some form of truth in them, and I wondered what that might mean about the man in front of me.

"And did anything out of the ordinary happen?" he asked, not responding to my admission. "That night, I mean?"

"No, of course not," I said, taken aback by his question. "Nothing at all." Then I thought of Lucy, our argument, and my breath caught in my throat. I was certain he had noticed it, by the way his eyes narrowed. Still, after a few moments of silence, when I said nothing further, he nodded, thanked me for my time, and turned, as if intending to leave.

I began to close the door, anxious now for the man to be gone — but then he paused and turned back, his face pinched in concentration. "Forgive me," he said, "but what time did you say he left?"

I crossed my arms tightly across my chest. "Sometime in the afternoon. I'm not sure exactly. Perhaps late morning," I said, unsure just how long I had actually stayed in bed the day before. It had felt like ages and only seconds, all at once. I shook my head, looking up at the man now staring intently into my face. "I don't know, I'm afraid."

He frowned, as if my uncertainty displeased him. "I see," he said. "Well. If you hear from him." He withdrew a card from within his suit pocket. "Please be in touch."

I took the proffered card and frowned, thinking again of that morning's dream. "Is he — has something happened?"

234

He fixed me with an odd expression. "Do you think something has happened?"

"What?" I felt my face flush. "No, I only thought, I mean, I thought you were implying —" I stopped, waiting for him to speak. He didn't. Instead he pointed to the card in my hand and then started to leave once more. "Wait," I said, my voice trembling. "Should we — I mean, shouldn't I telephone the police?"

His brow unfurrowed, the scarred white stretch expanded, and his mouth slipped into a wide grin that made me want to do nothing so much as shut the door between us, firmly, not waiting for his response. "I don't think there is any reason to do that," he said, his voice low, placating. "After all, we wouldn't want to involve the locals in our business, would we?"

I heard the force, the threat, implicit in his words, despite the odd smile that clung to his lips. He turned, and at the sound of his retreating footsteps, at last I closed the door.

John wasn't in Fez, then. Wasn't with his friend Charlie. Surely the man — I was unsure whether he had given me his name, and looking at his card realized it was nothing but a telephone number — had already spoken with him. I thought about ringing Charlie, just to make sure, before realizing I didn't actually know how to get in touch with him. I had met Charlie only a handful of times, at one party or another, and in those moments, I had been convinced that he did not have a sense of who I was, not really. He knew that John had married, knew that he was bringing his wife with him to Tangier. But my name, my face — both of these were a mystery to him, and ones I suspected he was not intent on solving.

I moved to the living room, to the desk that John rarely used, the drawers transformed into a receptacle for papers and pens. Surely John had written down Charlie's contact information somewhere. I sorted through each, flinging paper to the ground around me, not caring about the mess that I was making, frantic to find something, anything at all, so long as it would help dispel the image of John's lifeless body from my mind. As long as it would stop it from becoming a reality.

"What are you looking for?"

I jumped at the sound of her voice, slipping in the process, my already bruised knees connecting with the hardwood floor. Lucy stood above me, her hair hanging loose around her shoulders, the long strands trailing down her soft white blouse, which seemed to glow in the morning light.

She gave a small laugh. "You're too easily startled, Alice."

I blinked. It wasn't a trick of the light, a trick of my mind. She was there, still. I shook my head — it wasn't possible. I had asked her — no, *told* her — to leave, just the other night. I remembered standing there, staring in at her, asleep in the bed, knowing that I could no longer allow my fear to persuade me to remain silent. And so I had spoken the words, had finally released them, at last.

It had happened.

"Lucy," I sputtered. "What are you doing here?" They were similar to the words that I had spoken to her the first day she had arrived in Tangier. My head felt fuzzy, weighted down — my mind filled with nothing but the certainty of her presence and the terrible implication of what that might mean. I placed my hands on the floorboards beneath me, used the force of my arms to push myself upward, grit pressing into my skin. "I told you to leave."

Lucy gave a quick, short laugh. "Don't be silly, Alice. We were tired, we had a bit too much to drink." She gave a slight shake of her head. "You don't have to worry. I'm not going anywhere."

I could feel it, that all-too-familiar sensation of fear, in the very center, in my very core, pushing and pulling. My limbs trembled, and I was convinced that just one more moment in her presence would undo me completely. I pushed past her, walking — practically running — back to my bedroom, back to safety. I bolted the door, my fingers fumbling over the lock.

I sat in the corner of the bedroom, waiting.

Earlier, I had heard her footsteps as she had approached the door, heard the slight creak of the wood as she had leaned on it, presumably listening for me, just as I listened for her now. The symmetry of it made me shiver. My eyes roamed the space of the room, searching, though for what I could not explain — a way out, a trapdoor, something that would let me escape from what was happening around me, a nightmare I could not wake from. My eyes fell on the telephone next to John's side of the bed.

It had been an extravagance, something we had not needed — two telephones in one small household, it was absurd, I had told him — but John had insisted, telling me he wouldn't be dragging himself out of bed and down the hall each and every time my aunt decided to check in on us. An excuse, I soon realized. What he really meant was that he wanted to be able to conduct meetings while still in bed, so that I would have to turn away, a pillow pressed against my ears in an effort to block out the sound. As I crawled toward it now — pausing every so often as a board shifted under the weight of my frame, listening, waiting, frightened at what might happen if she were to realize what I was about to do, as if Lucy could already sense my plan, as if my thoughts were able to slip from my mind, porous and unreliable as it was — I silently thanked him for the decision.

Once next to the bed, I clasped the cold Bakelite between my hands, the one and only number that I had ever managed to commit to memory, ready on my lips.

At the sound of her voice, I grasped the telephone tightly between my fingers.

"Alice?" Aunt Maude asked, sounding for one moment as if she were there in the room with me and not thousands of miles away. "Alice, what is it? What's happened?"

I wondered briefly how she had known — that it was me, that something was wrong. If she could somehow feel it, despite the distance between us. But then I remembered the operator and I shook my head, embarrassed. "It's John," I began, realizing that she was waiting for me to speak. "He's —" I hesitated.

"He's what?" she demanded, her voice, so typically calm and measured, now sharp with panic. I thought I could feel it, vibrating through the phone.

"He's missing," I finally managed, the words coming out cracked, broken. "Someone from his work showed up at the flat this morning, looking for him. I told them he was supposed to be in Fez, with his friend Charlie — but now I don't know if that's true." I took a deep breath. "They told me not to go to the police, but I think something has happened. And I think — I think I know who might have been involved."

There was no response.

"Auntie?" I whispered, worried that I might have only imagined her voice a few moments before.

"Yes, Alice, I'm here." There was another pause. "I want you to listen carefully to me, now. I am going to have my secretary book a flight to Spain, and I'll board a ferry from there. I'm not sure how long it will take to organize, but I am going to do my best to be there by the end of the week. Do you understand?"

"Thank you." I breathed. "Thank you so much, Auntie." I thought, then, of Aunt Maude, sturdy and solid, of her uncanny ability to take a complicated mess and sort it into something orderly and structured. I felt relief wrap itself around me, tight and comforting in its insistence.

"Alice," she said, her voice cutting into my thoughts. "I want you to promise me something."

I nodded. "Yes, of course."

"I want you to promise me that you won't speak to the police. You said they don't know about John's disappearance yet, and I want you to promise me that you won't go and tell them."

I nodded again, though she could not see me. "Of course," I promised. I knew that it would not be hard to keep, for the thought of going into the station on my own, against the advice of that man with the scar from earlier, of reporting John's disappearance and trying to explain everything that had happened, caused me to pale. "I promise, Auntie."

"Good," she said. "And if they come to question you, I want you to tell them that you won't speak without your guardian."

Again, I nodded. I still had several months left of my guardianship, and though I had felt the chains of it rankle at times — eager to be in charge of my own finances, my own life, to feel as though I was no longer a child — now, I was grateful to still be tied to Maude in a way that was legal and binding. For while I knew that she was my aunt, that she was my family, I had always sensed a distance between us, a confusion on Maude's part toward the girl she had been forced to raise upon her brother's death. She had never wanted children, and though she had never complained about her duties as my guardian, a part of me often wondered whether she had resented having to take me in. I brushed aside my concerns. We made a plan to speak soon, and I was just about to place the telephone onto the receiver when I heard her voice again: "I said, did your friend ever get in touch with you?"

I frowned. "My friend?"

"Yes, what was her name? I noted it here somewhere." Aunt Maude paused, and I thought I heard the rustling of papers. "There. Sophie Turner. I ran into her on the streets of New York, oh, it's been months now, but she said she was trying to get ahold of you. Did she ever manage?"

My fingers grasped the telephone. I had never spoken a word to Sophie Turner during my years at Bennington. And there was only one person who would have recognized Aunt Maude. *Lucy.* She had admitted, just the other night, that she had worked at a publishing company in the city. It had to have been her. I had wondered how she had found me, but then, Lucy had always managed things that others couldn't.

"Alice?"

"Yes, yes, she did," I replied. My voice dropped to a whisper as I looked around the room, convinced that she was listening. It was as if I could feel her presence, breathing, just there, on the other side of the door, so that I shot a quick, harried glance over my shoulder. I turned back to the telephone, still clasped between my fingers.

At first I had thought to warn Aunt Maude about Lucy, to tell her that she was in Tangier and that it was happening all over again — that the fog had lifted and I had remembered everything I had wanted to forget. But the words felt too dangerous to speak aloud, the walls too thin, too tenuous. I worried that even the telephone connection might not be safe, that it too held the possibility of being altered and changed. After all, there

**241**

were telephone operators stationed in Tangier. Perhaps Lucy had befriended one and convinced them to keep her apprised of any conversations that might pass between me and others. I shook my head. It was mad — and yet. I paused, an idea growing. Perhaps if I told Aunt Maude about Sophie Turner, a sort of code for the real Lucy, the explanation would come easier once she was in Tangier. She would be able to see, then, just how devious, how manipulative Lucy Mason really was, for there would be nowhere to hide.

I took a deep breath and said, "In fact, she's here now."

"What, in Tangier?" my aunt questioned. I could hear the surprise, the confusion, evident in her voice. "I hadn't known she was planning a visit. She didn't mention anything of the sort."

"Yes," I replied. "It was all very sudden. I was quite surprised as well."

There was a pause. "Well, I suppose at least that means you're not entirely alone there. Sophie must be a great source of comfort to you at the moment."

I squeezed my eyes together. "Yes, Auntie, of course." I hated to lie, to make her believe something that wasn't true. But it was necessary, I told myself.

"Don't worry, Alice," my aunt said, her voice once more slow and measured. "I'll be there soon enough and I'll take care of everything. I promise."

I thought of the words she had once spoken to me at Bennington, how eerily similar they were to the ones she had said just now.

When I placed the telephone back onto the receiver, my hand hovered for a few moments in the empty space above, shaking.

# CHAPTER
# TWELVE

## LUCY

She was an impostor. The thought came as I lay on the bed, a cigarette held between my fingers, the hot ash threatening to spill onto the sheet below me. It was a strange idea, a ridiculous one, I knew, and yet my mind lingered over the possibility, thinking once more of the look she had given me only moments before — as if I were a stranger, someone she didn't know, someone she was frightened of. Before, I had attributed her words, her behavior, to John's presence, to his influence, but now that he was gone, there were no more excuses.

I sat up, ash scattering onto my blouse. I brushed it away, impatient.

Perhaps that was it — the reason for her curious behavior. She did not yet know that he was gone, not for sure. Perhaps I had only to tell her — what I had done, for her — and everything would go back to how it had been before. But then something pulled, something tugged, and I wondered what that word *before* actually meant and just how far back we would have to go — before John, before Tom, before all of the madness that had encircled us.

The sound of voices interrupted my thoughts.

Creeping to the door, I placed my ear against the wooden frame, curious. It was Alice, her voice unmistakable, but she was not singing, like she had that first night, was not simply muttering aloud to herself in the empty space of her room. No, it sounded as though her words, a steady stream of them, were directed toward someone else, as if there were another person in the apartment with us.

The telephone, I realized.

Opening the door — hesitantly, at first, so that the turn of the brass knob was all that I could hear, my ears ringing with the violence of it — I made my way carefully out into the hallway. My feet bare, I stepped over the damaged floorboard just outside my bedroom door, its texture stained and weathered. Her voice was clearer now, though still muffled. I frowned and moved toward her bedroom door. She was quiet again and I waited, my breath held, before — yes. I could hear her, though the shape of her words were still hidden. A second passed and then another, my frustration mounting before I remembered the telephone that I had seen in the sitting room, tucked away just behind the sofa. I did not hesitate, fearful that even a fraction of a second lost would be enough to lose the conversation.

Lifting the telephone from the receiver, I placed one hand firmly across my mouth, determined they would not hear my intrusion. There was a pause and for a second I worried that I had been caught out. But, no — there was Maude, I realized — speaking to her niece in a plaintive tone, demanding to know what was wrong, what had happened.

I listened, eager to hear how Alice would respond.

John was missing. Those were the words she spoke next, so that I was lost, momentarily unable to follow their narrative thread, puzzling over the fact that Alice knew, that somehow already she had known. She mentioned, then, a man at the door, someone looking for John. I cast a hurried glance toward the hallway, as if he might still be there. What man? I wondered silently. For while it was true that I had spent most of the morning in bed, I had always slept lightly, had always woken at the slightest of sounds, and there had been nothing, nothing at all that had alerted me, that had warned me of another's presence in the flat. I thought of Alice when I had found her earlier that morning — eyes wide, hair matted and tangled — digging through John's desk drawers, obviously looking for something, though I hadn't dared ask what.

And then I heard her whisper the words: *I know who did it*. I heard her mention Sophie Turner, and I knew all at once what it was that she had realized, knew what it was that she was intending to do — for I knew her, Alice, better than she knew herself, could anticipate every action and reaction before they had ever occurred to her.

I sunk to the floor, my fingers grasping the Berber carpet beneath me, my nails turning white against the pressure as I clutched at its frayed edges. I remained there, unable to move, though I became aware, at some point, of the closing of the front door, of Alice's absence from the flat, of the telephone operator, still in my ear.

"Miss? Are you still there on the line? Miss?"

I remained kneeling, feeling, savoring the burn of the carpet against my knees.

"Yes. Yes, I'm still here," I replied, my mouth dry.

"This is Information again. Is there anything else I can help you with?"

I hesitated, but only for a fraction of a second.

"Yes, can you please reconnect me with the last number requested?"

"The same number, miss?"

"Yes, please."

I waited, listening to the clicks, imagining the wires being plugged and unplugged as the operator worked to connect the telephone in Alice's sitting room to one miles and miles away. I focused on this image, working hard to keep it in my mind, to not think of anything else, if only for one moment longer.

It rang once, twice, and then — "Alice?"

I knew already that it would be Maude who answered, had heard her voice only seconds before, and yet there was something different, a finality in the act that made me shiver, my body chilled despite the blazing heat of the afternoon.

I moved to replace the telephone onto the receiver but stopped, and bringing it back to my ear began, tentatively, "Miss Shipley?"

There was a pause. "Yes?"

"It's Sophie Turner here."

"Sophie?" I could hear the surprise register in her voice.

"Yes. I'm awfully sorry about reaching you this way, but I needed to speak with you, urgently." I stopped, held my breath, counted in my head. "It's about Alice."

She did not hesitate to respond this time. "Is everything all right, Sophie?"

I willed my voice to shake, to sound unsteady as I whispered into the telephone: "No. No, I'm afraid, it isn't."

I had to be quick. There was still one more thing to be done, one more telephone call to be completed before Alice returned — and one that couldn't be made from inside the flat, just in case they ever tried to trace it. I wasn't sure how it all worked, but I knew that there were records, little cards that the telephone operators were responsible for and that logged who had placed what call and where and for how long. There could be no evidence of this next one, not if my plan was to work.

As I walked, my steps steady and sure, I hoped that it would.

That the plan I had conjured up out of despair and desperation only moments earlier would be enough. I had not anticipated this, after all, had not foreseen this turn — and it stung, this change in the narrative that I had not consented to. I had already worked it out so perfectly, and she had gone and erased it all.

The public telephone box sat at the end of the street, just as I remembered. Once inside, I waited to hear the click, waited for the greeting of the operator before I began to speak, my accent molded in some proximity after Alice's own. "I'd like to be connected to the local police, please." I paused. "Yes, yes, I'll wait. My name? Alice Shipley."

It was done. There was no turning back.

I hung up the telephone, my thoughts distorted. Everything had shifted in the course of an hour. It seemed impossible, ridiculous even, that an entire life could be altered by a few brief words. My mind tried and failed to keep up with it, to understand the consequences of what I had just set in motion. But then, no, I reminded myself, it had not been me — it had been Alice. She had been the one.

I turned to exit the telephone booth, but a figure stood there, blocking me. Youssef.

"Oh, please, just leave me alone," I murmured, suddenly aware of the sweltering temperature of the little glass booth. My blouse clung to my back. "We have nothing to say to each other."

He smiled. "But I only wish to speak, to try and make things right between us once more."

I looked at him, knowing that he did not mean what he said, knowing that there was something else, another reason for his visit today, for his visit the other night. Our encounters were not merely coincidences, I knew. There was something that he wanted from me — no, it was more than that. Something he thought he could get — perhaps deserved, was owed. I wondered what it could be, how it could ever matter, in light of what had happened already. The police would arrive soon. I had little time left, which meant I needed to return to the flat. But I paused, wanting a few more minutes, a few more hours, in which I could pretend that everything was just as it had been the day before. And so even though I knew that it was not the smartest decision, that I should shoo away the mosquito before me and continue with what I needed to get done, I leaned heavily against the frame of the booth and consented.

"I suppose," I said, ignoring, even as I did so, the dangerous smile on his face.

Pushing aside the venomous words that he had spoken to me that night in the street, I followed him to Café Hafa and beyond, through one of the numerous unmarked doors that signaled the dwellings of the local community. I even agreed to the ridiculous proposition that he eventually put forth — a request for a portrait — wanting, needing to know in that instant just what it was that lurked behind his smile, both tired and angry that he was the second person in my life who had decided to try to put something over on me that day.

Once inside, I noted the dozen or so canvases lining the room, and moving silently among them, I wondered whether any of the work actually belonged to Youssef, or if these too were part of his facade. Perhaps the paints and brushes were just props on a stage, the canvases completed by another hand — that daughter that either John or Alice had once mentioned, though I could no longer recall who had spoken the words. The paintings themselves were adequate if unremarkable. A sunset, an ocean, the market on a busy day. Everyday

250

life in Tangier, I noted, though the colors were bright and cheerful, dispelling the notion that anything untoward ever ran through the veins of the city. All trace of filth, of grime, swept away. I was struck with the sudden desire to laugh.

There was one, though, that caused me to pause. It was of a series of rooftops, nothing remarkable, but the vibrancy of the paints struck me. Perhaps it was the broad careless strokes, or the clashing colors — clotheslines, I could decipher, a tenuous link that held each building together, a jumbled mess that made it impossible to pick out where one began and the other ended. It was horrible, in some ways, going against everything they taught you in class — and yet, there was something else there as well, something that reminded me of Tangier, as if I were already gone. Whatever it was, I slowed, my fingers resting lightly on the frame.

"This one is beautiful," I said.

Youssef nodded, directing me toward a stool that he had set in the center of the room, a beam of natural light illuminating the space, his easel and canvas only a few paces away. "Please," he said.

I sat, grateful for his suggestion, for the opportunity to let my mind relax, to wander, to not dwell on all that had happened over the last few days, on all the things that would have to happen still. My eyes began to flutter in the calmness of the room. I felt the warmth of the sun against my face and I sighed, my body relaxing.

"You know," Youssef said, his voice cutting through the air, "I saw you."

I frowned, my mind still slow from the heat. I had not expected him to begin so quickly. "You saw me?" I repeated, opening my eyes to look at him.

His face emerged from behind the canvas, his eyes strangely bright. "Yes. I saw you the other day. By the tombs."

I stopped. My hands twitched in my lap, but I stilled them. "With my friend, you mean?" I replied, working to keep my voice light, breathy — though I was awake now. "Yes, I took her up to Café Hafa. I thought she would enjoy the view."

"Yes." He nodded. "I saw that too."

Ah. So here was the truth of it at last — he had been following me, tailing me, like some heroic detective in a third-rate film. It seemed I had not given Youssef enough thought. He had faded into the background, a mosquito to be flicked away, but now, thinking about it, recalling his expression when I had brushed him aside that night — irritation, yes, but something more as well — I felt his buzzing return. Anger. That's what it had been. An anger that ran wide and deep, and that was, I knew, directed at far more than just me. My mind raced. If he had been following me, that would mean — my breath caught in my throat — he *knew*, I realized. He knew, and he had decided that he would try to trap me with it.

"Yes," he continued, speaking slowly, with confidence, with ease — confirming my suspicions. "I saw you with him." And then, just so that there was no misunderstanding between us, he added, "I saw what you did."

252

I did not move. "I have money," I said evenly, as though it were not a great thing, but thinking, even as I said it, of my nearly depleted account.

Youssef nodded, though his face was twisted, as if insulted by my words — even though they were the ones he had wished me to speak. I thought that I understood his disgust, his hatred. And I was willing to forgive him, in light of his situation, willing to overlook the fact that he had just attempted this con on *me*, his sole supporter and defender. After all, I understood desperation, understood what it could do to you, what it could force you to do in return. We were, Youssef and I, not so dissimilar from each other. But then I thought of the money. I clasped my hands together tightly, feeling the pain as my nails dug into flesh. I ignored it, ignored the bright red blood that rose from my skin. One payment would not be enough. No amount of money would ever be enough, I suspected.

No — I needed a way out.

And then I remembered. The first time we had met, all those days ago now, outside of Cinema Rif. Youssef thought my name was Alice.

It hadn't been a conscious decision, when I had first arrived in Tangier and given him her name instead of my own. It had only been a hesitation, an uncertainty about the man before me. He was someone used to wearing masks, and so I had, as I had done many times before, adopted my own. There had been nothing beyond that initial instinct. But now, now I could see the advantages. I hated to do it, felt my whole body rebel at the thought. But then, I reminded myself, there was nothing else to be done. I had been trapped, backed into a corner, and the only thing that mattered any longer was survival — my own survival. They had, Alice and Youssef both, left me no other choice.

# CHAPTER
# THIRTEEN

## ALICE

After the telephone call with Aunt Maude, I felt relieved, buoyed even, knowing that she would soon be in Tangier, that she would set things right. And yet as I stood in the living room, as I took in each and every little item that belonged to John, I felt consumed by guilt for the thoughts that I had entertained only hours before, wondering whether I wanted to remain in Tangier, remain with him. It felt like a betrayal, and one far more dangerous than anything he had committed. I left the flat then, desperate to be away from the tight enclosure that was filled with him, walking down one street and then another, passing by the market that we had once gone to together, ignoring the overpowering smell of leather, of meat, though it threatened to turn my stomach. I passed by a café I recognized from our early days, where we had sat and laughed together. As I increased my pace, tripping over my own feet as I hurried, with no real direction, no real purpose, I realized that each and every corner of this city was marked by my memories of John. It did not matter where I went, there was no escaping them.

At some point, I became aware of being watched.

He was smart, kept himself well hidden, so that I saw him first only out of the corner of my eye, the wide brim of his hat obscuring his face. I had shaken my head, had told myself, sternly, to stop imagining things, but then — there he was again, the same man from earlier that morning. The one with the scar. He was just to the side of me, first to the right, then to the left, sometimes a few paces ahead. Careful never to let me see him — not entirely. He was smart, but then, I reminded myself, if he worked with John, for the government, I supposed he had to be. I felt my heart begin to beat faster, wondering what it was that he wanted, what answers he could possibly think I held. I increased my speed, turned down one alley and then another, but it did not matter.

I could not manage to lose him.

By the time I returned to the flat, I was out of breath, my heart beating hard and fast, my hands shaking as I fumbled with the lock. At some point my hair had fallen from its clasp, and I could feel the strands as I made my way to the sitting room, tickling around the edges of my face, so that I brushed them away, quickly, intently, trying to free myself from their maddening touch.

I came to a sudden stop.

Lucy was there, sitting on the sofa — but she was not alone. Two policemen stood, one on either side of her, clothed in the familiar tan uniform and peculiar hat, the one that sat on top of, rather than on, their heads. Their rifles, I noticed, were balanced against one of the bookshelves. I blinked, wondering if they were truly there, wondering whether I had only imagined them.

"Alice," Lucy began, her voice filled with concern. "The police have come to ask about John, about his disappearance. They wanted to speak with you, but I told them I wasn't sure where you were. At the market, I supposed."

I must look mad, I realized, clutching at the bookcase beside me, desperate, in that moment, to feel something real beneath my fingers. "I'm sorry," I murmured, not knowing to whom I had even addressed the apology.

One of the policemen stood. "*Est-ce que tout va bien, madame?*"

"*Oui,*" I struggled to answer. My breath, I noticed, was short and raspy.

"*Elle a l'air malade,*" the other policeman observed.

He made as if to start toward me, but I held up my hand. "*Non,*" I declared firmly. "I'm not ill."

There was a silence, during which the policemen both eyed me with something that was not quite concern. "We received your telephone call, Madame Shipley," one of them eventually said.

"Telephone call?" I looked around the room, at the expectant faces watching me. "But I didn't ring anyone."

The same officer frowned, consulting the notebook he held between his hands. "We were informed, earlier this morning, by a Madame Alice Shipley, that her husband was missing." He paused. "That is not you?"

"No," I said, my gaze sliding over to where Lucy sat, wondering how long the policemen had been there, and just what she might have said to them in the interval. My thoughts flickered to the man with the scar then, and his insistence that the local police not be contacted.

"So your husband isn't missing?"

"What?" I asked, turning my attention back to the officer. "No — I mean, yes, yes, he is."

"Your husband is missing, but you didn't call to report him?"

I nodded, cheeks blushing. "Yes, yes, that's right."

There was a silence as both the officers frowned, and then Lucy said, "I was thinking," sounding as though she were resuming a conversation that I had interrupted with my entrance. Her eyes scanned the room, resting, eventually, on me. It was only for a fraction of a second — one, two, three — I didn't know how long exactly, but I could see, already, what it was that she was doing. I knew her as well as I knew myself — knew the way her mouth curved into an O when she was embarrassed, knew the sound she made when startled, or the way her pupils dilated when she was pleased. I knew her. And I knew in that instance that whatever thoughts were turning in her mind, they had arrived upon some sort of conclusion when she had glanced my way.

"There was a man," she said. "Youssef."

I frowned, feeling something begin to prickle at the back of my neck.

258

"Youssef?" The policeman paused, scrolling through his note-pad. "Who is this?"

Lucy shrugged. "He's just a local. A grifter, really. He also goes by the name of Joseph." She shook her head, as if to clear her thoughts. "I don't even know why I mentioned him."

It was a lie, I thought.

She turned to me. "I think Alice knew him. I seem to remember her mentioning him when I first moved here. I always thought it was strange, that she would know someone like him, but now, I realize that Tangier is a small city. It's quite easy to know everyone." She stopped, and then added: "He wears a fedora, with a purple ribbon. That's how most people know him — he never goes anywhere without it."

There was no accusation in her voice. She was smarter than that. But the policeman — I could see the light behind his eyes flash, just dimly, but enough such that I knew his interest had been piqued. I could see it in the way his body seemed to expand, to fill the room.

I could also see what she had done — made a connection, a link, between Youssef and me. A trail, scattering the bread crumbs.

"*Merci beaucoup*," the officer said, making a slight nod with his head. "We will look into this and let you know whether anything more has been found. Chances are, he is where most Tangerines end up — drunk somewhere, sleeping it off, or . . ." He let his words trail.

"Or what?" I asked, my voice not quite the challenge I intended.

**259**

He only shrugged. "In the meantime, madame, let us know if you hear from your husband."

I nodded, ignoring the way the words sounded like a reprimand, as if I were the one to blame for John's disappearance. I tried to think of the other reasons he had left unspoken. A fight with a local gambler gone wrong, a stabbing perhaps. A disagreement at one of the nightclubs, with one of the men in charge of the women there. I shook my head; they were wrong. But before I could tell them, they were gone, a jostling of thick fabric and heavy boots.

"Where have you been?" Lucy asked, her voice cutting through the silence.

I watched as she stood from the sofa, as she moved to perch on the ledge of the window. She was dressed in dark trousers and a plain light blouse and I was struck with the thought: *this is her*, watching as she brought a lit cigarette to her mouth. The long, elegant lines, the absence of frills and bows. She was still the most beautiful woman that I had ever met — but in a way that made me shiver with fear.

"It's so dark," I observed, realizing that the sun had begun to set, that the room had fallen into darkness since the departure of the police. I moved toward one of the lamps, desperate, suddenly, for the light.

"Don't," she instructed, her voice firm, resolute. "I want to watch the sun set."

There was a challenge there, and I fought the urge to disregard her words, to flip the switch anyway, so that it would send us both, momentarily blind, into the light. I thought of Aunt Maude, now on her way to Tangier, and my fingers twitched again, eager for the moment she arrived.

"It's unlike anything at home, isn't it?" she asked then, not bothering to turn her head toward me.

I looked out of the window, the sky awash with stripes of pink and white and blue. Yes, it was different, I thought. Maybe even beautiful. But at that moment, I saw only something ominous and warning, a threat that I could never quite manage to elude. I had promised my aunt that I would not involve the police, and yet somehow they had turned up on my doorstep. And even though I was certain that I had not called them, that I had not been the one to summon them, my mind sought and failed to remember those moments after I had hung up the telephone with Maude with any sort of precision. I had been overwrought, surrounded by this place that was entirely John's, the apartment and the city belonging to him in a way that I could not understand. I would have given anything, in that moment, to return to the dark, rainy skies of my childhood.

She turned to me. "You never go out."

There was no accusation in her voice. She spoke as one did when reciting facts — and it was a fact, I thought. Once, I had never gone out. Once, I had been so afraid of what might lurk in the corners of the alleyways, in the back rooms of bars and cafés. But that was before, I wanted to tell her. Before she had arrived, before John had disappeared, before everything had changed and I had begun to suspect, begun to remember, that the true danger did not lie entirely within my own mind.

"Where did you go?" she asked.

I watched the plume of her cigarette smoke as it crowded her features, and I wondered whether she might know and whether it was possible that she was asking only in order to see if I would be truthful. "To the market," I lied.

She looked around the flat. "And what did you buy?"

"Nothing." I shrugged, although I was unable to determine whether she could see the gesture in the darkness that shrouded us. "I only wanted to look."

"It's quite late for the market."

My voice was too insistent as I replied, "I went there first, and then out for a walk."

She nodded, and then said, her eyes boring into my own, "I was surprised that you didn't tell me. About John's disappearance, I mean."

I held her gaze, and though my voice trembled, I asked, "Did I need to?"

The question, the implication, hung between us, unanswered.

She turned to the window and said, "We could still leave, you know. The two of us, together. We could go to Spain. To Paris." She paused, turning to look at me slowly, so that I could hear the rustle of her trousers as she moved. "It's not too late. This doesn't have to be the end."

I could see it — the desperation glinting in her eyes. And part of me, though I knew it was absurd, that it was wrong, wanted to say yes. It would be easier to close my eyes and give in, to close the distance between us and leave this nightmare behind. And perhaps she sensed it too, this relenting, for she reached out, as if to touch me. But then I thought of Tom, of John, of what she had most likely — *No*, I whispered fiercely to myself, *had* absolutely *done* — and I felt myself pale. I knocked her hand away with a force that surprised us both. I could see it — the shock, the disappointment, and yes, the anger. "You can't blackmail me into loving you, Lucy," I spat, unable to stop myself. "It doesn't work like that."

Her face froze, so that it seemed as though her features were contracting, shrinking. And then, through the darkness, I saw the start of a smile beginning at one corner of her mouth. It seemed like her lips were tilted, jerked upward. The look of a cat toying with a mouse.

My skin began to itch, knowing that something was about to happen, sensing, already, the danger in her next words.

"When will you tell the police?" she asked.

I grew still.

"About what you know."

"What do I know?" I whispered, trying to ignore the trembling of my body.

A smile now — a real, genuine one that could not be hidden. "About Sabine."

I placed my arms around my waist. I did not want to be there any longer. Not in that room, not in Tangier, not anywhere on the continent of Africa. It was not my home. It had never been my home. All I had done was create an enclosure that I had trapped myself within. I had created the lock and I had given Lucy the key. My stomach lurched and I thought for a moment that I would be sick, there, in the living room, surrounded by John's things and Lucy's Cheshire grin.

"Sabine?" I repeated.

"Yes." She turned. "The police will want to know about what happened that day, at Café Hafa."

I could feel it then, could feel myself contracting, could feel myself stalling in terror — no, not terror, horror. I remembered that day, the woman, the shattered glass — the blood on the stairs glistening underneath the afternoon sun. The conviction that she was somehow familiar, though I could not place her, but then, of course, I could — the image of her face from that first night, those seconds before I had fainted, the truth of John, of our relationship, laid bare. I could not move, could not speak. I stood there, frozen.

"What are you talking about, Lucy?"

She let out a small laugh. "Alice. I know you pushed her."

I could feel my blood rushing, could hear the noise whooshing through my ears, pulsing against my eardrums. "I didn't, Lucy. I didn't push that woman."

"You mean Sabine?" she asked.

My stomach dropped at the mention of her name, but I forced the panic down.

I had puzzled over that day already, wondering at what had happened a dozen or so times, never arriving at any explanation. I had seen it play out in my mind, over and over, sometimes imagining that I saw her face in the moments before she fell, the look of terror that shrouded her features, knowing what was happening and unable to stop it. Had I relished it? I wondered, trying to conjure up that feeling again, knowing somehow that I had realized who she was, even then. I looked at Lucy and I fought for words that would not come.

"I don't blame you, Alice," she said, moving away from the window. "I would have done the same. After all, when someone betrays you like that . . ." she said, letting her words trail off, her eyes glowing in the darkness.

I felt my pulse quicken, felt the shadows in the corners begin to grow.

"I'm headed to bed now," I said, feeling my voice as it reverberated throughout my body. "I'm afraid I have a terrible headache."

That night I locked the door to my bedroom. I pushed and pulled the heavy wooden dresser from its regular place beside the door, listening with satisfaction as its wooden legs scraped and scratched at the floorboards beneath, thinking about the absurdity of the situation, of the circularity of the whole wretched thing. It took me the better part of an hour — pushing and pulling — but I did not stop, not until at last it formed a barrier, a divide between my room and the hallway, between Lucy and me. I looked down — deep rivulets were now carved into the floorboards beneath. I was glad for the marks, for the permanency of my actions, a record of my resistance. I would show them to Aunt Maude when she arrived, so that she could see

**265**

everything I had done in order to free myself from Lucy's grasp.

She would understand then — and together, we would find a way out.

# CHAPTER
# FOURTEEN

## LUCY

I waited several days before returning to the place where I had hidden his body.

I made the journey as much to reassure myself that it was real — that it had happened, that John was well and truly dead and would not somehow reappear, a specter sent to haunt me — as to ensure that Youssef had not meddled with it in the meantime. I waited until Alice was asleep, until the city at last began to doze, before moving quickly through the darkness. My head full, my ears ringing, the humidity seemed to rise with each and every step, ones that brought me, inevitably, closer to him.

And yet, despite knowing that I would find him where I had last left him — his body wedged beneath a boulder so near the cliff's edge that not even the locals dared to stray there — it was still a shock to see him, the visceral evidence of my anger. I tilted my head. Under the fractured moonlight, he could almost be mistaken for a tourist sleeping peacefully under the Tangier moon. After it had happened, time had swept by curiously fast, so that I had found myself unusually unsettled, panicked as I strove to move him, his body, toward my intended hiding place — a spot that had once seemed perfect but in that moment felt too far away, too exposed.

I stood, looking down at him — my former opponent, now defeated, now vanquished. He posed a threat no longer. The ringing in my ears began to ease and the feeling of fullness began to dissipate, as if with my previous thought went all the worry, the anxiety, that had plagued me since my arrival in Tangier.

I moved closer and, averting my face, began to pull — trying now to unwedge what I had so determinedly wedged only a few days before. I gave him a hard shove, his body already rigid, putrid. My eyes resisted gazing at his skull, at the hollow I imagined there, from the rock that I had hidden behind my back that night, its edges sharp, filled with intention.

It had made a dull thud when it landed on the crown of his head, the movement itself forcing me to reach up — up and up and up, it seemed, beyond my natural height — so that I had wrenched my shoulder in the process, so that afterward I had reared back, unsteady, worried I had just given him the upper hand. But no, he had already fallen to his knees — in surprise, in hurt, I didn't know, couldn't recall, that insistent buzzing had, by then, grown to deafening heights, so that even if he had said something, anything, I most likely wouldn't have heard it at all. His last words, if there were any, were lost. Only Tangier knew, and I suspected she would keep her secrets.

Afterward, I had looked at the rock in my hand, at the cold mass smeared in blood, and wondered whether it was a rock at all, or a piece of a tomb that had once housed the dead. I had been forced to suppress a laugh.

John had stirred then, his face contorting with rage at the realization of what was happening, the ferocity of his emotions somehow managing to knock us both to the ground, so that the rock slipped from my hand. Perhaps he did speak then, my memory suggested. A couple of short declarative sentences, nothing worth remembering — his speech had been slurred, as if he had had too much to drink.

He had taken the rock, holding it high above his head so that he looked like some grotesque version of a dancer, trying to execute a pirouette. He had started to move toward me, unsteady, the gash on his forehead bleeding heavily, streaming down the side of his face, cloaking him in a slick darkness.

It happened quickly then. I was up, prying the rock from his fingers — he offered little resistance, as if realizing the futility of it. I brought the rock down, hard this time, and he did not stir again.

Pushing his body now, my arms shaking with the effort, I wondered at what it had all been for. I stopped at the cliff's edge.

We had come to the end.

Leaning down I gave one final push, the strain, the effort running through each and every part of my body, every sinewy muscle, as if it were required, necessary in absolution of my crime. I stood still, covered in dirt and grime, listening for the splash below, waiting to hear the heralding of the end.

There was nothing.

Afterward I stood on the edge of the cliff, looking out at the ocean below, trying to read my future. Alice would not be coming with me, I knew. We would not be traveling to Spain, would not be eating tapas or drinking wine under the setting sun. Paris, I realized dully, would never happen. I saw clearly, for perhaps the first time, that the life that I had envisioned for us would never come to pass. And what was more, I saw why — it was Alice. She was the one who had run away to Tangier, who had left me, alone and broken, in the cold streets of New York. It had been her choices, her decisions that had led us here. The only thing I had done, that I had ever done, was try to do what was best for us, to create the life that she had claimed to want. Only she hadn't wanted it, not really. I thought back to her words the other night at the bar and the realization hit, full and hard, so that I heard the ringing, tasted the coppery, metallic tang of it — the truth — in my mouth. She had never wanted me.

I turned away from the ocean, from what I had done.

I was not one for last rites and I knew there was nothing to say that would be honest and good. The most I could muster, as I walked away from the breaking light of morning, was that he was with a woman he had loved, for better or for worse, and whatever that love had meant to him, he would be with her, Tangier, for the rest of time.

In that, John was the luckiest one among us.

# CHAPTER
# FIFTEEN

## ALICE

I arrived at the door, out of breath. That morning had been spent at the bank, trying to withdraw what money was left in the account that I had shared with John, before it was time to leave Tangier for good. I had been dismayed, at first, to find out just how much John had run through, the number causing me to start in confusion as I puzzled over what he had done with the allowance that Aunt Maude had wired each month. At first I had thought of Sabine, had wondered whether she had been another beneficiary who had profited from my parents' trust. The idea had made me ill, but then I remembered the sight of her face — about what Lucy had claimed — before she had fallen, so young, so frightened, and I no longer worried about how much she may or may not have received.

I turned the key into the lock, moving quickly, wanting to make sure the flat was tidy before Aunt Maude arrived. I had received a telegram from her only the day before, and though I had planned to meet her at the dock, I had been met with a firm refusal, Maude insisting that I needn't trouble myself, that a taxi would be suitable and she would meet me at the flat.

I only hoped that Lucy would be out.

We had fallen into a pattern, over the last several days. Lucy rose early, disappearing for most of the afternoon, returning only after I had already secured myself behind my locked bedroom door each night. I had worried, at first, wondering whether I should be wary, whether I should be concerned that she did not seek my company as she once had but rather seemed to run from it, anxious to pass the day away from me. It was strange and so unlike her, but I had decided, in the end, that my time would be better spent cleaning, packing, preparing myself for my aunt's arrival and my ensuing exodus from Tangier. For the moment when I would no longer have to concern myself with Lucy Mason, ever again.

I stepped into the hallway and stopped. There were voices coming from the living room. A bit of laughter and then a rushed word or two, spoken in a tenor that I recognized as belonging to Aunt Maude. My stomach lurched as I moved quickly, wondering how on earth Lucy had known, wondering too what she had done, what she had said to make Aunt Maude laugh like that — a sound I could not remember hearing in all the years I had known her.

They sat together on the sofa, the two of them, as if it were the most natural thing in the world, a tray of tea and biscuits before them.

"What's going on?" I demanded.

Aunt Maude looked up, startled. "Alice, there you are." She stood, crossed the distance between us, and gave me a brief, perfunctory hug. "I was early, but

272

Sophie was here to let me in." She frowned at my expression, which was, I knew, frozen in fear, in terror — at finding Maude here, with her, and all the implications that hung around that one simple fact. "Alice, what's happened? You've gone pale." She began to step toward me, saying, "The police have told you, then?"

I looked at Lucy, sitting there, perched on the edge of the sofa. She was, I noticed, wearing that same black, belted dress she had first arrived in. Her disguise, I realized now. "That's not Sophie Turner," I replied, ignoring my aunt's question.

Maude frowned. "What on earth are you talking about?" She turned around, toward Lucy. "Do you have any idea?"

Lucy's face collapsed with concern. "I think perhaps it's the stress of the situation. As I said on the telephone, she hasn't been herself since John's disappearance."

"She's lying," I snapped, so that Maude turned to me in surprise. "Everything Lucy says is a lie, it always has been."

"Alice," Maude began, quietly, "I think you're confused, dear. I think you're mixing up what happened with John with what happened before, with Tom."

"No, no, I'm not," I said, shaking my head.

"Yes, dear," she replied, her hands clutching at her throat, that same gesture of worry, the one trait that we shared, the one visible proof that the same blood ran through our veins. "You told me yourself about Sophie staying with you, only a few days ago. Don't you remember?"

I shook my head, unable, in that moment, to find a way out of my own lies. And then I remembered her earlier words. "Have the police told me what?" I asked.

She stopped, confusion sweeping her features. "I assumed that was why you looked so upset. That you had just come from the police."

"What's happened?" I demanded.

Lucy stood. "Alice, the police were here earlier. I've told your aunt what they came to see you about — a group of fishermen found him, down by the port. John, I mean." She paused, her face a picture of concern. "They've been looking for you."

"For me?" I asked.

"Yes, Alice," Maude replied. "They need you to identify him."

I had been right, then. John was dead, just as Tom was dead.

I crossed the distance between us in only a few short steps, ignoring the shock on my aunt's face, the amused surprise on Lucy's own.

I grabbed at her handbag, tearing it away from her.

"Alice," Maude cried, "what are you doing?"

I ignored her, rummaging through the bag, searching for what had to be there, knowing that not even she could have foreseen this. "Her passport," I said, my hand grasping onto the small booklet at last. I tossed the handbag aside, watching Lucy flinch as it clattered onto the ground, a silver compact landing facedown, its powder crumbling, covering the tiled floor. "Here," I

274

said, thrusting the booklet toward my aunt. My hand faltered, though only for a moment, remembering as I did so the incidents at Bennington with the bracelet, with the photographs. I brushed away a stray piece of hair that clung, stubbornly, to the sweat on my forehead. It did not matter, I reminded myself. That was a different time, a different circumstance. Back then Lucy had planned it, plotted each and every step, so that there was nothing I could do but fall into the trap she had set for me. Now, she was acting only on instinct. She was reacting to my refusal to yield, the denial of which had caught her off guard, unaware. I could see it, written plainly across her face.

"Open it," I commanded my aunt. "Open it and you'll see she's lying. You'll see that she's not Sophie Turner. That she's someone else entirely."

"And who is that?" Maude demanded.

"I've already told you," I said, my voice pleading. "Lucy Mason."

She let out a noise of frustration. "Oh, Alice." She shook her head. "How are we back here again?"

"No," I said, refusing to listen. "You'll see, this time you'll see that I'm right. Just open it."

Aunt Maude sighed, holding the bundle between her fingers, as though she dreaded to open them, dreaded even to touch them. But why, I wanted to shout, why when they would prove her niece right, when they would cast suspicion and doubt onto the woman, the stranger sitting beside her, instead of on her flesh and blood?

"Auntie, please," I whispered, hating her in that moment for forcing me to ask her to choose her own niece.

"Very well." She sighed, opening the pages.

I waited — for the frown of confusion, the inevitable anger once Maude realized she too had been taken in by the seemingly innocuous girl sitting on the sofa before us.

And yes, there it was. I smiled in relief — watching as a frown stole over her features, the lines between her eyes folding, deepening. I watched as she handed Lucy the papers — wanting, I knew, an explanation. My body arched toward them, eager to hear the excuses that Lucy would produce, knowing that there was nothing she could say, nothing that would save her this time.

But then Lucy was placing the papers into the pocket of her dress, and Maude was settling back onto the sofa.

"What's happened?" I demanded. "What has she done?"

Maude shook her head, as though disappointed. "Sophie hasn't done anything, Alice."

I struggled to breathe. "Why are you still calling her that?" I shook my head, trying to understand. "You saw her passport, you just looked at it."

Maude nodded. "Yes, Alice, I did."

I looked from Maude to Lucy and back again. The two of them, the pair of them, sat gazing up at me, their faces steely and hard. It struck me then just how similar they were — strong and sometimes distant, hard and oftentimes unyielding. I wondered how I had never seen it before. And then, the thought flickered across my mind, even though I knew it was nonsense, that it was a thought of desperation, of madness, and yet still, looking at them, together, I wondered whether it was possible — whether they were in on it together. If this, all of this, wasn't for the sole purpose of driving me mad, of putting me away forever. It would make Lucy glad to know that I would never belong to another, that locked away, no one would ever touch me. And Maude? I thought of the trust that would be mine within a short time, of her role as my guardian. It was insane, it was madness, and yet I could not help but think that it all made sense.

"Why are you doing this?" I whispered, my voice cold and still.

"Doing what?" Aunt Maude asked.

"This," I said, willing my voice to remain steady, calm. "What was on that passport?" I demanded, realizing that I had not seen it myself, had not seen the words written beside the photograph.

Maude watched me, coolly. "What do you think was on it, Alice?"

I wasn't sure if it was the way she looked at me — detached, as though we were no longer bound together by blood — or her voice, low and challenging, and which in that moment I could only read as a threat. Or perhaps it was the simple realization that the one woman I had always trusted, the only real family I had left, had abandoned me, betrayed me. The knowledge of that threatened to smother me, such that I let out a strange, demented cry as I lunged toward Lucy once more — this time, toward the pages in her pocket.

I had to know, I told myself, pushing away her hands that she held up in self-defense, my nails sinking into her flesh. I had to know what was on the passport, whether my aunt simply did not believe me, or whether she was working with her, with Lucy — whether it was my best interest or my fortune that she had on her mind. And so I pushed and pulled. I scratched until I felt the blood, her blood, beneath my fingernails. I did everything I could until I tasted copper, until I felt two powerful arms pull me away.

"Alice." Maude was crying, her face drained of color.

I stopped. I looked up into my aunt's face, into the fear that flooded her features. Her hair had started to come undone, strands of it falling down her face. I turned toward Lucy and saw that she looked equally affected, her pinned hair now falling around her shoulders, her dress askew, her stockings torn, the evidence of my violence written there, across her body. An apology rose on my lips but I stopped, feeling the weight of her papers between my hands. I had to know. And so I cast a hurried glance at the words written on the passport now grasped between my fingers. SOPHIE TURNER. I struggled to breathe.

She was, I realized with a sinking feeling, still one step ahead.

# CHAPTER
# SIXTEEN

## LUCY

It was easy enough to convince Maude Shipley that her niece was going mad.

After that initial telephone call, we had spoken a handful of times before her arrival in Tangier, and I had reported on her niece's movements, her state of mind, remembering all the while the words that Alice had once spoken to me — about the fear, after her parents' death, that her aunt had wanted to commit her. The fear that her aunt thought she was mad, the fear that she might just be right.

Alice's episode that afternoon had only helped. I had almost pitied her, watching how confident she had been, convinced that she was about to best me. As she stood before us, her eyes wide, dazed, her fingers turning the same pages of the passport back and forth, over and over, as if it would somehow change what was printed there, I had been half-tempted to rush to her, to take her in my arms and forgive her for everything that she had done. Instead I had looked away, brushed the instinct aside.

She couldn't have known that I had already switched passports. That the idea had come to me while sitting in

Youssef's studio, that day he had tried to blackmail me. I had sat still in the moments afterward, afraid to move, to betray any indication of weakness. Only when I had worked it all out in my mind at last did I allow myself to smile, to shift. And then, steeling myself for his response, I had said, "Before I give you the money, I need you to do something for me first."

Youssef's eyes had narrowed, surprised no doubt by the audacity of my request.

I held his gaze. "I need a new passport."

"And why would I do that?" He laughed. "So that you can disappear without paying me?"

"You'll be paid — and in advance. But if I don't get new papers, well, what would be the point of paying you to keep quiet? The police will figure it out sooner or later. New papers are my only way out of Tangier. Otherwise I might as well spend my money on enjoying my final hours." I held my smile, though I could feel it, shaking against my teeth.

Youssef paused, considering my words. I could see him weighing them, carefully, as I had known he would. After all, what did he care if I left Tangier, as long as he got something first? Yes, he would have preferred a longer con, one that continued to earn him something over time, but if forced to choose between nothing and something — he was smart, and I knew where he would fall.

"All right," he conceded. "I know a man who might be able to help." He pointed his brush at me. "But only after I have been compensated."

I nodded. "Agreed."

280

His eyes narrowed. "Any tricks, and our deal is off."

"Understood." I stretched out my hand toward him. "Shall we shake on it?"

He laughed then, an amused sharp noise that let him indulge in his triumph over the helpless American girl. And I had wanted to give him that before I did what I had to next. His hand felt rough in my own, but I clasped it and shook — as if I had lost, as if he had won, as if the gesture was an acknowledgment of defeat.

Later, out in the streets, I had laughed, marveling that I had once ever doubted his worth.

I waited until Maude had convinced her niece to rest, until she had tucked her into bed, as though a child, and emerged a short time later, looking troubled and worn.

"You were right," she said, her body sinking into the fabric of the sofa. I sat beside her. "Thank you for telephoning me, Sophie. For letting me know what has been happening. I'm afraid Alice has always been prone to such — episodes." She reached out, placing her hand on top of my own.

Her touch was dry, cold, as if she were immune even to the heat of the desert, as if not even the elements of nature could threaten to overwhelm her. She was implacable. Unmovable. She was, I could not help but think, a woman wasted on a girl like Alice. I imagined what I might have been, the things I might have accomplished, had fate chosen to bestow upon me a relation such as the woman in front of me.

I quickly pushed the thought aside.

"Of course."

"I'll confess I had hoped that John was just off with his friends, on a silly little adventure of some sort. It wouldn't have been surprising, knowing him." She fixed her gaze on me. "You were here when he went missing. What do you think happened?"

I considered my words carefully before I responded, casting aside those pieces of information that did not serve a purpose here. "I don't know. They seemed fine, at first, but then it started to become apparent that something was wrong. And then Alice confided in me, about the other woman." I shook my head. "The last time I saw John, they had a terrible fight. I don't know what happened after that. I just don't know," I whispered, forcing all the emotion I could into those final words, so that they sounded ominous, haunting, so that both of us could feel them refusing to disappear.

She nodded. "The question now, I suppose, is what should be done."

I affected surprise. "With Alice, you mean?"

"Yes." She sighed. "I confess, I've never really known what to do when it comes to Alice, what the right thing is. She's rather like my brother, in that respect. I never knew what to say to him either." She shook her head, a shadow sweeping across her features. "It all seems too much, in a way. That such misfortune should fall upon one girl, so many times. First her parents, and then that boy in Vermont. Now this." She shook her head. "And this silly business with her old roommate. I don't understand it at all. She was adamant, you know, that the girl had something to do with the accident at Bennington too. It took all my powers of persuasion to convince the police there that she was out of her mind, that she was just confusing it all — the accident, the girl's disappearance."

I felt the weight of her words — of Alice's accusation — deep within my stomach. "Was it the police who suggested it to her?" I asked, and seeing Maude's confusion, I continued on, unable to turn back. "About her roommate, I mean. I imagine they could be rather forceful, if necessary."

Maude shook her head. "No, this was Alice entirely. Why do you ask, dear?"

I blinked, my vision seeming suddenly hazy — obscured, I thought. But then, no — I shook my head, the fluttering in my ear strong and persistent. Unrelenting, I decided. "It just sounds so fantastical," I said quickly. "So unbelievable. Almost like —" I paused, casting my eyes downward. "Forgive me for asking, Miss Shipley, but has Alice ever been committed?"

Maude's eyes cut to mine, hard, hesitant. "No. Why do you ask?"

"She seems so — fragile. And you mentioned about the episodes." I shifted, slightly. "I know we weren't always the greatest of friends, but there was always something that seemed rather delicate about her," I continued, thinking back to the day I met her, letting the words become truth. "I worried for her, about her." I paused. "I had an aunt who was in quite poor health. She used to — well, she used to claim things that

**283**

weren't really true. That someone had come into her house and touched her lamps, that someone had moved her furniture. My parents, they decided in the end that it was kinder to put her someplace where she could be looked after."

Maude watched me now, her eyes sharp, missing nothing. "I had considered it," she said, breaking the silence. "After her parents died. She was inconsolable, you know. Beyond normal grieving." She glanced at me, hurried and quick, so that I knew her next words would be important. "She had convinced herself that she was to blame for their deaths."

I remained silent, letting the idea grow in the light between us: the image of the poor orphaned girl whose presence had wrought so many deaths. And then, though I couldn't explain why, I felt as though something had been decided. As if Maude had used the time, the silence, to question, to ponder, to decide. She turned to me, and I no longer saw a lost and confused woman but rather one with a purpose, with a plan.

Her eyes narrowed. "I was sorry to hear about your family's misfortunes. I had meant to tell you that earlier."

"Oh?" I asked, eyebrows raised, eager to see what it was that she seemed to have arrived upon — and what part Sophie Turner would have to play in it.

"Yes." She paused. "You see, I have an idea, but it would require some assistance." When I did not object, she continued, "I would need you to do something for me, in Spain, if you thought you could manage it. And you would be compensated, of course, for your time.

284

Alice receives a small monthly allowance from her trust, and I could have this sum forwarded to you there, in the meantime. The bank would handle all the details, so you wouldn't have to worry about a thing."

"Yes, I see," I said, though I didn't quite, not just yet. But I knew that I would soon, that Maude trusted me completely, that she believed the woman who sat before her, Sophie Turner, was good and decent and worth helping. And while it was true that I had already made a plan, I was intrigued to see where Maude was heading, if her plan might be more beneficial in the long run.

I weighed the risks, considered the odds — brought to mind that sad, anonymous room in the boardinghouse — and quickly agreed.

Maude nodded in acknowledgment. "Her behavior today has convinced me what must be done." She looked away, toward the window. "Of what should have been done, long ago."

# CHAPTER
# SEVENTEEN

## ALICE

The police came early the next morning.

I had expected them to, of course, knew that the time between when they would knock on my door and when I would be left in peace — in quiet, in that in-between state where I could still pretend that something horrible hadn't happened, that it was all just a dream — was inching closer and closer.

John was dead. They had told me the day before — Maude and Lucy — though it had still failed to become real, to work itself into my mind as the truth, something concrete and unwavering that could not be challenged, changed, or altered. I had lain in bed, Maude tucking me in as though I were a child, an invalid, a problem she could never quite manage to shake, and I felt the word reverberating in my mind. *Dead.* It was all too familiar, and yet somehow foreign. It couldn't be true, I wanted to tell my aunt, feeling her tug and pull at the sheets. John couldn't be gone, couldn't be dead. He was the one, I wanted to explain to her, the one who was supposed to pull me up and out of the depression, out of the darkness that had swirled around me ever since that bitter cold night in Vermont. Since before that, even. He couldn't be gone, couldn't be dead.

My mind simply would not accept it. Not even later, when they showed me his body under the harsh, glaring lights of the coroner's office, the color draining from my face as I stepped backward, staggering, conscious all the while of Aunt Maude beside me, of the officers' eyes evaluating my every movement, every intake of breath. I felt them — all of them — waiting, watching, for the tears, for the hysterics. For a performance that I did not seem to have the energy to enact.

I turned away, setting my face to stone.

"Madame?"

I looked up at the two officers, their faces hesitant, uncertain — as if they were afraid, I thought. I wanted to laugh then, for what on earth had they to fear from me? I wanted to know. I was moved to ask them — but then the weight of the moment, the emotions that I was supposed to be feeling, that they were expecting me to display, became all too much. I nodded at the men — a clipped little gesture, something like a bow — and started to back away, heading toward the door. It was the same feeling I had experienced at Café Hafa, at countless other moments in my life, when the panic had started rising in me, the feeling of being trapped threatening to overtake me so that I needed nothing so much in that moment as to be able to leave the space I was confined within. Despite this, I paused, looking to my left, to my right, convinced that there was something missing, something I was forgetting.

It was Lucy, I suddenly realized.

I had been looking for Lucy.

This time, I did laugh.

"Madame." I heard the officer speak again, could feel Aunt Maude's sharp eyes on me, but still, I could not respond, could not do anything but turn and walk away, out of the coroner's office, out into the hallway filled with doors, though none of them seemed to hold the exit I was searching for. I pushed up against one, and then another, each of them refusing to yield. There was no way out — I was trapped, stuck in this labyrinthine hall.

A figure emerged in front of me. "Madame McAllister?"

No one had ever called me by my husband's name. I thought about the absurdity of it: hearing it for the first time while standing only steps away from his corpse. "Shipley," I whispered, my voice trembling. "My surname is Shipley."

The man frowned. "All right, Madame Shipley." He paused, indicating the door next to him. "Follow me, please."

The man standing in front of me was not particularly large, his eyes reaching just a fraction above my own, and yet there was something about him, something that made me pause, something that made my heart begin to pound in fear. He was quite obviously of a higher rank than the two previous officers that I had spoken with, and I wondered what he wanted. I looked at the door that he had pointed toward, filled with panic at the thought of what might be hidden just behind it. There was too, somewhere at the back of my mind, the vague realization that I should ask exactly who he was and what he wanted, but the only question I could manage was, "Where are we going?"

"To my office," he answered simply, offering no more explanation than that.

I felt a hand on my shoulder and turned to find Aunt Maude, a light sheen of sweat breaking just above her lip. "You heard the man, Alice," she said, her voice terse. "Let's go inside."

The man frowned, disappointed, it seemed, that she would be accompanying us.

His office was sparse, little else dotting the walls besides the thin layer of yellow paint that seemed to be peeling, flaking in the corners. I settled into one of two chairs placed in front of his desk, Aunt Maude taking the other.

Once we were seated, the officer lowered himself into his own chair behind the desk and leaned forward. "Madame Shipley," he began. "Do you know of any reason why a man by the name of Youssef might have been in possession of your husband's articles?"

I shook my head, surprised by the question, for whatever it was that I had been expecting, it was not this. But then something poked, needled, and I remembered what Lucy had said the other night to the policeman, about Youssef.

"No," I whispered, my voice low and hoarse. "I have no idea."

He frowned, watching me. "Are you quite all right, madame?"

I considered telling him then. About Lucy, about how she had deliberately mentioned Youssef to the policeman, how she had, more than likely, been responsible for whatever it was that they were talking about. I considered telling him this and everything else that had happened — but then I noticed the way that he was looking at me, his features sharp and narrow, and the words died on my lips.

"Could I have a glass of water, please?" I asked instead.

He looked irritated at this request but nonetheless signaled to one of his officers standing just outside the door. A few moments of silence passed until at last a glass of tepid water was placed in front of me.

"Thank you," I murmured. I placed the glass back onto his desk, watching as a small puddle formed, the ring that encircled it eventually sinking into the wood beneath. I could feel Aunt Maude's eyes on me, but I could not bring myself to return her gaze. Not just yet.

"I'm sorry, what did you say your name was?" I asked the man, stalling.

He sat back in his chair and sighed. "My apologies, madame. I am Officer Ayoub," he said. "Now, I understand you knew the man."

I frowned, placing a hand to my temple, wondering if anyone else had noticed just how stuffy and confined the office was. "Who?" I asked, not knowing, in that moment, who he was referring to.

"Youssef," he responded, his voice curt, the word overenunciated. "Or perhaps you knew him as Joseph.

He is the man responsible for your husband's death, madame."

"No," I responded, shaking my head at the impossibility of the idea. No, they had got it all wrong. I could feel Aunt Maude stir beside me.

"No?" Ayoub raised his eyebrows. "Do you mean that you do not know him, or that he is not the one responsible?"

"No, I don't know him," I said, wanting, and failing, to say the other as well.

"That is not what my men reported to me." Ayoub's eyes narrowed. "They say that you were well acquainted."

"No, that isn't true," I protested, worried that it had already progressed to this — from knowing him to well acquainted. There was a difference, I was well aware. "I knew of him, but not him personally. John —" I stopped, my voice halting for a moment, stumbling over his name. "He warned me about him."

"Warned you — why?" Ayoub asked.

I shook my head. "I don't know. To watch out for him, I suppose. To be careful if I ever ran into him, while I was on my own."

The officer seemed to consider this. "Your husband had met him, then?"

I shook my head. "No." But then I thought of Sabine, of the other life that he had lived apart from me. "I don't know," I found myself admitting. "I mean, I don't think so. Not that he ever mentioned." I reached for the glass of water again.

The officer watched me, his face still, revealing nothing. "I'm confused, madame. If you had never met Youssef, and your husband had never met him, then why were you both scared of him?"

"We were never scared," I replied, quickly.

"No?" He frowned.

"No," I repeated, frustrated now. "I don't know. John had told me stories, about Youssef, about how he had conned some tourists out of money."

"And you were afraid he would do this to you as well — con you out of money?"

Again, I shook my head. "No, not really. It's just —"

"Just what, Madame Shipley?" he snapped.

I felt a flush, could tell that it had broken out across my chest, its redness most likely unmistakable even in the grim, darkened setting of the room. I cleared my throat, but before I could speak, Aunt Maude stirred. Leaning forward, she placed a hand on the officer's desk. "What is this about, please?"

Ayoub tilted his head, clearly unsettled by the interruption but doing his best to hide it. "Nothing at all, madame," he finally said, with what seemed a reluctant smile. "We are only trying to establish a link between this young woman, her husband, and the perpetrator." He turned back to me. "So you never met Youssef?"

I shook my head. "I've told you this already. I have never met him."

"That is interesting." He sat back in his chair, a smile emerging on his previously blank face. "You see, we've

292

spoken to the suspect and he claims to be very well acquainted with you, Madame Shipley."

I stilled at his words. "What do you mean?"

"He says that you know each other, that you met a few weeks back, in a café, outside Cinema Rif."

"But I've never been to Cinema Rif," I protested, but even as I said the words, I realized — it was Lucy. She was the one he was describing. She was the one who had somehow planted this idea, this trap, so that I had ended up here, in this particular office. "Lucy," I breathed.

A frown stole over Ayoub's face. "Pardon, madame?"

"It's Lucy," I said again, only louder this time.

"I don't understand," Ayoub said, glancing toward Aunt Maude.

I hesitated, feeling my aunt's icy stare, her disapproval, but I brushed them aside, pushing ahead. I could remain quiet no longer, not when everything had become twisted and jumbled. They would need my help to sort through it, so that it made sense at last. Maude didn't see yet, she couldn't — but she would, eventually.

"Lucy Mason," I said, though my voice trembled. "She's my old college roommate."

The frown remained. "And how does this relate to what has happened here?"

"Lucy only just recently arrived in Tangier," I began, "and I believe that she might be involved."

Ayoub shook his head. "Perhaps I am not understanding. Involved with what, exactly?"

"With all of it," I said, leaning toward the officer. "With John's death, with this silly idea that I somehow know Youssef, that I might somehow have something to do with it myself."

Ayoub was quiet for a moment, but then he smiled and said, "It's interesting that you mention this — the idea that you might be involved. Yes, you see, Youssef has also claimed that someone else is responsible. A Tangerine, a woman." He paused. "His good friend, Madame Alice Shipley."

"What do you mean?" I demanded.

"I mean, that the man claims he is innocent." Ayoub shrugged. "He says that you, Madame Shipley, came to him, asking questions about a woman, someone your husband had been seeing on the side. And then, not shortly after that, he claims he saw this same woman attack and murder her husband. Your husband, Madame Shipley."

A scoff from beside me as my aunt demanded: "And you believe him?"

Ayoub waved away the question. "We know about Youssef, we've been watching him now for years. Of course he's only dabbled in petty theft before, little schemes of no real consequence." He paused. "This was quite surprising, and yet —"

"What?" I asked, my voice trembling.

"I can imagine it," he said, pointedly. "If there was perhaps, shall we say, a persuasive force," he paused. "Did you, Madame Shipley," he said, emphasizing the latter word, "know about your husband's affair?"

294

I froze, but before I could respond, Aunt Maude placed a hand on my shoulder. She leaned forward and whispered in a low, forceful tone, "Monsieur, are you charging my niece with something today?"

He seemed to consider her words carefully. "Not at this moment, madame. This is only an informal chat, a chance for Madame Shipley to tell us anything she might know."

"But I've just told you," I said. "I had nothing to do with this man. And he didn't have anything to do with John. It's Lucy, not him."

"No?" He removed several items from his pocket then and placed them onto the table between us. I saw the leather wallet that John had purchased in the souks, a wallet that smelled of the city and conjured up memories and images that I would rather leave behind. It had been purchased the same day I had lost John in the market, had grown angry and confused and scared — but then no, I realized. That hadn't been the same day at all, those two had been separate and distinct. I shook my head, focusing my eyes, my mind, instead on the other object Ayoub had produced.

A small silver item that I couldn't place at first. But then I heard its familiar clatter, saw its shape and detail, and I knew what it was, knew that it could only be one thing and nothing else.

My mother's bracelet.

The officer was watching me expectantly — a look of triumph already spreading across his features. "You recognize these, yes?"

The room was hot, suffocating. "Yes," I replied, "the bracelet belonged to my mother." But even as I said the words, I struggled to understand how it had come into his possession, to understand what sequence of events had placed that bracelet — one my mother had once held in the palm of her hands, had once worn around the curve of her wrist — into the rough, calloused hands of a stranger, miles and miles away from where I had last seen it.

"But it was most recently in your possession, yes?" the officer pressed. "That is, before you gave it away."

"Yes," I continued, but then I shook my head. "No. I mean, it belongs to me now, but no, I did not give it away," I said, my voice low and hoarse.

He looked at me. "If that is true, madame, then how do you think I have happened to come into possession of it?"

I struggled to speak. "I don't know," I said, turning toward my aunt at last, my words spoken more to her than the officer. "I haven't a clue. I lost it when I was at Bennington. I thought at first Lucy had stolen it, but then she denied it. I haven't seen it since."

The officer leaned back in his chair. "Shall I tell you where I found it?" His eyes narrowed. "Though, I suspect you already know."

"I don't," I said. "Auntie." I reached out to take her hand. "I promise I have no idea."

Aunt Maude said nothing.

"Your good friend Youssef was found in possession of this bracelet." He paused. "Payment," he said, the word long and drawn out.

I started, turning back to him. "I beg your pardon?"

"Payment," he repeated. "That's why he claims you gave him the bracelet." He gave a short laugh. "He seemed to have no idea that it was worthless, a piece of metal and paste."

Maude shifted. "Payment for what, exactly?"

The officer turned toward her. "Papers, madame. According to Youssef, Madame Shipley suggested that the police would know what she had done, sooner or later. She wanted to make sure she was able to leave, undetected, before that happened."

Papers. Lucy had obtained new papers from someone recently, and Lucy was the one who had befriended Youssef, all those weeks ago. Perhaps — though I didn't know why — Lucy had planned it all. But no, why on earth would this man ever agree to any of it when he had landed in jail? There would be no reason for pretense now. But then, perhaps he did not know that it was pretense, perhaps he believed it — believed that she was me, that she was called Alice.

I started.

"Madame?" The officer frowned.

"The name," I gasped. "What was the name on the papers?"

"I beg your pardon?"

"The new passport," I said hurriedly. "What was the name on the new passport?"

The officer looked down at his notepad, turning a page or two calmly, carefully, leaving me to lean forward, gripping the handles of my chair until my knuckles were white.

"Alice, what is it?" Aunt Maude asked. She looked down at my shaking fingers and I released them, quickly.

"The papers," I whispered, not wanting to disturb the officer. "It's the papers, don't you see?" She frowned and I hastened to explain. "Lucy. She had new papers made, ones with Sophie Turner as the name."

"Alice —" she began, the frown deepening between her brows.

"No," I interrupted, shaking my head. "I'm right, I know I'm right. It makes sense. It's the only thing that makes sense." I turned back toward the officer. "Have you found it yet? The name?"

The officer looked up. "He did not know the name. He said madame was insistent she be put in touch with the forger personally, so as not to incriminate him further."

I fell back against the chair.

"Madame," the officer began again, though his voice was distant now. "We also went to speak with your husband's mistress. She was, however, not to be found. It seems she left the country — fled, rather, in fear of her life. It was, it appears, with the help of your husband, the night before he went missing. And from what we understand, he had plans to eventually join her, in Europe."

I shook my head, feeling the words as they were absorbed, one by one, into my body. "I didn't push her," I whispered, knowing as I did, that it was the wrong thing to say.

298

Both Ayoub and Maude leaned forward quickly, words spilling from them both, loud and rushed, though I did not hear them, did not register them. Instead I felt the blood drain from my face, felt the knowledge of it all hit me — sharp and accurate, so that it seemed my breath had been knocked out of me. I realized then, for the first time, what was happening — why this man was asking these questions. I turned to look at Aunt Maude, to see if she too had realized. Her stony demeanor told me that she had, and I found myself wondering just how long she had known — whether she had figured it out from the beginning, from the moment the officer had pointed us through the door. My skin prickled. "I need to be excused," I said, the words dulled so that I did not recognize them as my own.

The officer watched me with those hardened eyes, any trace of kindness long dissipated. "There is just one more thing," he said.

I hesitated. "Yes?"

He peered up at me. "Why did you not go to the police, when you knew your husband was missing?" When I did not respond, he continued, "Or perhaps you did. That is also unclear. You see, my men claim that someone by the name of Alice Shipley telephoned the station, only when they paid her a visit, she denied having made the telephone call."

I blinked. "It wasn't me. And I didn't know. Not at first."

He frowned. "You didn't know that your husband was missing?"

"No," I said, shaking my head, knowing how the words sounded, that no explanation would ever suffice. Still, I hastened to explain: "He was supposed to go somewhere. With a friend."

"What friend?"

I hesitated, suspecting what his next question would be. "His name is Charlie," I responded. And then, when he did indeed follow up by asking how he could get in touch with him, I answered, shaking my head: "I don't know."

"You don't know how to get in touch with your husband's friend?" he asked, suspicion, doubt, flooding his voice.

My heart began to pound as I admitted, "No, I've only ever met him a couple of times. Charlie, I mean."

"But that still does not explain how you knew."

"About Charlie?" I asked, puzzled.

"No, madame," he shook his head. "That your husband was missing."

"A man came to tell me. Someone that John works with." I paused, knowing, once more, that his next question would demand specifics I could not provide. "I don't know his name."

"He didn't tell you?"

"No, he didn't."

He grimaced. "Pardon me for saying so, but there is a lot that you don't seem to know, madame. A lot that you don't seem to have answers for."

I considered this as I began to stand, turning away from the police officer. I felt Aunt Maude rise beside

**300**

me, felt her at my back as I pushed the door open and we were, at last, released into the hallway.

"Madame?" came the officer's voice again.

I stopped but did not turn.

"We have been made aware that you recently closed your account with the local bank. With this in mind, we ask that you please surrender your passport before leaving the station today."

I nodded stiffly and let the door close behind us.

Aunt Maude insisted that I accompany her back to the Hotel Continental.

One of the oldest hotels in Tangier, its expansive white facade sat higher than the rest of the buildings it surrounded, as if in recognition of its significance. I had always thought it looked like something out of a fairy tale, only instead of a moat, there was the harbor, instead of pillars, there were dozens of palm trees, and instead of royalty, there were artists and writers — all the names that were famous and meant something *out there*, beyond Tangier. It was strange, but I found that I could no longer imagine it: a world outside of this place, Morocco. One that existed at the same time, concurrently. It seemed as though everything, each and every strand of my life, was tied to this place, would always be tied to this place, no matter how much distance I were to put between us. I tried to remember if I had felt the same about Bennington before I left, but it seemed so far away, as if that too could no longer exist under the blazing sun of Tangier, as if the hot, dusty city held the power to wipe clean the green forests, the rolling hills, the smell of damp leaves underfoot. I was certain, in that moment, that I would never see it again.

"Are you feeling ill?" My aunt's voice cut through my thoughts. We sat across from each other, an elaborate tea service between us, on the patio overlooking the harbor. Up until that moment, we had remained silent, our unspoken words a divide I could not figure out how to cross.

"No, I was only thinking," I began, setting my teacup down with a clatter.

She held up a hand to silence me. "It's fine, Alice. You needn't say anything. We will figure out a solution, just as we did before."

I frowned, realizing she meant Bennington. "Maude," I started again, the sound of her name causing her to look up, startled. "You have to believe me, about Lucy."

"Alice —"

"No," I cut in, refusing to listen. "You have to believe me, you have to trust me when I tell you that she is the one responsible for all of this, just like before. You have to."

She shook her head, setting down her own teacup with an exasperated sigh. "Enough, Alice," she commanded, though her voice was not as harsh as I believe she intended it to be. Instead she sounded sad, tired — as if she had been having this same conversation for the entirety of her life. "No more of this Lucy Mason business, I beg of you."

"But if you would just listen —"

"No, Alice," she cut in. "I can't. I can't go back there, not again." She shook her head. "After all that wretched business in Vermont, all you would talk about was Lucy. It was like you were obsessed." She paused. "There were girls who came forward, afterward. Girls who said they heard you fighting, that you said something — that night."

I tried to remember. "What did I say?"

Aunt Maude looked away. "That you wished she would disappear." She paused. "And then she did."

"It was —" I began to protest.

"Alice," she cut in again, "you must see how it all looks."

I shook my head, not understanding what she was saying. "Lucy did it, Lucy is the one responsible — just like before."

"Alice," she began again, lowering her voice. "There is no evidence of that. There is no evidence that anyone is responsible at all. It was just an accident, something that no one can be held accountable for. It was tragic, yes, and I can see how you're still struggling with the injustice. It's entirely understandable. But blaming someone else, a girl who no one has seen since —" She let her voice fade.

I frowned, struggling once more to understand her aversion to the topic, to understand why instead of choosing to listen to her niece, to what she offered as truth, she preferred instead to sweep away all mention of Lucy entirely.

And then I remembered her words, after the accident. *I will take care of everything.* I inhaled sharply. That was it, then, the truth of the matter. The one that had always been there but that I had refused to see until that moment. I looked up at my aunt, made sure to catch her eye, to hold it. "Maude," I said, my voice level, even. And then I asked the question that had been floating between us, I now realized, for the past year: "Maude, what do you think I've done?"

She paled. I waited for her to deny it, to tell me that I was being absurd, hysterical even, but then she broke my gaze, looking out to the port, to the sea just beyond and whispered, "I don't know, Alice." She turned back to look at me. "And what's more, I don't know if you do either."

I could feel them then — the shadows — threatening. I remembered those days, after my parents died, how everything had seemed heightened but also dull and distant at the same time. Time had passed strangely. Hours had felt like days, and days had felt like hours. Most of that I had spent in bed, my mind exhausted and racing, the lack of sleep causing me to blink rapidly, my dry and tired eyes struggling to determine what was real, what was tangible, and what had only been imagined by my fervent mind.

This could not be how it all ended.

I pushed the thought of my parents, of their death, from my mind. I ignored those dark spaces at the edges of my vision, the ones that seemed to grow, minute by minute.

There had to be something left that I could do, something that might help to right the horrible, wretched mess that Lucy had once again created.

I stood, knocking over my teacup as I did so, the light brown liquid running down the sides of the table, onto the ground. "I'm so sorry," I murmured. "Please excuse me, Auntie."

As I walked away from the Hotel Continental, leaving behind Maude — who looked stricken and confused at my hasty exit — I thought about what the police officer had said back at the station. Yes, there was a lot that I did not have answers for, that much was true.

But I also knew the one person who did.

# CHAPTER
# EIGHTEEN

## LUCY

I peeled off my dress, the imposing belted black one I had worn on my first day in Tangier and again, recently, for the sake of Maude. I did not imagine a girl like Sophie Turner wore trousers. The dress clung to my back, slick with sweat, as if reluctant to leave my body. A few minutes passed and I wrestled, furiously, until I heard a slight rip, a slight give of the fabric and then it was off and I was free, the defeated dress lying in a heap on the ground. I sighed. Part of me wanted to leave it there, to toss it out the window and into a trash heap, but I stuffed it into the bottom of my suitcase, hoping, as I did so, that the need for such pretense would soon be over.

It was almost time to leave now.

There was a part of me that had hesitated, earlier that day, that had felt guilty even as I moved inside Youssef's empty studio. He had waited his entire life to see Tangier free and he was so close to it — it was only a matter of weeks now, until that moment when Tangier would be entirely its own. I was aware of the injustice, even as I had placed John's bloodstained wallet onto the ground, behind one of Youssef's paintings, the bracelet already there somewhere, a down payment of my gratitude. It was not fair, I knew. He would spend the rest of his life in prison and simply because he had done what I had always done myself — scratched and clawed, fought as hard as possible, in order to get his own in a world that refused to give it to him. Once again I was struck by how similar we were, Youssef and I. Oppressed by the same forces, by men like John. And while we should have been allies, while this defeat of John should have made us partners, coconspirators, we would be nothing but enemies now.

My hand had paused at the sight of the painting resting on the easel. I had not asked to see it, had not bothered to look at it, the last time I had been in his studio. A part of me, later, had wondered whether he had even been painting at all, whether it had truly been my portrait his brushstrokes had created. But about this, at least, he had been honest.

A strange mix of blues, the shades of which I could not name, the painting displayed my features in startling clarity. It betrayed, I thought, just how closely he had been observing me these past weeks — for surely he had not seen all this in just the few moments that I had sat for him. There was something intimate, something that suggested a relationship existed between the artist and the subject. I knew little about art, but I had the sense that it was something that should make one feel, should make one think.

It was already approaching evening, and I struggled in that moment, watching as the fading light cast its beams across the painting, caught between the desperate need to get away, from the studio, from Tangier, and yet hesitant to leave. It seemed all too sudden, as if I hadn't had time to prepare, to allow myself to mourn. Part of me wanted to leave it there, as a reminder, proof that I was once there, that I had loved Tangier, had loved Alice, in that moment. That it had all meant something. But then I thought of the painting remaining there for Youssef to look at, believing he had bested me — even if the illusion would last only for a moment or two longer. The idea unsettled me. I thought too of the police, who would find it, who might pause long enough, particularly if Youssef decided to point in my direction, when he realized his Alice was not *the* Alice. It would not do, I realized.

I had reached out and taken the painting.

I now paused before lowering the blouse over my head, my eyes flickering to the mirror, to what I saw reflected there. A young woman, handsome enough, but nothing that clamored for attention. I thought of Youssef's painting — of the shrewdness that he had captured. I relaxed my face, watching, working to soften my features, to rearrange myself into a girl called Sophie Turner, though I had already begun to suspect that she would not fit for much longer — her worth, her purpose diminishing with each and every step that I took.

I reached for my suitcase, taking one last look around the apartment.

We could have been happy here, I thought sadly.

I closed the door and exited onto the streets below.

\* \* \*

I inhaled, taking in the scents of Tangier, reminding myself, even as I did so, that it might be the last time I found myself on her shores again. As I moved through the markets, my eyes trailed over the tall mounds of spices, from the brilliant shades of squash-colored turmeric, to the crushed rose petals and overflowing baskets of whole peppercorns. If I were a painter, an artist, this is where I would spend all my time, I decided. There was no better place to observe Tangier.

And then, though I knew it was silly, that it was entirely too sentimental, dangerous even, I made my way toward the Kasbah, toward the tombs and the cliff and the water beyond, one last time. In the end, I could not stop myself.

Standing atop the cliff, determined to take in one last view of Tangier, I was struck by her beauty, by her mystery. I thought of the tale that Youssef had told me. The one about the beautiful woman luring men to their death. Perhaps it wasn't some mysterious woman at all, I thought now, perhaps it was simply Tangier, Tingis. For in a way I too had experienced a sort of death upon her shores. I had come to her as one thing and was now leaving as another. This metamorphosis, it seemed, was dependent on rebirth, and so death must also be a part of it, the two inherently linked.

I removed the painting from under my arm, gave a quick look around to make sure that no one was watching, and released it into the water below.

Lucy Mason had outlived her usefulness at last — though she had never been particularly useful to begin with, I thought with disdain. Born poor, uneducated, to

**309**

a family that couldn't be bothered to care, in the end her survival past the age of ten was a miracle in itself. That she had found a way to survive, in that garage, alone with her father, with the other men, that she had picked up one book and then another, teaching herself to read, to write, to earn a scholarship that promised her something more, something better — it should never have happened. She should have died long ago, just like her mother, another forgotten life, another forgotten death. With no one left to mourn, to remember. I stood for a moment or two longer, imagining the waves as flames of a fire, watching as they lapped, as they drowned and devoured the last and final traces of Lucy Mason.

I moved away from the cliffs, realizing that time had been slipping away from me, that the ferry would soon be arriving. Heading toward the port, I kept my eyes focused, kept my gaze averted as I walked, avoiding those very same spots where only moments before I had walked, eagerly, greedily, hungry for a reminder, a souvenir, of Tangier. I thought of that first day, of the sellers that had greeted me, called out to me, trying and failing to get me to part with my money. I saw them again as I moved toward the port and then — yes, I knew it was him — that very same Mosquito who had pursued me through the streets as I had sought to find Alice's flat that first day, who had slipped away only moments before I had stood beneath her balcony, watching her from a distance.

He moved toward me now, a smile emerging on his face. "Madame needs a tour guide?" he asked eagerly.

I shook my head and indicated the boat, just beyond.

He nodded in response and opened his jacket, revealing a hidden layer of cheap, shiny bracelets and rings, the kind that would no doubt stain one's skin green within a few days. "A trinket, madame," he offered. "To remember your journey."

I nodded, reaching for my last few francs. "Here," I said, handing over the coins.

He rewarded me with one of the bracelets.

"A reminder, madame," he said, smiling. "Of your time in Tangier."

I thanked him and headed toward the port. As I boarded, I let the trinket drop from my hand into the Mediterranean, though I did not bother to watch as it sank. Letting out a small laugh, I thought of what I had wanted to say to the Mosquito. That the bracelet, or any other of his treasures, was unnecessary. That I didn't need anything to remind me of Tangier, of her.

After all, I was a Tangerine.

I would never forget.

# CHAPTER
# NINETEEN

## ALICE

In some ways, Malabata prison was not so grim as I had anticipated.

Sitting on the eastern outskirts of the city, it stood, a vast grand building rising up in front of me so that I was immediately reminded of the Hotel Continental. I felt a chill run through me. The two structures could not have been more different, and yet there was something in them that felt strangely familiar, a sense of the imposing stature that radiated from both.

Inside I was conducted through a series of hallways before passing at last into what appeared to be some sort of makeshift cell, held apart from the rest of the prison.

Youssef stood when I entered. "I am so famous now they decided I must have my own room," he said by way of greeting, indicating his surroundings. He smiled, watching as I assessed the tiny enclosure, the prison within a prison that they had created for him.

I smiled weakly in response, though I suspected he knew the truth. For while Tangier could most certainly be a dangerous place, I had learned from John that most of the criminals within the walls of Malabata were thieves and pimps, the most common offense the smuggling of kif from the mountains and into the city. A dangerous criminal like Youssef would not sit well with either the prisoners or the guards. And so they had cordoned him off, creating a room that held him apart from the rest of the populace, with only one solitary window for company.

I cleared my throat. "I wanted to speak with you, about Lucy Mason."

Youssef, who occupied the room's only chair, tipped the frame of it against the wall in what seemed a dangerous balancing act. "You are not the first person to mention that name to me," he observed, shaking his head with a short laugh. He let the chair fall back onto the ground with a clatter. "I am sorry to disappoint you, madame, but I do not know anyone by that name."

"She was the woman whom you met, several weeks ago, in the Grand Socco," I said. He inclined his head, an indication, I thought, that was meant to let me know that he was listening, that I should continue. "You see, monsieur, *I* am Alice Shipley."

His eyes widened at this, his eyebrows raising just an inch or two. He remained silent, though his eyes sought, appraised. Finally, he said, "I see."

"The woman you met," I continued, eager now to have it all out in the open, "used my name, though I'm not sure why. But I think it was for this reason, because she planned this, all of it, somehow, from the very beginning." I waited for a response, and when there was none, I said, "So you see, you have to tell them."

He smiled. "Tell what to whom, madame?"

"The police," I replied, confused that he did not understand, that he did not see. "You have to tell them what I've just told you."

"That a Tangerine lied to me? Gave me a false name?" He shrugged. "That is hardly news."

I shook my head. "You must tell them that I am not Alice, or rather, not the Alice that you know. That I am not the one you saw that night — that night when John was killed."

"Yes, I could tell them this." He paused. "But why would they believe me?"

I sputtered, confused. How could he not see it? I wondered, that this was not only my way out but his as well, his one chance to clear his name and be free of the shackles that her lies had imposed upon him. "They have to," I said.

He shook his head. "Madame, let me tell you what the police will say. That you came here to convince me to lie. After all, why would you visit a man in prison you did not know? For what other reason than to ask him to save your life, since his own is already lost?"

I stood, speechless.

"They will twist everything," he continued. "Your words, your intentions, until they fit their own. This is their way. Nothing will change that. So you see, it is an impossible situation."

"But, it's not right," I said, though the words came out soft, meek. "She can't get away with it. Surely this place won't let her get away with it."

He raised his eyebrows. "This place?"

314

"I didn't mean," I began hastily, anxious to explain. But then I fell silent, wondering if I hadn't meant exactly that. Tangier. This place. This strange, lawless city that belonged to everyone and no one.

Youssef settled back into his chair. "Let me tell you something a friend once told me. He works at the Hotel Continental — do you know it?"

"Yes," I replied, a blush starting on my cheeks at the mention of it. Looking at the man in front of me, I wondered how often he had sat down to tea there or passed through its doors at all. It struck me as odd, the idea that he belonged to this city, and it to him, and yet the places, the spaces of the city, did not. "Yes," I repeated. "I know it."

He nodded. "My friend there is the manager of the hotel. He told me once about a group of tourists that had come to stay, Americans, he said. Upon departing the ferry, one of the first things they asked him was if Tangier was safe."

Youssef paused then, affixing me with a gaze that made me grow uneasy. For at his words, all I could think of was John, of his body on the metal table of the coroner. No, I wanted to say, to shout. No, Tangier was not safe. Nothing I knew about it suggested otherwise, and nothing Youssef, a son of Tangier, could say would change that. But then I looked at him, sitting there before me, imprisoned for a crime he did not commit, and I felt I could not say the words aloud. "I don't know," I offered instead.

"Well," Youssef said, shifting in his seat. "He asked them this — when at home, if a strange man was to

**315**

approach you, one with a jagged scar on his face," he began, indicating his own visage, as if the deformity could be viewed there, "would you stop to see what he wanted?" He leaned forward. "Would you?" he demanded, the last words spoken more harshly.

"No," I answered quickly.

"No," he repeated. "No, of course not. So why would you stop to talk to such a man here, only to be surprised when something bad happens later?" He shook his head ruefully. "If you are not smart at home," he said, tapping his head, "you will not be smart here. If you run into trouble at home, do not be surprised to run into trouble here. You are still the same person. Tangier can be magic, but even she is not a miracle worker."

I nodded, refusing, in that moment, to consider the implications of his words, of the truth I suspected that they held, of what they might mean for me — no, about me.

"But what will you do?" I asked, realizing that all other questions were lost to me.

"I will survive." He shrugged. "Nothing is forever, Alice Shipley."

The taxi back to the flat could have dropped me outside the front door, but I found myself restless to be outside — to be walking in the fresh air, though it felt thick and languorous already. Still, it was nothing compared to the temperature in the backseat of the taxi, the windows shut tightly, as if the driver feared the air itself.

**316**

I puzzled over Youssef's words, could not help but feel the sharp sting of them, as if they had been a rebuke intended solely for me. After all, he was right — how could I blame this place, Tangier, when I had brought the problems myself? They had not manifested out of the cracks and corners of the sidewalks around me; no, they had been born and bred somewhere else, had followed me here because I had ignored them, had allowed the fog to hide what I already knew.

It was my fault. What had happened with Tom, with John — all of it. There was no one else to blame. Only myself and Lucy. She had taken everything from me — but I had let her.

The realization stirred something, so that as I made my way back to the flat, I increased my pace, desperate to confront her on my own at last. Feeling, in that moment, as though this is where we had been headed for some time now, the two of us, standing before each other, all our secrets and lies exposed. I walked faster, turning one corner and then another, stumbling against locals, against the vibrant blues, pinks, and yellows of doorways, stopping and starting several times over in confusion. I realized soon enough, my heart hammering in my chest, that I was lost.

And that there was someone following me.

It hit me in the chest as I struggled to breathe, as I increased my speed, my eyes scanning over every building, every landmark, searching for something that looked familiar, that whispered of home. I thought of the man with the scar, positive that it had been him, only a few days before, following me through the streets. I had been frightened then, and though I was still frightened now, I was tired of running.

And so I stopped, quickly and without warning.

I felt the force of another body smack into my own. My handbag was knocked from my arm, and its contents went scattering across the pavement: a tube of lipstick, a container of rouge, the few coins that had fallen to the bottom. I had forgotten about them until that moment, and my gaze fixated on them as they fell, the bright silver flittering like leaves in the air around me.

I turned, expecting to find the man standing there — but no, it was a woman, it was her — Lucy. "What do you want?" I demanded, scurrying to grab my purse, my belongings, to place a few feet of distance between us. I fumbled, wondering how long she had been following me, whether she knew about the police station, about the horrible thing that Aunt Maude had confessed afterward. I imagined her listening around the corner, smiling, taking pleasure in my displeasure. Hoisting my handbag onto my shoulder, I began to move away, but that monstrous grin of hers — the same one that she had fixed on me the other night — was all that I could see. I thought of my father, of his teasing voice, *my little Alice in Wonderland*. "Why are you doing this?" I shouted now, ready at last, feeling the rage course through my veins.

But when I looked up at her, what I saw made me stop and blink.

It was Lucy, I had been certain. But no, I could see now that I had been wrong. That it was a woman, yes, but not Lucy — not anyone who even looked like her, not really. This woman was older, taller — she was fair where Lucy was dark — and she was watching me with concern, her hand pressed up against her mouth, her eyes wide with an expression that I could not manage to read.

I shook my head.

"I'm sorry," I murmured. "*Je suis désolée.*" I continued, moving my head oddly, I thought, though I could not stop the gesture, a funny tilt that looked as though I were bowing to her. She started to speak, to say something, but I walked — no, *sprinted* — away, imagining that she, whoever *she* was, remained there, watching me with derision. I could almost hear it, her laughter pressing up against my back as I hurried from one street to the next, not paying attention to where I was going, needing to lose myself in the crowd, to put as much distance between myself and that grinning face as possible.

By the time I returned home, Lucy was gone.

At first I could not believe it, assumed that she was only out, somewhere in the city. But then, stepping into her room — slowly, at first, as though I expected her to emerge at any moment — I could see that it was true. Her suitcase, her clothes, her toiletries, everything was gone. As though she had never really even been there.

I felt the realization, dully, felt the knowledge of what her absence truly meant begin to sink in, slowly, trickling, bit by bit.

Youssef would not speak up. Aunt Maude did not believe me. Worse still, she thought *I* was the one responsible. I thought of the officer from earlier — his questioning, his disappointment and simultaneous glee as he realized just how many of the questions he put before me I was unable to answer. I knew then that it would not be long before they came.

I leaned up against the wall and felt the bracelet in my pocket, solid and heavy.

At the reminder of it now I felt the rage well up inside me. It erupted in that moment, so that its release felt almost violent, such that I could actually feel it leaking from my pores.

I tore the plates from the wall first, the force of the movement wrenching my shoulder. I ignored the pain, ignored the trembling of my hands, desperate to have them gone — wanting, no, *needing*, to destroy this place that had once promised safety, a new chance, a new start. It had been lies. And in that moment, I wanted nothing more than to destroy it.

When my own strength failed me, I ran to the kitchen, my hands encircling the sharpest knife that I could find. This I plunged through the cushions on the sofa, through the leather poufs on the ground, pulling down on the knife's handle with such force that the fabric had no choice but to yield at last, pulling apart at my insistence. My hands were shaking, my breath short and fast. I could feel my heart thudding loudly against my chest as I wiped away the sweat that had collected on my forehead.

**320**

I had an image then of what I must look like — face wild, teeth and claws bared.

Dropping the knife, I collapsed onto the ground amid the tattered room, now torn into jagged strips, the remains scattered around me like some macabre version of snowfall. And I waited, for the feeling of comfort, the feeling of triumph to wash over me. I looked down at the mess that I had made — but there was nothing. Only the feeling of emptiness at the thought that she was gone. That I might never know for certain — what she had done then, what she had done now. That all I would ever have were my own suspicions, my own convictions, which suddenly did not seem like enough at all.

And there was something else too.

It was absurd, grotesque even, but there was something like a physical ache, just there, behind my rib cage. I remembered the moment at the police station, earlier, when I had turned to look for her. Almost as if there were some missing part of me that only Lucy's presence would ever truly complete. For even though I blanched at the idea, without her, I knew from experience, my resolve diminished, my voice disappeared. Whatever symbiosis existed between us was real, tangible, and now, without her presence I could feel the absence of it, as if she were an extension of my own person. She was, I realized, that awful, wretched part of me that should be locked away and boarded up forever — like Jane's madwoman in the attic. She was the unfiltered version, the rawness that no one should ever see. She was every wicked thought, every forbidden desire turned real and visceral. I held up my hand and saw that the dye from the leather had stained my skin. I laughed, whispering the words to myself, *See, you will never be rid of her*. I looked down once again, willing myself to feel something, anything.

But there was nothing. Nothing at all.

I heard my name being called, muffled, from the other side.

It was the police, I knew. They had returned at last.

I looked at the walls of my apartment, desperate to be swallowed up by them, to be consumed, once and for all, by the shadows lurking in the corners.

I should have known that I would never be able to outrun them.

That I would never be able to outrun *her*.

I moved from my place on the floor. Strips of leather, of fabric, now stuck to my arms. There was a small piece affixed to my cheek. Pulling them away, gazing down at the strips of canvas, I was gripped with the conviction that none of it, what happened with Tom, with John, with anything in between, mattered. Not really. This had always been about her, about me, about the two of us. And it was always destined to end this way.

There was an ache in my head, and I pushed my fingers into my temple.

The knocking grew more insistent.

I thought about the last time I had heard someone knock on the door like that, the morning that John had disappeared. No, not the morning of his disappearance, but the first time I had learned of it, from that strange man with the scar. I wondered then, and not for the first time, who he had been and why he had been so reluctant to contact the police. If he truly had been the person following me that day in the streets. If what the police had said, about John leaving with Sabine, had been true. It made me realize that I had never really known John, only the hazy mirage he had presented to me that summer we first met, a shimmering beacon of hope that I had clung to in my darkest moment. I turned toward the door, toward the sound of someone fumbling with the knob. It was locked. They would not get in so easily.

I moved quickly, toward the bedroom.

They had come for me at last, my invisible shadows, which Lucy had made real. But this time, I knew, they would not go away. After all, the police believed that I was responsible for John's death — if not the actual physical act, then at least in the collusion of it. A Lady Macbeth whispering that could not go unpunished.

I thought about John's body, wondering whether they would bury it here or whether they would return it to England. I thought of his eyes, empty — or at least I imagined they were empty, for they had been closed when I had seen them last. It seemed strange, the idea of returning him to his birthplace. He had loved Tangier, and she had loved him, for a time. It didn't seem right for them to be parted. No, it made sense for him to remain with her, forever. I hoped they would realize that.

I grasped the knife that I had picked up from the floor.

In many ways, this too seemed to make a certain sort of sense. As if all the years in between now and my parents' death I had only been waiting, for this. For the end that I was meant for that night, that I perhaps would have succumbed to, if not for some strange miracle. Or perhaps it had not been a miracle after all. Perhaps it had only been a mistake. Perhaps I had not been meant to survive, and the shadows were simply warnings, or time, watching over me, waiting, for my impending death.

Perhaps I had always been moving toward this day, all on my own.

There was a comfort in the thought, I realized as I moved onto the bed. I crawled, pulling the duvet back and slipping under the sheets.

It sounded now as though a large body was pummeling the wooden frame, over and over, so that I worried the sound of it would never stop, that it would go on and on forever.

But then, I remembered, looking down into my hand, it *would* stop.

All of it. Soon.

And nothing that had come before would matter ever again.

# CHAPTER
# TWENTY

## LUCY

In front of her, the queue was finally moving. "Ticket, please," the man commanded, opening his hand in expectation. For a moment, she considered turning back. Pushing through the line she had waited in for nearly an hour, making her way through the port and into the heart of the city, just as she had done the first day. She could almost feel it, the heat of the medina pushing up against her, the frenzied excitement that ran through it, as though a vein that kept the city alive — pumping and rushing, working relentlessly so that the rest of Tangier could survive. She longed to be in the midst of it again, suspecting — no, perhaps already knowing — that she never would be. That Tangier would be a stranger to her, now and forever. Well, not really a stranger, but a piece of her past. One that she might take out and examine from time to time, holding it up to the light — but one that she would never revisit. That was impossible.

If only Alice had not called Maude.

If only Youssef had not blackmailed her.

Lucy handed over her ticket to the attendant and found a seat toward the back, away from the screaming children, their faces sticky with sweets, their parents already wearing the resigned look of those who know they are facing a losing battle. It was an expression they no doubt shared — for Lucy also knew that this was the end for her and Alice as well. There would be no more chances between them.

She felt the fabric beneath her shift, and she half turned, surveying the occupant of the seat beside her. The woman was older, perhaps a decade or more than Lucy's own years, but there was something soft and inviting in the way that she smiled and nodded her head. Just a slight tilt, nothing too intrusive, but Lucy found herself returning the easy gesture, suddenly eager to leave her heavy thoughts behind.

The woman sighed loudly. "It's a relief, isn't it?"

Lucy frowned. "What is?"

The woman gestured to the window beside Lucy, which had grown hot and hazy from the afternoon sun. Already she could feel the force of it pressing up against her cheek.

"Leaving this behind," the woman said. She let out another sigh, moving farther into the cushion. "Not that I don't love Morocco, of course, but it's always such a relief when it's time to return home. Like I'm, oh, I don't know, shedding my skin, or something. Like suddenly I can breathe again." She turned back to Lucy. "Isn't there some saying about it?"

"Saying?" Lucy repeated. She was staring at the woman more intently now. There was something about her, in the way that she moved — theatrical, Lucy thought — with an elaborate flourish of her gloved hands. There was a sturdiness to the woman's voice, a confidence that Lucy found herself enthralled with, and she found herself wondering whether the woman did this often, talking to strangers as if it were the most natural thing in the world. Her tone confident, self-assured, as if she was already certain that such a quote existed and that the question she put to Lucy of its validity, its existence, was nothing more than a mere formality.

There had been a time when Lucy had been that certain — when everything had seemed easy and fitted into place. But then the world had tilted upside down, and when it righted itself at last, she had stood in front of the burning wreckage, suddenly unsure of everything. This time more of a change would be required, something more than a simple relocation and fabricated résumé. She thought of Tangier and its many names and alterations. Of the people who had claimed it as home over the centuries — a vast array of nationalities, of languages. Tangier was a city of transformation, one that shifted and altered in order to survive. It was a place where one went to be transformed. And it had, in a way, changed her. Gone was the girl, the young woman who had loved so carelessly, so blindly, that she was willing to do anything to keep that love. For while she still believed that Alice had loved her once, she could no longer pinpoint the exact time in her mind.

Lucy turned back to the woman — to the present — and smiled. "I don't think I know that saying."

The woman raised her eyebrows. "No? Well, perhaps I'm just imagining it then." She stuck out her hand, still gloved. "I'm Martha."

Lucy took the outstretched palm, the sweat on her own transferring to the starched material. "Alice," she said, trying it out, shifting her voice just a bit, so that the a was higher, more rounded.

Martha frowned. "Now, am I wrong, or do I detect a bit of a British accent?" she asked, leaning in. Her own vowels were long and drawn out, like the lazy flies that circled overhead, so that Lucy imagined hot, dusty weather, with mud the color of burned ochre.

Lucy smiled. "My mother was American, but my father was British." She paused, feeling the gears of the boat as they began to churn at last. "Though I was raised by my aunt in London."

"By your aunt?" Martha questioned.

"Yes," Lucy said. She felt the boat pull away, but she resisted the urge to turn and look out of the window. She had already said her good-bye to Tangier. "My parents died when I was young."

Martha's hand flew to her cherry-stained lips. "Oh, my dear, that is awful."

Lucy lowered her eyes. "Yes, yes, it was." She let out a deep sigh, feeling the movement as it made its way through her entire body, until she was no longer certain whether it was the exclamation of relief or the churn of the mechanics that rumbled there. "But that was a long time ago now."

"Of course," Martha said, nodding eagerly. She started to speak, but then hesitated. Lucy thought that she could read the conflicting emotions there — politeness and interest, the two of them fighting within the woman. Her back pressed against the window, refusing to look backward, Lucy waited to see which one would win.

The boat surged then, and the woman gave a sudden lurch, slapping Lucy lightly on the shoulder. "I've got it!" she exclaimed.

Lucy frowned, startled. "What?"

"The saying," Martha replied, shaking her head, as if she couldn't believe that Lucy didn't know what she was referring to — as if they were already fast friends. "There is a local saying here — or there, rather," she said, indicating over Lucy's shoulders, toward the retreating image of Tangier and her shores. Martha paused, watching Lucy expectantly. And then she said: "'You cry when you arrive, and you cry when you leave.'"

# Epilogue

# SPAIN

In her dreams, she's sitting at Café Hafa. There is a glass of mint tea before her, only recently delivered, and she marvels at the colors. A rich forest-green on top, a golden amber on the bottom. It is one of those perfect Tangier days, she thinks. The skies are a deep blue, the clouds a startling white. She wishes, not for the first time, that she was able to capture it all somehow — perhaps with words on a page, or paint on a canvas — just so she can keep it with her, always.

Her reality upon waking isn't entirely different. The sun still shines, set against an azure sky. Only instead of the sapphire blue of the Mediterranean, she faces mountains — green and budding in the first days of spring.

Today is Tuesday, her favorite day of the week.

On Tuesdays, she wakes early, ladles out coffee grinds into a cup — just enough for one, as she has somewhere else to be. Afterward, she climbs the stairs and drinks her coffee on the balcony, which overlooks the street and one of the town's many steep inclines. She is high up enough that she can see the vast stretch of it, the mountains beyond — at night, when most of the town falls quiet, she can observe those places that stay awake, their lights pulsing in this otherwise darkened mountain town.

Today someone has moved into the flat across the street. She can, from her vantage point, see into the belly of it as they move around, pulling sheets from the furniture, shaking the dust out the window and onto the street below. One of the pieces is an old piano, pushed up against the back of the room. As she is finishing her coffee, music begins to drift out of the window. *Two drifters, off to see the world, There's such a lot of world to see.* She sits and listens, smiling, drawing out the moment as long as it will stretch.

Today will be her last day in the house.

She waits patiently at the bus stop, nodding to the other faces that have since grown familiar to her. There is the couple who owns one of the three restaurants in town and who serves her cerveza with a small tapa, fish that she doesn't recognize but that is always oily and salty and satisfying; there is the tramp who has taken up residence in the abandoned shack behind the doctor's house; and more, other familiar smiles. She nods at them all but does not speak. No one, it seems, understands English or French in this little town, and so she remains apart from them, happy in the barrier that exists.

She climbs onto the bus, pausing in front of the driver. "Málaga," she says, handing over the required coin.

It is an hour's ride away, but a pleasant one. She sits alone, looking out the window, watching the dips and

**331**

curves of the mountains as they rush past — a sprinkling of flowers, purple and yellow, coating the green fields. There are moments when she wishes that the drive would go on forever as she rests her head against the window, her eyelids fluttering. She feels nearly content in these moments, almost at peace.

In Málaga, the noises seem to assault her — she has grown used to the quiet of her little mountain town. Here, there are too many people, moving frantically from one place to another. It is too hot somehow, though it is most likely the same temperature. Still, it is uncomfortable here, so that after she walks a block or two, her shirt sticks to her back and her breath comes hard and fast. She pushes her sunglasses farther up the bridge of her nose, trying to shield herself from the sun.

Once there, she finds her sitting in the corner of her room, alone.

Maude would, she knows, prefer to have Alice somewhere in England. So far, however, the doctors have advised against such a move, and so she has had to be content with sending over a personal nurse, a young redheaded girl who looks frightened at the prospect of spending her time in Spain indefinitely. At least it is not Tangier, Maude had said, months ago now, shaking her head. She had told her then about the state that Alice was discovered in, and the arrangements, the arguments, that Maude had endured before finally convincing the police that the best place for her niece was an institution in Málaga, not a jail cell in Tangier. That everything had already been arranged, at her behest, by a friend of Alice's, a capable young woman named Sophie Turner. Eventually they had relented. It had all become too difficult, too messy for their taste. Independence had arrived and they were eager to start again, to focus on their own, to leave the problems of expatriates to their own countries. They were only too happy to expel the British girl from their shores, in the end.

She stands next to the bed, looking down at what remains of the girl she had once known, had once loved. It is a curious thing, she has thought often, over these last few months as Alice's caretaker, how the feelings she once had have slipped away, dried up, so that she knows it is time to leave at last.

There is a slip of paper on the bed, and reaching down, she sees her own name written there. The nurses had warned her of this some weeks earlier, that this obsession with the name has only increased, along with the torn pieces of paper, hidden throughout Alice's room.

She slips it into her pocket.

Leaning down, she places a kiss on the girl's forehead and leaves. She does not look back. This will be the last time they see each other.

Her steps are heavy as she heads to Banco de Málaga.

Behind the counter, the tellers are startled by her appearance — usually the courier is sent to deliver the allowance to Alice Shipley, in care of Sophie Turner. She shakes her head and smiles, explaining that she is better now, that her caretaker has returned to England and that she has come to withdraw funds from the trust she now has full access to, her birthday only the day before. At their frowns, their confusion, she places a hand to her cheeks and asks, "Oh dear, didn't my aunt leave a note with instructions?"

"No, *señorita*, nothing," they say, blushing.

They do not speak much English — but this is to her advantage.

They hover around her, smiling at the sweet foreign English girl who watches them with wide and trusting eyes, so that they are aware of how alone, how vulnerable she is, here in a country that is not her own, where she does not even speak the language. They think, with worry, of their own daughters, and in the end, they relent. After all, the girl has her passport — Alice Shipley — the same surname as the imposing older woman who had first opened the account. The connection can be no coincidence. The woman set up the payments to care for her niece while in the hospital, and though they did not ask for what ailment, they can see now that she is cured.

And the trust is in her name, so there is no reason to deny her.

On the street, she smiles, feeling comfort, feeling the future, alive and throbbing, in the heft of her suitcase. She is not a thief, she reasons, for she has not taken everything, only what she is owed. For all the promises Alice made and broke. For the life she had whispered into being one cool, autumn night and that she had set alight in the bitter cold of winter.

334

Afterward, she makes her way onto Alameda Principal and to Antigua Casa de Guardia, where she has developed a taste for *lágrima transañejo*. She will have one last taste, in celebration, she has decided. And so she strolls slowly down the road, watching as families, couples, walk along the middle of the street that runs through the city, a pulsing vein of activity. They stop at a flower stall just there, and then another one a few feet down, inspecting, haggling, before any purchases are made.

Inside the bar, her mind relaxes.

She watches as the chalk marks that the bartender leaves in front of her grow from one to two to three. In the past, on bad days, she has ordered a small cask to take home with her. On the worst days, she paid for a hotel room in the city. Today she feels the weight of her luggage and knows there will be no more such days.

She signals to the bartender. Her bus leaves in little over half an hour and she cannot miss it, the city name printed on her bus ticket a hope, a dream she can no longer postpone. She hands over the coins, which the bartender counts quickly, before reaching into his pockets and handing her the correct amount of change. She shakes her head, indicating that the man should keep it as a tip, knowing that she can afford such things now. He dips his head in thanks.

Lucy watches as the bartender takes out a cloth from his pockets, wiping it across the wooden countertop, the number of her drinks disappearing, until at last the counter is clean and it is as though she were never there at all.

# Acknowledgments

I would like to thank my agent, Elisabeth Weed, for picking *Tangerine* out of the slush pile and seeing the potential hidden within my original draft. She has read this book countless times over the past year, in all its many variations, and has always remained incredibly encouraging throughout the process, something for which I am eternally grateful. My deepest gratitude to the rest of the team at the Book Group and, in particular, Dana Murphy, another early reader of *Tangerine*, for all of her insightful notes. I would also like to thank everyone at Ecco for their continued enthusiasm, and of course, in particular, my editor, Zachary Wagman. This novel would not exist today without his support and editorial guidance, all of which ultimately shaped *Tangerine* into the book you are reading today.